Praise for **Front Page Fatality**

"Author LynDee Walker sure knows her way around a plot twist. She kept me turning pages late into the night, following the roller-coaster adventures of her fashionably feisty heroine….*Front Page Fatality* is smart, funny, and loaded with surprises. A terrific debut mystery."

– Laura Levine,
Author of the Jaine Austen Mystery Series

"*Front Page Fatality* is delightful, with engaging characters, a crackling good mystery, and of course, high, high heels. LynDee Walker writes with wit and intelligence and the confidence of a newsroom insider. What fun!"

– Harley Jane Kozak,
Agatha, Anthony, and Macavity-Award Winning Author of *Dating Dead Men* and *Keeper of the Moon* (March 2013)

"This is a joy to read: Nichelle is a likeable character who does put her nose into whatever seems curious to her…the book can be read in one sitting thanks to the easy and casual language the author has employed in writing the book. Highly recommended to the fans of cozy mysteries!"

– *Mystery Tribune*

"Gives those designer shoes a workout! Nicey's adventure kept me guessing. Goes down as smooth as hot chocolate with whipped cream."

– Alice Loweecey,
Author of the Falcone and Driscoll Investigations

HENERY PRESS

FRONT PAGE FATALITY
A Henery Press Mystery

First Edition
Trade paperback edition | January 2013

Henery Press
www.henerypress.com

Cover design by Fayette Terlouw
Author photograph by Sarah Dabney-Reardon

ISBN-13: 978-1-938383-12-0

Printed in the United States of America

For my mom, who was my biggest fan.
I hope there are bookstores in Heaven. I miss you every day.

ACKNOWLEDGEMENTS

So many people had a hand in making this book a reality, and each one has my eternal gratitude. I'm sure I'll forget to mention someone, though I've been working on this list for a while. If you find that your name was left off, know that it was inadvertent, and accept my thanks.

Richmond is a beautiful city that has truly become home for my family. Thank you to the gracious people of central Virginia. This is fiction, and I took liberties, but I tried very hard to capture the things I love about this place. I hope I was successful.

All of the amazing journalists and police officers I've worked with: thank you for doing what you do. Thanks to my favorite forensic lab tech, Corrie Meyer, who graciously answered my questions no matter how crazy they seemed.

No manuscript is ever perfect, but they're much more imperfect in various drafting stages. This is why writers love their beta readers. Thank you Courtney Loveday, Allison Ward, Pam Walker, Lane Buckman, Becky Durfee, Jennifer Walkup, Maer Wilson, Dee Garretson, Ramsey Hootman, and Danielle Devor, for reading some version of this for me.

My writer friends have propped me up and poured virtual drinks on bad days, and cheered like no one else on great ones. Thank you, my purgy buds, especially Kris Herndon, Lisa Brackmann, Alice Loweecey, Gretchen McNeil, Sue Laybourn, Kelly Andrews, Amy Bai, Elizabeth Loupas, Alex Harrow, Rick Campbell, Rebecca Burrell, Elysabeth Williams, and Jenn Nelson. Special thanks to my late-night title brainstorm buds, Jan O'Hara and Clovia Shaw.

My fellow Hens: I couldn't be more honored to be in such

talented company. Thanks Terri L. Austin, Larissa Reinhart, Christina Freeburn, Susan M. Boyer, Gigi Pandian, and Diane Vallere, for being so welcoming and supportive.

My amazingly talented, fabutastic (why yes, I did just make up a word) editor, Kendel Flaum: thank you for your unending patience and support, for seeing "a gem in the slush pile" (and telling me that—I'm going to frame that email as soon as I have time) and for not getting annoyed with me for breaking the rules and emailing you back. Most of all, thank you for making this a better book. I cannot tell you what a pleasure it is to work with you.

Big thanks to marketing guru Art Molinares for keeping your finger on the pulse of Internet trends, and for your availability, support, and help.

Every writer dreams of what the cover of their book might look like if it's ever published. Thank you to the insanely talented Fayette Terlouw for making this one more beautiful than I ever imagined.

Great teachers inspire us to achieve great things. Thank you to the talented teachers who made me think I could do this: Carol Mendez, Lynnda Roselle, Margie Howeth, Keith Shelton, Jacque Lambiase, Richard Wells, and Frank Feigert.

Years of front line experience as a reporter went into Nichelle's story. Thanks to the folks who made it fun: Sally Ellertson, Lisa Hermes, and Joy E. Cressler. My very own "chief," James Moody, thank you for taking a chance on me. Photographer extraordinaire Darlene Moore, I still miss the armadillo eggs.

I am blessed to have great friends. Sarah Dabney-Reardon, many thanks for the author pictures that make me look pretty, even to me. That's not an easy feat. Thank you for your endless encouragement and your boundless optimism. Nichole Dwire and Nichol Vogel, thank you for believing in me.

My big-hearted, funny best friend, who read every page of the rambling rough draft and saw something there that made her say nice things, who listened to me talk about plot points and publishing until I'm sure she could've cheerfully taken a hammer to me (but never let on), who put up with my neuroses, and who taught me to walk in heels: thank you, Julie Hallberg, for being you.

My supportive and all-around fantastic husband, Justin, who was an evenings-and-weekends single dad for almost a whole summer while his wife went a little crazy after being bitten by the fiction bug. Thanks for believing in me even when I didn't. And my monkeys, who don't complain too much when mommy is holed up with her imaginary friends — thank you for being the light in my days, and the very best things that ever happened to me. I love you.

1.

So many bodies, so little time

Thinking about blood spatters and ballistics reports before I'd even finished my coffee wasn't exactly how I wanted to start my weekend.

"More dead people? Really, guys?" I asked, as if the beat cops whose chatter blared out of the police scanner in my passenger seat could hear me. They, of course, kept right on talking. Apparently, this dead guy had lost a good bit of brains to a bullet, too.

I reached for my Blackberry, keeping one hand on the steering wheel and my eyes on the morning traffic. A body before I'd even made it to the newsroom was usually a good thing—but not that Friday. If I'd had to pay by the corpse, my MasterCard would've been maxed out by Wednesday that week. Especially given the eBay charge for the new heels on my feet.

I glanced at the clock and stomped my sapphire Louboutin down on the gas pedal, thumbing the speed dial for police headquarters.

"Aaron, it's Nichelle," I said when I got the department spokesman's voicemail. "I hear y'all are having a party out on

Southside this morning, and I seem to have misplaced my invitation. Give me a call when you get a minute."

Tossing my phone back into my bag, I turned into the parking garage of the *Richmond Telegraph*. I had been hoping for an idiot crook who'd opened an account with his real address before he'd robbed the video store. Anything but another body.

I flashed a semi-grin at my editor as I strode into his office a few minutes later.

"I've got another dead drug dealer on Southside. They just found him this morning." My words dissolved his annoyed expression to one of interest, his perpetual aggravation with my last-minute arrivals for the morning staff meeting forgotten at the mention of a homicide.

"Another one, huh?" He leaned forward and rested his elbows on his massive mahogany desk. "Do we know if this homicide is related to the guy they found out there a couple of weeks ago?"

"Aside from the bit about him being a dealer I caught on the scanner, not really." I dropped into my usual seat. "I left a message for Aaron White on my way in. I should have something for you by this afternoon."

Bob nodded, appearing satisfied and moving on to the sports section. "What's going on in your world this morning, Parker? Anything worth having an opinion on, or am I paying you to make stuff up yet?"

Our sports columnist (and de facto sports editor since the real thing was still on leave with his wife and new baby) raised his voice over the round of laughter and began a rundown of the day's sporting events.

"And I'm writing my column on the women's basketball coach over at the University of Richmond," he finished. "She's in the middle of treatment for breast cancer, and she still led the team to the playoffs again this past season." He glanced at his notes. "This makes four years in a row."

"Nice," Bob said. "I love a human interest story on a woman in the sports section."

The international desk was following an uprising after yet another questionable election in the Middle East, and the government reporters were still covering the bickering between the senate candidates who were gearing up for the fall race.

Political jokes fired faster than a drunken celebutante's antics circle the blogosphere, and I chuckled at the warring punch lines as my eyes skipped between the faces of my colleagues—my family in Richmond, really. They adopted me the second I'd stepped into the newsroom without a friend in a six-hundred-mile radius, the ink still wet on my degree from Syracuse.

"Bawb." The drawling soprano that belonged to our copy chief came from the doorway as if on cue, chasing away my warm fuzzies and twisting my smile into a reflexive grimace. Every family needs at least one annoying cousin, and Shelby was happy to fill that role for me. "Could you please make sure everyone has their copy in by deadline tonight? My staff would like to leave on time, since it is Friday and all."

It wouldn't be morning if Shelby wasn't trying to crash the news meeting. Maybe I could at least stay far enough under her radar to avoid the trademark backhanded compliments she was so fond of throwing my way, especially in front of Bob. *Or not*, I thought as she swung her phoniest smile on me. *Here it comes. I left out a comma, or a hyphen, or there's an extra space somewhere.*

"Nichelle, what a great job you did on the murder conviction!" Shelby put her hands on her tiny hips and stuck out her inversely-proportionate chest, straining the cotton of her simple cornflower t-shirt. "Though I'm pretty sure the prosecutor was approaching the bench, not the beach."

My temper flared, but before I opened my mouth to tell her that quickly pounding out the day's lead story was different than writing up the garden club meetings she covered before her big move to the copy desk, Bob cleared his throat.

"That one's on me, since I edited that story, Shelby," he said, before he dismissed her with a promise that deadlines would be adhered to by all.

"Sorry, chief." I shrugged at Bob as Shelby's spiky black hair disappeared into the maze of cubicles. "Bench, beach. Potato, tomato."

Bob chuckled before he turned to the features editor. I tuned out what they were talking about. For the most part, I preferred hard news writing to any other kind.

I had grabbed the police report on the first drug dealer murder from my file drawer on my way into the meeting, and I pulled it out and read it again. Noah Leon Smith, age twenty-six, had died the Friday before Memorial Day of a massive head injury inflicted by a .45 caliber bullet. He'd been found sprawled across his own sofa in a neighborhood that saw more than its fair share of violence. The easy assumption was that he'd been killed by another dealer, or maybe a desperate customer. But now did a second victim prove that easy assumption faulty?

My eyes scanned the detective's narrative with that in mind, and four simple lines jumped out at me like a pair of old sneakers at a Manolo collection debut.

Bathroom sink, lower cabinet: four kilograms beige powder, two large plastic bags dried, green leafy substance. Upper cabinet: fifteen large bags containing tablets, various sizes and colors. Lab results: powder: heroin. Green leafy: marijuana. Tablets: Oxycontin, Vicodin, Zoloft, Effexor, Ritalin. Kitchen, freezer compartment: three paper grocery sacks containing a total of $257,400 in large bills.

I'd dismissed it before. Sure, a business rival or a junkie would have stolen the drugs and the money—if they had time, knew where to find it, and weren't already flying on a sample of Noah Smith's pharmaceuticals. But another dealer with holes where he shouldn't have them made me wonder if the crime scenes were similar. If the new victim still had a house full of smack and cash, now that was a story.

My fingers wound around a lock of my hair, my thoughts hijacked by scenes from old Charles Bronson movies as I considered the possibility the shooter was more interested in payback than a payday. That could be a very sexy story.

Bob's endearingly cheesy dismissal snapped me out of my reverie. "All right, folks," he said every morning. "My office is not newsworthy, so get out and go find me something to print."

I paused outside Bob's door, where Grant Parker was chatting with the international editor about the baseball season. I couldn't remember ever having spoken more than a dozen words to Parker, an almost-professional pitcher who was regarded around Richmond as just slightly less than Zeus' son, but the column he'd talked about in the meeting caught my attention.

I cleared my throat lightly and he turned his head, his bright green eyes widening a touch when they met mine. He was tall, but in my heels, I was almost nose-to-nose with him.

"What can I do for you, Miss Clarke?" He flashed the smile that made most women here channel their corset-bound ancestors and swoon—and sold a fair number of newspapers, too.

"I wanted to say thank you," I said, shifting my file folder to the other arm. "For the column you're doing today. My mom is a breast cancer survivor, and it's nice you're writing about it. The sports section isn't usually where you'd look for a breast cancer story. So thanks."

"You're so welcome." His eyes dropped to the square-toed perfection of the shiny blue stilettos I'd shoved my feet into between my early morning body combat class and my mad dash to the meeting, then raised back to mine. "Nice of you to say so. I didn't know you read my column."

"I don't." I smiled. "But I will tomorrow."

"I guess I'd better be on my A game, then." He ran a hand through his already-messy blond hair and grinned at me again.

"I guess you'd better." I took a step backward. "I'm told I can be tough to impress."

"I do love a challenge." He raised his eyebrows and twisted his mouth to one side.

"I bet you do." I shook my head, making a mental note to call my mother as I turned and headed for my ivory cubicle, Parker and his too-perfect smile forgotten. Charles Bronson. Dead guys. The nagging feeling there was something beyond the obvious on the murdered dealers got stronger the more I thought about the scattered details I'd heard on the scanner.

My hand was already on the phone to call Aaron again when I snatched up the pink slip on my desk, but the message was from my friend Jenna. She was probably looking for my input on which restaurants had sufficiently-stocked bars for our every-other-Friday girls' night, which I'd been looking forward to roughly since the opening gavel banged on Monday morning.

Before I could pick up the phone to return her call, my favorite detective returned mine.

"Why didn't the shooter take the drugs and the money in Noah Smith's house? The dead dealer, from last month?" I asked, barely bothering to tell Aaron good morning. "And was the murder scene this morning the same?"

He sighed, and I felt my eyebrows go up. That would be a yes. I fumbled for a pen.

"It was," he said after a pause. "And we're not sure."

"You think it was the same shooter?"

"I don't know. Maybe."

I could almost hear the wheels turning in his head as he weighed what to tell me. The uncomfortably symbiotic relationship between police departments and the media was an odd line to walk: I needed him for stories, and he needed the stories for the key witnesses they sometimes brought in his door. I didn't have to file a Freedom of Information request for every routine report, but Aaron's job was to let out only the information the department wanted to release. Mine was to get my readers as much as I could. Most days, we struck a decent balance.

"We rushed the ballistics, but it still won't be back for another few hours at the earliest," he said. "Maybe not 'til Monday. I don't know how busy they are. You want to come by this afternoon?"

I asked for the first half-hour he had available. "Bob wants something on this for tomorrow, and it is Friday. I'd like to leave at a decent hour one night this week."

"I hear that." Aaron laughed. "We've been busy down here lately, too. Too many bad guys out there. I saw your piece on the conviction in the Barbie and Ken case this morning. Such a sad story."

I murmured agreement as the mention of the capital murder trial I'd spent the whole week chronicling called up unwanted impressions of the poster-sized, high-resolution crime scene photos the prosecutor left on display for the jury the entire day before.

It had been nearly two years since budget cuts (and a little finagling on my part—trial stories were bigger and often juicier than initial crime reports) had added the courthouse to my list of responsibilities as the crime reporter. It meant insane hours, but

I didn't mind, considering almost a third of our news staff had been laid off and I still had a job.

I'd dreamed of being a journalist ever since I could remember. It paired my love of writing with the ability to do good in the world. I hadn't yet developed the intestinal fortitude covering the Richmond PD often required, though, and the trials were worse.

Aaron promised I'd have my interview with him in time to make the first Metro deadline.

Lacking anything pressing to do, I called Jenna back to see if she had her heart set on anything special for our dinner date. I was in the mood for Mexican food. And a margarita. That damned trial had made for a long week.

"Nicey!" Jenna practically shouted the nickname I'd reserved for those closest to me since preschool, when a playmate's speech impediment had dubbed me "nee-see" and my mom had turned it into an endearment.

"Anything good going on in the news today?" My friend's tone came down a few decibels.

"There's seldom anything good in the news I write," I said. "But I think I might have something interesting. And Grant Parker is working on a great story about the women's basketball coach at U of R."

"Oh, yeah? And how is Virginia's hottest sportswriter this morning?"

I laughed. "He seemed all right. And you're still, you know, married."

"Married. Not blind," she said. "Speaking of my darling husband, I told Chad not to wait up, so we have no curfew. Have I told you how glad I am the baby isn't nursing anymore?"

"Just now, or the other fifteen times I've heard that this week?"

"Only fifteen? And I thought I was excited about this."

"I believe the word you're looking for is 'thrilled,'" I said. "Possibly even 'euphoric.'"

She laughed again. "Euphoric. Yes. Has a nice, festive ring to it. Anyway, what do you feel like doing tonight?"

"Margaritas?" I knew Jenna was more interested in libations than food that particular day. "I want Mexican if that's okay with you."

It was. I returned the phone to its cradle after promising to meet her at six-thirty, and went to tell Bob to save me a little space for my drug dealer story. Even he hadn't escaped the cost-cutting, inheriting the metro editor's job duties when she'd quit the year before.

His door was open, as usual, but I tapped the doorframe before I walked in anyway.

"Hey, chief," I said, sticking my head around the corner. "Got a minute?"

"Just one." He turned from his monitor to face me, tucking a pen under the tuft of thinning salt-and-pepper hair that peeked over the top of his left ear. "Anything on your dead guy yet?"

I took the same high-backed orange armchair I'd occupied at the morning meeting. Bob's office décor was heavy on Virginia Tech's sacred maroon and orange, his walls cluttered with a hodgepodge of framed copies of his favorite *Telegraph* photos and our best front pages. I flipped my file open.

"I think I have something coming from the PD this afternoon." My roaming eyes lingered on Bob's Pulitzer, centered on the far wall in an impressive bronze frame, before I focused on him. "Or, I know I have something. I'm waiting to see how good it's going to be. I'm going to headquarters this afternoon to talk to the detective who's working on this morning's murder.

Both murder scenes had hundreds of thousands of dollars in drugs and cash left behind."

He raised his thick white eyebrows. "They think there's a vigilante on Southside?"

"Maybe. That's kind of what I'm thinking, but Aaron hasn't said much. They're waiting for ballistics to come back on the second bullet before they assume it was the same shooter."

"Sounds like you have at least a promise of a decent story there."

"We'll see. A vigilante is definitely sexier than a broke addict looking for a fix. I might only have a short write-up on the murder tonight, depending on when they get the ballistics results, but we'll have it in there tomorrow. And I'll have more if anything comes of it."

"Sounds good, kid."

I would've bristled at the last word from anyone else, but I knew he meant it affectionately, and the feeling was mutual. I didn't make it all the way to my feet before he picked up the newspaper on his desk and spoke again.

"You know, you really have turned into quite a reporter since the first time you walked in here, hugging your little college portfolio, afraid I wouldn't give you a job," he said, his voice a little softer than I was used to hearing it. "I wasn't at all sure you could handle both cops and courts when you came in here begging, either—"

"Hey! I can be accused of doing a lot of things for a story, but I have never begged," I objected.

Bob grinned. "Beg, wheedle; 'bench, beach.' Call it what you will, I know wheedling when I hear it—I was married for almost thirty years. My point is, I made a good call. Both times." He thumped my final report on the Barbie and Ken double homicide case, which was destined to become an overdramatized TV movie. "We sold more newspapers this week than we have in any single week since the end of the '08 election. And what's good for the bean counters is good for the news department nowadays. Good job."

Well, hot damn. To say Bob wasn't terribly forthcoming with compliments would be like saying John Edwards was a little unfaithful to his wife. The journalism equivalent of a decorated war hero, my editor expected excellence from his staff and rarely commented on anything that wasn't a shortfall. My week suddenly seemed less taxing.

Upside down pictures of the victims smiled at me from the newspaper on Bob's desk. It was the sort of story that wasn't much fun to write, but everyone wanted to read—the essence of my love/hate relationship with covering crime. The cops and courts beat was among the best places to begin building a career, though, and I told myself that reporting on crime kept people aware of their safety, and what was going on around them, which was a good thing. It made the parts of the job I found less than fun easier to take, especially with stories like that one.

All the elements that drove producers (I'd counted five at the courthouse the day before) to stalk heartbroken couples who'd just buried their children were there: a crime of passion perpetrated against beautiful people, a lopsided college love triangle, and a conviction that left the last man standing facing Virginia's electric chair, probably before his thirtieth birthday.

The TV folks, ever fond of their graphics-friendly catchphrases, had dubbed the case "the Barbie and Ken murder" in homage to the victims' perfect, flaxen-haired good looks. I had twenty bucks in the courthouse pool those words would appear somewhere in the movie title.

The usual sandpapery scratch returned to Bob's voice as he dropped the paper and smiled at me. "Go get your dead dealer story. And then go have a good weekend. Treat yourself to a new one of those crazy puzzles of yours, or a pair of shoes. I believe you've earned it this week."

Still glowing with pride twenty minutes later, I fit my back against the trunk of an ancient oak tree at a tiny, hidden park on the banks of the James River. It was my preferred place to ponder a story, write, or just sit and think when I had the chance. The water whispering over the rocks and the postcard-perfect downtown skyline were still enough to make me wonder if being on the east coast would ever stop feeling like a vacation to me.

Vacation. The word roused unexpected images from my memory: the beauty of roadside seas of bluebonnets in the spring, succumbing in the summer to flat, oppressive heat that browned the landscape and shimmered off the streets in visible waves by noon. My last trip to Dallas had been more of a vacation than a visit home.

It's probably nice to know where home is, even if you can't go there again, I thought. I supposed my cute little stone craftsman in the Fan—the historic neighborhood named for the way its tree-lined streets fan out from downtown Richmond like the paper and lace creations that once aided Virginia ladies with everything from cooling to courting—was as good a place as any to feel like I didn't belong. But I wished there was someplace I did.

The rootless feeling was unsettling. I shook my head as though I could clear it like an etch-a-sketch and shifted my thoughts back to the comforting familiarity of the dead dealer and the detective I was interviewing in a couple of hours.

Home or not, I would've been on the first plane back to Texas if I had any idea what that particular dead guy was about to get me into. But that's the thing about dead people: they can't warn you to keep your nose out of things that are going to put your ass in danger.

2.

Pieces of the puzzle

"Have a seat." Aaron cleared a stack of paper off a black plastic chair in his cluttered closet of an office. An ever-changing collection of maps, photos, and notes made it impossible to guess the color of the walls, and the small metal desk was buried under piles of manila case file folders. Judging by the detectives' offices, Richmond was a downright dangerous place to live.

His gray upholstered chair rocked backward as he settled into it and looked at me expectantly, the genial manner that made him the department's king of confessions evident in the smile that lit his round face. Aaron's charm was his central talent. He had a real gift for getting people to talk to him, and was nearly as good at keeping his own hand close. Often, reporters left his office with little or nothing, and felt like they'd somehow been done a favor. Not me. Usually, anyway. Aaron and I had a nice little groove where he tried to bullshit me, I called him on it, and then we bantered until I talked him out of some actual information.

"Who is our unfortunate friend who was shot in the head?" I asked.

Aaron flipped a page on a legal pad. "Darryl Anthony Wright, African-American male, age twenty-five. Formerly a resident of cellblock seven at Cold Springs."

I jotted that down and pulled the police report on the Noah Smith murder from my bag.

"Are you guys looking for some kind of Charles Bronson wannabe?"

He pinched the bridge of his nose between his thumb and forefinger and chuckled. When he looked up, his hand slid down his face so his fingers rested over his lips and muffled the first part of his answer.

"Not pulling any punches today, I see. But I think so." His hand dropped to the desk and he shook his head. "I can't say anything for sure without ballistics."

"When is the report supposed to be back?" I smiled as I scrawled his words into my notes. That was easier than I thought.

It took about thirty-five seconds to figure out why.

Ignoring my question, Aaron cocked his head to one side and grinned. "This whole damned thing is about to turn into a giant pain in my ass, isn't it?"

I arched an eyebrow. His Detective Adorable routine was usually reserved for the TV crews. I waited, eyebrow up, for him to go on.

"In a lot of ways, a vigilante is going to be harder to prosecute than just another dealer or a junkie." He widened the baby blues just enough to smooth out the lines that were really the only evidence he was pushing fifty. "The public tends to sympathize with vigilantes. I don't suppose you want to keep that part out of the newspaper for me, do you?"

I felt my mouth drop open, and the other eyebrow shot up. "You've got to be kidding. I talked to my editor about this before I left the office. He'd fire me. Between what I have here," I brandished the report, "and what I heard on the scanner, our copyeditor-cum-aspiring-cops-reporter could figure this one out. I can't sit on it, Aaron. Not unless you're offering me something pretty damned amazing in return."

"What would it take?" He sounded like he meant it.

I sat back in my chair and studied him. Aaron's people skills had contributed to the soft edges on his average frame, making him the obvious choice for department spokesman and thereby trapping him behind a desk in a building with too many Krispy Kreme boxes for too many years. His face looked as puppy-doggish as it ever did, but my inner Lois Lane was hopping up and down, hollering there was something else in play that I didn't see. Why on Earth would he care so much about keeping something that, in the grand scheme, was pretty insignificant to him, out of print?

"Are you serious?"

"Don't I look serious? When you get past the dashingly, heartbreakingly handsome, that is?"

I snorted and shook my head. "How could I have missed it?"

I felt my fingers wind into my hair as I focused on the roof of my house on the aerial map behind his head. A vigilante was a sexier story angle, but not having it didn't preclude me from writing about the murder. And if it turned out the killer was on some sort of *Death Wish* trip, I'd get it at the trial anyway. Letting my hand fall back to my lap, I met Aaron's eyes and nodded.

"All right, detective. I don't know why you care, but I can keep the word 'vigilante' out for now. It's going to cost you, though. One all-access pass, to be used at my discretion, on the story of my choice. No arguments, no negotiations, nothing held back."

He rested his chin on his left fist and twisted his mouth to the side.

"That it?" Aaron was rarely sarcastic, and it sounded funny in his cheerful tenor.

"No."

His eyes widened. "I was kidding!"

He wanted this. And badly. And I didn't like not understanding why.

"I'm not. All access. Story of my choice. To be determined later. And someday, you're going to tell me why you made this deal with me."

"Done. Anything else you need today?"

"Just the report on this morning's murder. I'll leave out the vigilante hoopla, but I have to have something. Bob knows I'm here. Speaking of, how are you going to get around the TV guys?"

Aaron grinned. "Not worried about it. You and Charlie are the only ones who've even asked about the other guy so far. There's a new girl at Channel Ten. Green as a March inchworm. And Kessler over at RVA…" he rolled his eyes and I laughed.

"If the report wasn't on his makeup mirror, he didn't look at it for more than ten seconds," I said. "But what'd you tell Charlie?"

Charlotte Lewis at Channel Four was my biggest competition, usually one step ahead of or behind me on any given story. If she was going with the vigilante, Aaron would just have to get over it.

"Hey, if I can handle you, I can handle Charlie." He laughed. "She left about an hour ago. She didn't ask for nearly as much as you did, but she did make me swear on my grandmama's grave I'd call her if you were running it. So you just made my afternoon a bit more pleasant. Thanks."

"You're welcome. When can I have my report?"

"It's waiting on forensics, but I asked Jerry to bring it in with him. He won't be too much longer."

He didn't get the words out before the door flew open and a disarmingly handsome detective who looked like he was good at hiding from those Krispy Kreme boxes in the gym rushed in. His sheer mass made the small space feel crowded.

"Jerry," Aaron said, "this is Nichelle Clarke from the *Telegraph*. Nichelle, this is Jerry Davis, the detective working on this morning's shooting."

I smiled, extending my hand and shaking his firmly. "Nice to meet you, Jerry."

"Nichelle." Jerry nodded, offering Aaron a folder full of papers and photos. He shot a sidelong glance at me, then focused on Aaron, who was reading something he'd pulled from the file.

An eight-by-ten glossy from the scene lay on top of the stack in the open folder. Darryl Wright, lifeless eyes staring at nothing, was sprawled across his sofa in a relaxed pose that mimicked the first dead dealer. Part of Darryl's baseball cap was gone; the shot had come from the front and blown the hat and its contents across the lamp on the table next to the sofa and the wall behind it. I swallowed a curse, averting my eyes.

"Ballistics worked fast today. Same gun." Aaron dropped the report over the photo and tapped it with his pen, raising his eyes to mine. "So, yes, Nichelle, we can't say for certain that it's the same shooter, but it's looking that way. Jerry can answer some questions for you."

Jerry folded his big frame into the other chair and rested his elbows on his knees, facing me.

"How does that change your investigation?" I asked, pen poised over my notepad. I prided myself on the fact that I'd never once been accused of misquoting anyone, especially since my inexplicable disdain for gadgets extended to tape recorders (and pretty much everything else with a battery that wasn't my laptop or my Blackberry). I'd invented my own form of shorthand after I'd gotten frustrated trying to learn the real thing, but the accuracy of my notes would've made them admissible in court.

"Well, we can combine resources on the cases since we're likely not looking for two different killers," he said. "The more heads you've got looking at it, the better."

"And what are you looking for? You have any working theories?" I asked.

Jerry glanced at Aaron and Aaron shot me a warning glare I pretended to ignore.

"We're not ruling anything out yet. We have officers canvassing the neighborhood, and we're waiting for all the relevant information to come in before we construct likely scenarios."

Wow, that was a long way of saying a fat lot of nothing. I scribbled anyway. I was long-since fluent in cop doubletalk, and figured it would serve me well if I ever made it to covering politics.

"So you've stepped up police presence on Southside?"

"Yes. The number of uniformed officers on the streets of that particular neighborhood has been doubled and will stay that way until this is resolved. We don't want our residents living in fear."

I nodded. It wasn't much, but I had two dead guys killed with the same gun. Not exactly Son of Sam, but worthy of a little space.

"Anything else?" Jerry asked.

I finished my notes and asked for the report, looking for contact information for the victim's next of kin.

"Thanks for your time, guys," I said as I stood up. "Aaron, you'll call me if anything comes up?"

He nodded. "Always a pleasure, Nichelle. Have a good weekend."

Not even my favorite CD could get the dead drug dealers out of my head on the way back to the office. I wondered if the victims knew each other as I sat at a red light, my mind attempting to order the jumble of information by creating a puzzle. A lot of the pieces were blank, though. Two drug dealers, living in the same part of town. It wasn't such a stretch. I reached for my phone, but before I could hit the speed dial for the PD, the startling effect of the beeping horn behind me sent my Blackberry clattering into the fissure between my seat and the console.

Gunning it through the green light I hadn't noticed, I managed to worm my hand through the narrow space to retrieve the phone just as I parked in the office garage, where there was never a signal. I rushed to my cubicle, drummed my fingers on the desk through the hold music, and blurted my question at Aaron as soon as he picked up.

He chuckled. "Nichelle, have you ever thought about a career in law enforcement? Jerry's on his way out there now to look for family members and neighbors, trying to figure out if they might have been friends—or enemies."

I laughed, and not just at the idea of the police uniform shoes. "I don't particularly care for people shooting at me."

He promised to call if Jerry managed to find anything interesting and reminded me about our deal.

"Oh, I won't forget," I said. "Just don't go getting amnesia when it's time for you to make good, okay?"

"I have a mind like a steel trap."

I killed the line momentarily, my laughter fading as I dialed the number on the report for Darryl's mother. I hated bothering people who just lost a loved one. It was the only thing about my job that felt like a burden. I let it ring a dozen times, sighing with equal parts relief and disappointment when I didn't even get a machine.

Turning to the computer, I started typing.

Richmond detectives are investigating the shooting death of a second convicted drug dealer in three weeks on the Southside, stepping up patrols in the area until an arrest is made.

"The number of uniformed officers on the streets of that particular neighborhood has been doubled and will stay that way until this is resolved," RPD Detective Jerry Davis said Friday. "We don't want our residents living in fear."

The latest victim, Darryl Lee Wright, Jr., was found early Friday morning in his home in the 2900 block of Decatur Street.

Wright, 25, was released from Cold Springs Penitentiary 18 months ago after being convicted of possession of a controlled substance with intent to distribute in 2009. Ballistics analysis found that Wright was shot with the same gun as Noah Leon Smith, who was found dead in his home last month.

I sketched out the few details I could and mentioned Wright's family wasn't immediately available for comment. Reading back through it twenty minutes later, I sighed. It would only amount to about an eighth of a page after they added a headline, but it was all I had. I pushed the key to send it to Bob for approval and went hunting for caffeine.

Wrinkling my nose, I strolled into the break room in the back corner of our floor. Proximity to the darkroom made the air in the narrow space perpetually reek of chemicals, even in the age of digital photography. Too many years of the smell seeping into the walls, I guessed. The old darkroom had become the photographers' cave, outfitted with computers and high-definition monitors for photo editing. They didn't seem to mind the smell.

I stared at the soda machine, debating between diet and not, then decided to save the sugar consumption for margarita mix. A third of the bottle was gone in one gulp. I was too thirsty to notice the artificial-sweetener aftertaste.

"Any more dead people pop up in your day?" Grant Parker's voice caught me by surprise and I inhaled part of my second mouthful of soda. Dropping the bottle on the orange laminate next to the sink, I grabbed the edge of the countertop for support while I tried to clear my lungs.

"Are you okay?" Parker stepped forward into my line of sight. "Sorry. I didn't mean to startle you."

I nodded as I coughed up the last of the soda, tears streaming down my face. I took a deep, hitching breath.

"I didn't assume you did," I croaked. "I just have the one corpse today. How about you? That column represent your A game, Mr. Baseball?"

"My A game, yes. That woman is amazing. I hope I did her justice. Your A game is probably in a whole different league, though. I've been reading your stuff on Barbie and Ken all week, and it was good. Really good. No matter what Shelby says. She's just bitter. She's been after the crime desk since the first time she set foot in this building." He shoved his hands into the pockets of his khakis and flashed me the million-dollar grin.

I wiped my cheeks one last time and faced him, vaguely remembering a couple of the sports guys bantering about Parker banging a brunette from copy a while back.

"Well, thank you. And I know. About Shelby, I mean. It took me forever to figure out what she had up her ass when I first came here, but I finally caught on. I've read some of her stuff in the archives. Her writing is solid. Given a chance, she might be good at this—if she could handle the crap and jump through the hoops. But I'd like for her to keep those skills at the copy desk for now." I tapped the bottle on the countertop and smiled. "Keeps me on my A game."

He nodded. "So, just the one dead guy? Is he an interesting dead guy, at least?"

"Yeah, there's something," I said, deciding to skirt the details of the deal I'd made with Aaron just in case Parker and Shelby still had a thing going. It didn't really sound like it, but better safe than sorry. "I'm not exactly sure how interesting it is, but I can do a little digging."

Parker's eyes narrowed as he listened to a synopsis of what I had on the presses that night, which anyone could have pulled off the server and read.

"So all the drugs and money were still in the house?" He laughed, but it wasn't the relaxed sound I'd heard in the meeting that morning. There was an edge to it I couldn't place. "That sounds kinda suspicious to me, but what do I know?"

"How many RBIs did Jeter have last season?" I grinned, pushing the subject away from my story. I wasn't in the habit of sharing the down-and-dirty of what I was working on before I finished an article. People talk, sometimes to the wrong person, even when they don't mean any harm.

"Hey, speaking of Jeter, do you like baseball? The Yankees are in town tonight." Parker's once-pitching-hero status and blinding grin had landed him the cushy star sports columnist gig, and though it didn't require evening hours, he still loved baseball and chose to spend his summer nights at the stadium covering the city's big league team. Bob, not surprisingly, didn't object. "Want to hang out at the ballpark with me and a bunch of over-opinionated sports guys?"

"Tempting." I laughed, not sure if I was lying or not, but relieved to have a better excuse than sitting at home with the dog and one of my ridiculously monochromatic puzzles. "But I have plans. It's girls' night. Margaritas and Mexican food."

He nodded. "Some other time, then."

Not likely, I wanted to say, but I kept my mouth shut. Parker was the kind of guy who dated the kind of girls who starred in beer commercials. And I generally preferred men who spent less time on their hair than I did on mine.

I smiled instead and turned toward the door.

"I need to go see if my story's set before it gets too much later," I said. "Nice talking to you."

"Back at you. Have a good time tonight."

"You, too. I hope they win."

I hurried to Bob's office and tapped on the doorframe.

"Yeah?" He didn't turn from his computer monitor.

"Did you need me to make any changes to my piece before it goes?"

"No. Not a lot of bite, but it looked like you didn't have much to share. What happened to the vigilante?"

I kept my eyes on my shoes. "They didn't have it. Not yet, anyway. Maybe Monday," I said, making a mental note to come up with a plausible story to put him off again before then. "The cops are trying to figure out if these guys were connected. Hopefully they'll get lucky this weekend."

"Just as long as Charlie Lewis doesn't have it Sunday." Bob's eyes never left the screen—I'd bet he didn't even lose his place in the story he was editing. "Have a good weekend, kiddo. See you Monday."

Not even sticking around to chat with Melanie at the city desk as I normally would, I called a goodnight to anyone who happened to be listening as I unplugged my laptop and slid it into my bag. Striding to the elevators, I waved at our features editor, a grandmotherly woman whose home cooked treats could've come straight out of Aunt Bea's kitchen. She carted in batches of various baked and fried goodies at least once a week (twice, if she was stressed or there was an upcoming holiday) and was thereby solely responsible for any widening of my ass that might occasionally occur.

"Have a good one, darlin'." The "g" disappeared into Eunice's native Virginia drawl. "Enjoy your Friday night."

"Friday night, hell, I'm out of here until Monday," I stepped into the elevator with a grin. "See you then."

The promise of a whole weekend with nothing to do was thrilling all by itself. I parked my little red SUV in the Carytown shopping district and melted into the collection of people who made up the city I had come to love in the six years since a stinging rejection from my dream employer brought me south to look for a job.

There were impeccably-dressed mothers pushing babies in hip strollers along the sidewalks, teenagers still high on the excitement of school letting out the week before, and couples walking hand-in-hand looking in the shop windows. The eclectic storefronts beckoned passersby with everything from toys and Christmas decorations to maternity clothes and jewelry.

A cobblestone sidewalk led to the heavy oak door of Pages, so picturesque it could have been conjured from the narrative of a nineteenth-century novel. The shop was housed in an old stone cottage, the door flanked by mosaic stained glass windows half-hidden behind climbing roses and jasmine vines, growing thick in twin shoebox-sized gardens and making the summer air sweeter with their perfume.

I turned the brass knob and shoved the stubborn old door, instantly overtaken by a very different fragrance. The smell of ink and paper and aged leather inside the little shop bordered on intoxicating. There were no maps, no sections, no pretty directional signs. Just tall shelves stretching from wall to wall and floor to ceiling in the small space, cluttered and piled with a fantastic collection of great stories. Jenna was the store's buyer, and she spent hours each day hunting down rare volumes and first editions. Pages was no generic bookstore; it was a book lover's haven.

"Hey." My friend waved from behind a stack of books perched on the sales counter. "You're early! How'd you manage that?"

"There was annoyingly little to be written of the story I spent the whole day chasing. I'll tell you all about it at dinner."

Shoving her reddish-brown curls out of her face, Jenna turned back to the MacBook that was the only evidence of the twenty-first century in the room and scooted her square, blue-rimmed glasses down the bridge of her nose.

At least she'd remembered them. I was convinced Jenna was going to go blind or kill some random blotch that was actually a person with her car, she forgot her glasses so often.

"Dying to hear all about it," she said. "Just let me finish one thing and we'll go."

I nodded and surveyed the nearest shelf, picking up a fat brown hardcover. My eyes widened when I checked the copyright page: MacMillan Books, May 1, 1936. A first edition of *Gone With the Wind.*

"Scarlett O'Hara was not beautiful, but men seldom realized it when caught by her charm as the Tarleton twins were," I recited the first line under my breath as I flipped the book closed and trailed my fingers along the cover, noting the missing dust jacket. But still, an actual first edition. I couldn't believe Jenna didn't tell me she'd found it. *There were only ten thousand of these printed*, I thought as I made a mental note to check the asking price with her. I was no rare books expert, but I knew enough about the one in my hands to land a guess in the ballpark, and that park had expensive seats. Even a thousand dollars—which might be a lowball for this one—was usually way above my price range, given that it was more than my rent. But it was *Gone With the Wind*. Maybe I could survive on Ramen for a few weeks.

I laid it on a high shelf and picked up a thick leather-bound Dickens tome. Shopping at Pages was like perusing some great collector's personal library. Every visit was an experience.

"Almost done," Jenna called, clicking her mouse and twisting up the corners of her lips, which were seldom more than a twitch away from smiling.

I admired the flowing simplicity of the wine-colored linen dress she wore. Like most of her wardrobe, it well suited her true passion: Jenna was a great book-buyer, but she was a better artist. "The bookstore definitely pays better," she said whenever I asked if she thought she'd ever buy the store from its retired owner, "and I love the thrill of the hunt in my job. But I will always be an artist at heart."

I owed her friendship, and by extension my sanity, to the abstract of a mother and child I'd talked her into selling me right off the shop's wall on my second visit. The painting had given us a reason to start talking, and once we had, we'd never stopped. I loved not knowing what I'd find when I popped into the store, and as I built a collection of books rivaled in my heart only by my shoe closet, Jenna and I had gone from casual acquaintances to the best of friends.

By the time her little boy came along the previous spring, I was planning the baby shower and driving her to the hospital when her water broke at a Friday night karaoke experiment (our unscientific method determined that lack of intoxication made singing off-key in front of strangers a lot less fun, and also that drunk people were surprisingly eager to help when you went into labor in a bar, some more appropriately than others). She was my non-newspaper family.

"Ready?" Jenna appeared at my elbow with her straw bag on her shoulder and her keys in her hand.

"Starving," I said, laying the book back on the shelf.

We were quiet for a half-block or so, until we reached the brick sidewalk to an old row house painted bright purple and converted into the city's best Mexican food restaurant.

"You ready to talk about your week yet?" Jenna asked. "You know I get all my thrills vicariously through you."

"My week started and ended with gross crime scene photos. I think that entitles me to at least one margarita, so I guess we'll just have to force ourselves to stay for a while."

"Ah, to not have to be home by the children's bedtime! Leave nothing out."

We followed the hostess up the narrow stairs to a square table covered in brightly-hued paint. The top was lavender and each leg was a different shade of the rainbow.

"Did you have time to actually read the paper today?" I asked, sinking into a ladderback chair just as colorful as the table.

She wiggled one hand back and forth as she popped a blue corn chip into her mouth with the other. "I started your story, but I only got through the part on the front page before I got busy looking through the ads."

Jenna found a lot of the bookstore's inventory at estate sales. She usually spent Fridays combing through the classifieds for the weekend and calling all the ones that mentioned books.

I filled her in on the gory details of the trial as we waited for our drinks. When I got to the part about the murderer confessing to his mom, the color drained from Jenna's face.

"So, this kid really just walked into his mother's kitchen splattered with other people's blood and sat down and told her what he did?" She gaped at me, her hand fluttering to her throat. "As a mother, you want your kids to trust you enough to tell you anything, but…Oh, my God. I can't even imagine."

"I know. That was the most dramatic part of the whole trial for me, when his mother testified. I felt so bad for that poor woman. Here her kid has done this horrible thing and she knows he did it and she kept looking at the victims' families and telling them she was sorry, but you know she still loves her kid and she's worried about what's going to happen to him, too."

"And she probably feels guilty," Jenna said. "I know I would. I'd never stop wondering what I did wrong. How my kid grew up to be the kind of person who could murder someone. It would drive me completely batshit insane."

The first round arrived and we nibbled chips and sipped margaritas (well, I sipped, Jenna gulped) as we studied our menus, the usual hum of other diners' conversations drowned out by the mariachi band that played on Friday nights.

We smiled thank-yous at the striking Hispanic waitress when she dropped off another margarita for Jenna and a glass of iced tea for me. She turned to the next table after she jotted down our order, and I raised my eyebrows at my friend.

"I wonder what it would be like to be one of those women people turn to look at when they walk by?" I asked, my eyes on the girl's bobbing ebony ponytail.

"You're pretty, Nicey." Jenna smiled. "I've never seen anyone with eyes like yours."

Neither had I, and I wasn't fishing for a compliment. I knew my striking violet eyes were my best feature. They always made people think I was lying when I said I wasn't wearing contacts. I also had long legs that were well-shaped by hours at the gym every week, and long, thick brown hair that didn't need much work in the mornings. I wasn't knocking my brand of unobtrusive, B-cup-and-brains beauty, just imagining how the chosen few lived. Maybe it was a reporter's curse. I often mused about what it would be like to be in other people's heads.

"So?" Jenna prodded as I watched the waitress sashay through a hot pink swinging door into the kitchen. She even had the pretty-girl walk. "What else is going on in the seedy criminal world in Richmond?"

The chips and salsa dwindled to crumbs and chunks of onion as I related the story of Darryl Wright and Noah Smith for the third time.

"I think it might be a vigilante," I finished. "Though, the cops wanted that kept quiet badly enough to give me a hell of a favor in trade for not running it tonight."

"My friend, the investigative reporter." Jenna sighed. "My life is so boring."

"Exaggerate much?" I snorted. "Investigative reporters bring down corrupt politicians and bust slimy, thieving CEOs. That's what I want to do when I grow up. I'm afraid I've just been working with cops for so long I'm starting to think like one. I think Aaron was only half-kidding this afternoon when he asked if I had ever considered going into law enforcement."

"Seriously?" It was Jenna's turn to snort. "Cops don't make enough money to keep you in shoes."

"Donald Trump barely makes enough money to keep me in shoes." I smiled, pausing to thank the waitress as she set a sizzling plate of fajitas in front of me, before I finished my thought. "If I paid retail for my shoe collection, I'd have been in bankruptcy court before I got out of college. Thank God for eBay."

I stuck my foot out from under the table and Jenna smiled at my barely-scuffed latest treasure.

"Ooh, pretty," she said. "Manolo?"

I lifted my foot to show off the red sole.

"Ah. That's the other one. Louboutin? I have kids. I have little frame of reference for overpriced, wobbly shoes."

"Louboutin is right, supermom. Less than a hundred dollars, because of a couple of scuff marks and a tiny wine stain that I took off with a Tide stick. I can't believe the number of people who wear these once and get rid of them. This pair was twelve hundred last spring."

Jenna shook her head. "Twelve hundred dollars. For a pair of shoes. If I was going to pay that kind of money for heels, George Clooney had better be in the box with them to give me a pedicure and a long foot massage."

I laughed. "I think George's rates for massage therapy would definitely price me out of those. But I do love my secondhand steals."

"You really have a talent for that. Somewhere, I'm convinced there's a market for it that you're missing."

"Ace reporter, professional bargain hunter." I held my hands up in a pantomime of scales and furrowed my brow. "I think I'll stick with the gig I have for now.

"In other news," I sipped my tea as she flagged the waitress down and ordered another margarita. "It's entirely possible that, at least in the most technical sense of the phrase, Grant Parker asked me out this afternoon."

Jenna's eyes got so big I could see white all the way around the brown.

"What? Where are you going? When?"

"I'm not." I laughed at her horrified expression. "Don't look at me like that. First of all, he's a has-been baseball player, not young Elvis incarnate. I told him thanks for the column he's running tomorrow on the basketball coach who has breast cancer, and I think he was trying to be nice by asking me to go with him to the game tonight. That's work, so it's not an actual date, but it's the closest I've gotten in longer than I care to admit."

"Who gives a rat's patootie?" Jenna slammed her glass down on the table for emphasis. "Going out is going out. You could have a t-shirt that says 'I went out with Grant Parker.'"

"Don't you use your 'mom voice' on me, missy!" I giggled at her chastising tone. "Though, I think you just hit on a viable business idea. There have to be a fair number of women around here who could use such a t-shirt. You could sell them at Pages."

Jenna carried on about how many women would jump at the chance for a date with Parker, and I drifted into my own world. It had been a long time since I'd been on a date with anyone, a fact that listening to witness after witness detail "Barbie and Ken's" undying devotion had brought to the forefront of my thoughts that week.

Someone sexy and exciting, who could hold their own in a conversation and knock me off my feet with a kiss—that's how my internet dating "what are you looking for in a partner?" would read, if I were brave enough to fill one out. I didn't think that was too picky, though all recent evidence said it might just be.

I didn't regret any of the big choices I had made, but my eighteen-year-old self had been so sure of her "where do you see yourself in ten years?" list: finish college, embark on a fabulous career as a political reporter for the *Washington Post*, and fall madly in love. And even though I was content most of the time, twenty-nine was just around the bend, and I couldn't help feeling I had fallen short of what that girl wanted her life to be.

I stared at a bright red tile in the middle of the sun mosaic on the far wall. Almost like I was back there, I saw Kyle's soft smile as I leaned my head on his shoulder in the front seat of my old Mustang, heard the huskiness that always came into his voice when he told me he loved me.

For a split second, it seemed like yesterday that he was the most important thing in my life. I'd nearly lost myself to the point of giving up on Syracuse and my dreams of the *Post*, which had scared me into a convent-like college existence. He'd walked away when I'd refused to stay, and I still couldn't bring myself to look him up on Facebook. Maybe some people only get to fall madly in love once.

Whether she was a tiny bit psychic or I was just easy to read, Jenna could almost always tell what I was thinking. She patted my hand, drawing me back to the bustle of the restaurant with a lopsided grin.

"Honey, you have yet to find the great love of your life. Kyle was a high school boy. You need to fall in love with a man."

I recognized her I-know-more-about-this-because-I'm-older-than-you voice and smiled. She thought being thirty-four made her positively wizened.

"I shudder to think what my life would be like if I had married the guy I was dating at eighteen," she said. "Last time I saw him he was standing on the side of I-64 wearing an orange vest and holding a 'stop ahead' sign. You're still looking for the right one. He's out there."

She spent two hours getting reacquainted with Jose Cuervo and helping me forget my lovelorn woes, her ability to make me laugh increasing in direct proportion to her level of intoxication.

"So, the light is green, but there's a big truck in front of us that's slow getting moving," Jenna said, her words already garbled by laughter as she started a new story. "I didn't say a word. I was listening to the radio, and all of a sudden from the backseat, I hear Gabby: 'It's the long vertical pedal on the right! What, are you waiting for the light to get greener? Some of us have places to go!' I thought I was going to wreck my car I was laughing so hard. Is that my kid, or what?"

I gasped for air and wiped at the tears streaming from my eyes. "Undeniably. And I'm going to pee my pants if you don't stop making me laugh."

Jenna giggled again. "I'm having a great time, hon. I love going out with you. You laugh at my stories, you love my kids, you drive me home—you rock!"

"I do, huh? Okay. I think you're sufficiently blitzed." I savored the last bite of a flaky white chocolate and caramel empanada. "I have done my job. We can't end the evening with a disappointed Chad."

I drained my tea glass for the sixth time and glanced around. The band had called it a night and the place was practically empty, the cartoon-colored walls not as bright in the soft yellow glow from the overhead bulbs. I pulled my phone out of my purse to check the time and frowned. It was coming up on midnight, and I'd missed two calls in the last hour.

I held up my index finger as I pressed the button to check my voicemail, skipping through a week's worth of messages, hunting for the most recent ones. I never listened to them unless I was looking for something specific, which had long-ago led Bob to order the receptionists to leave me notes.

"Someone tried to call me," I murmured as I finally got through the three from that afternoon. "Just a second."

Aaron White's voice froze me in my chair for an instant, and I listened to him make a crack about a free favor before I jumped to my feet, looking around for the waitress and reaching for my keys.

"What's going on?" Jenna lifted her glass again.

"I have to go back to work, and I guess you're coming with me." My words were clipped as I silently cursed the mariachis for drowning out the phone's musical tinkling, and myself for leaving my scanner in the car. "I have an accident to cover. Apparently there was a boat crash about an hour ago."

3.

Boats and ballplayers and brides, oh my

Jenna was still giggling twenty minutes later when we climbed out of the car by the river side a few miles south of the city. She was positively giddy from being forced to accompany me to an accident scene. Well that, and tequila.

I tried to look severe as I ordered her to do her best to appear sober and avoid making me laugh when I was supposed be working, but her twinkling eyes and eager grin reminded me of a little kid with a Toys "R" Us gift card, and it was damn near impossible to maintain decorum while I was looking at that.

"Yes, ma'am." she slurred, proving my point as she offered me a weak salute and then winced when I giggled. "Oops. Sorry. I'll try to be less funny. Damn you, Jack Daniels."

"You were drinking margaritas, honey. Wrong label." I chuckled as I tucked her arm into mine so at least she wouldn't fall. I knew I had no chance of getting her to stay in the car, not in her condition.

All the emergency vehicles had made it difficult to get the car within field-goal range of the crash site, and the flashing red and blue lights made the natural beauty of the riverbank unnaturally eerie. The shredded boats still burning on the black water in the distance didn't look promising for a happy ending.

I canvassed the emergency personnel for Aaron, but it was hard to even distinguish the policemen from the firefighters in the strange half-darkness so far from the accident scene.

The blond head bobbing just above most of the crowd, however, I knew instantly.

"It can't be," I muttered, even as I recognized the butter-colored polo I'd seen twice that day already.

"There you are!" Parker said when I caught up to him. "This is a madhouse. How do you ever get any work done at one of these things?"

"Hey, Parker." I stared, still unable to come up with a single logical reason for his presence. "I've never been to anything like this before. Boats don't usually blow up on the James. But I'm about to find a cop and see what's going on. Forgive my manners, but what are you doing here?"

"I know a little about what happened." He grimaced. "The coach got a call during my interview after the Generals game. The little speedboat belonged to Nate DeLuca, one of our pitchers. I don't know the details, but it hit a Richmond PD boat. Like you said, there was an explosion. The fire department is searching the river and the banks on both sides, but they don't think anyone survived. After I called in my story, I came to see for myself what happened to DeLuca. I'm going to write a feature on him for Sunday. He should've been at the ballpark tonight, but he had friends in town, and since he wasn't pitching, the coach gave him the night off."

"Sweet cartwheeling Jesus. Let's go see what else we can find out," I said. "Kiss your Saturday goodbye, Mr. Columnist. You're going to be at the office tomorrow." And so was I. So much for my leisurely weekend.

I turned to dive back into the crowd in search of Aaron and mid-whirl, I noticed Jenna standing there, still and surprised. Her eyes were doing that white-all-around thing again.

"People died out there?" she squeaked.

I patted her hand. "You want to go back to the car?"

"No." She squared her small shoulders and gripped my arm a little tighter. "I want to go to work with you."

I turned back to Parker. "Grant Parker, this is my friend Jenna Rowe. This wreck crashed girls' night. She drank too much tequila, but she's very excited to see the glamorous world of journalism up close."

"The best way to do that is after too much tequila," he said. "Nice to meet you, Jenna."

The thin fingers around my arm dug in tighter, and I didn't think their owner was breathing. I elbowed her lightly in the ribs, rolling my eyes. Her forceful exhale sounded like a sigh as she gazed at Parker.

"I really love your column," she lied. Jenna hated sports in any incarnation. She was already bemoaning the start of Gabby's soccer season, and it was three months away.

"Thank you." He smiled.

We moved through the crowd as a unit until I saw a familiar face.

"Mike!" I waved at Sergeant Sorrel from the narcotics unit.

"Nichelle," he said, turning from the water to face me when I stopped next to him. "Where've you been? You missed the TV crews. They all left about twenty minutes ago."

Damn. Charlie no doubt drank her margaritas with her scanner in her lap.

"I was out and I missed the call, but got down here as quick as I could. I didn't even take my poor friend Jenna home first."

Mike smiled at Jenna and held out his hand. "I guess you never know how your Friday night is going to end up when you're friends with Nichelle, huh?"

I started to introduce Parker, but quickly learned women weren't alone in their rambling worship of him.

"Hey! You're Grant Parker!" Mike said before I got a word out. "I watched you play ball when you were in college here, man. You had some arm. Too bad about all that, I guess—but I read your column. I'm a big fan."

Parker smiled and shook Mike's hand. "Thanks. I appreciate that."

I stared at Mike, and then at Parker. Parker had fans? I was impressed. And a little jealous.

"I guess you heard a baseball player was driving the little boat, huh?" Mike asked Parker.

Parker nodded, but I jumped in before he could say anything, impatient to get to the bottom of at least one story that day.

"Aaron's here, so he's taking point on this, right?" I asked.

"I saw him down closer to the crash site a little while ago," Mike said. "Let me see where he went."

He called Aaron on the police radio attached to his shoulder, and we all heard Aaron say he was about fifty yards downstream from us.

With Jenna and Parker in tow, I headed down the bank. It was tricky, navigating over the slimy rocks in the middle of the night. We'd had a wet spring, and the river had swollen almost to flood level, leaving the rocks along the banks coated with a layer of slippery goo once the water began receding. It was still fuller than normal and moving fast, judging by the bubbly whooshing that underscored the sounds around us. I wished I'd worn more practical shoes.

Aaron looked up at me with a grim half-smile when I found him. "Nichelle. Nice night to be out on the river. I can't believe this. Such a fucking waste."

"What happened?" I asked.

"Probably be several days, and even then we won't have the whole story because there were no survivors." Aaron talked, I scribbled. "It looks like the ballplayer and his buddies were going too fast, and when they came around that bend, they didn't have time to avoid our boys.

"The little speedboat came apart around the hull of the PD vessel," he continued. "Their gas lines and tank also shredded, and the sparks set it off, so our guys ended up basically wrapped inside the explosion."

Jenna whimpered behind me and I closed my eyes, as if that could somehow banish the image he just put into my head.

"Good God, Aaron."

When I had my wits about me again I returned to my questions. "Who was it? On the police vessel, I mean?"

"Couple of rookies." He shook his head. "Both under twenty-five, not too long out of the academy. This kind of shit makes me sick. Senseless."

I had never seen Aaron so upset. Not often at a loss for words, I laid a hand on his arm. He stared at the flames as he spoke. "I know. It's all part of the job, right?"

"I don't like it, either," I said, remembering some of the stories that had made me feel as bad as he looked. "What were they doing way out here? Isn't that the big patrol boat? Did somebody drown?"

"Yes, it is," he said, his shaking head seeming to contradict the affirmative answer at first. "And no, no one drowned. At least, not that we got a call about. I'm not sure what they were doing, and we still haven't been able to get the commander of the river unit on the phone. He's going to have a very unpleasant day tomorrow."

I nodded, still writing. "I'm going to need the names and records of the officers who were killed, and contact info for the next of kin. I'm sure Parker here will have a piece on the baseball player."

Aaron looked over my shoulder.

"Hey! Grant Parker!" Aaron's dark mood appeared at least partially forgotten.

Stepping forward, Parker shook Aaron's hand. Aaron gushed about Parker's golden arm, just like Mike had.

I waited for a break in the Parker-adulation, and when Aaron started stumbling around the inevitable apology for the way Parker's pitching career had ended, I took the opportunity to steer the conversation back to the crash. "When can I have the accident report?"

"We should have something Monday," Aaron said. "Probably not any earlier, though."

I made a face. Monday didn't do me much good when I wanted the story for Sunday's early edition.

He walked away after I thanked him, both for the phone call and the interview, and I tried to stand taller in my ridiculously unsuitable shoes, scanning the rest of the crowd for another familiar face.

Jenna was still wobbly and still silently hanging on my arm, and my teetering attempt to see better was all it took to throw her off balance. She probably would have ended up with a broken ankle if Parker hadn't reached for us, his hand catching my elbow as I started to fall with her. Leaning on him, I grabbed Jenna's left arm with both hands and pulled. She weighed next to nothing, and my grip was enough to help her get her feet back under her.

"Nothing like nearly busting your ass on a big rock to kill a buzz," she said.

I twisted my other hand around and grabbed Parker's forearm, jerking my heel out of a crevice between two rocks. I imagined the blue stilettos I'd so painstakingly cleaned wouldn't look quite as fabulous after hiking along the waterfront.

"Thanks." I smiled at Parker as I regained my balance and let go. "Turns out my shoes aren't suited for traipsing around slimy rocks in the dark."

"Shoes like that are only suited for one thing: making a woman's calves look good," he said, the grin that garnered thousands of readers three mornings a week making his eyes crinkle at the corners. "That's what my mom always says, anyway. Were you looking for someone? Before, I mean. I am a little taller than you. Maybe I can help."

"Oh, I…no one in particular. I was just checking to see if there was anyone else here I wanted to talk to."

He nodded, stepping up onto a bigger stone and surveying the riverbank himself. The rocky shoreline dissolved into overgrown grass, and the grass gave way to mammoth trees, their hulking outlines creeping right up to the water's edge a few hundred yards downstream.

"Hey." Parker stepped down and pointed through the crowd. "That's Katie DeLuca. She is—was—Nate's new wife. They got married in March."

I followed his gaze to a striking young blond woman standing near the crash site with two uniformed officers and an older man in a Richmond Generals baseball cap. She nodded at the officers as they talked and gestured toward the river, her face frozen in a mask of horror.

We picked our way toward her and as we got closer, I could see the tears streaming down her face. The patrolmen walked away, deep in conversation themselves, before we reached the little huddle.

"I hate this part of my job," I grumbled, my stomach lurching as my foot slipped a fraction of an inch on another rock. "I can get on a tight-lipped cop like a duck on a June bug, but just exactly what are we supposed to say to this woman who went from star pitcher's bride to twenty-something widow in the past hour?"

"Beats the hell out of me," Parker said. "This is your gig. I've met her a few times. You want me to try first?"

I started to say no, but a closer look at the young woman made me think twice. Maybe a familiar face would be a good thing, for her and me both.

Jenna bumped into me when I stopped short, motioning Parker ahead of me as we approached Katie. *She's probably not even as old as I am*, I thought. Parker nodded at the man who had his arm around Katie's waist and I thought I recognized him from the sports section as the Generals' head coach.

"Katie?" Parker's voice was low and smooth; soothing. "I'm Grant Parker. We met at the team's playoff celebration last fall. Do you remember me?"

Katie looked lost. She tilted her face up, gazing at Parker like he might tell her the way out of this nightmare.

"Aren't you from the newspaper?" she asked.

"Yes, I work at the *Telegraph*," he said.

It put me in mind of the way you would talk to a frightened child, surprising coming out of Parker. Ultra-confident and a little smartassed is how I'd describe his normal conversational tone. I stepped forward so she could see me, and Parker continued seamlessly into an introduction.

"This is Nichelle Clarke. She works with me at the paper. We're handling the coverage of the accident tonight."

Katie furrowed her brow as if she didn't quite understand why he was telling her that. Her eyes were red and swollen from crying, and flicked from one group of people to another with almost manic speed, as if searching the riverfront for something, anything.

We watched for a long minute, but she gave no indication she wanted to talk.

"Can you get me a phone number where I can reach her tomorrow, Bill?" Parker asked finally, exchanging a sad look with the coach over Katie's head.

I might have protested under more ordinary circumstances, but it would've taken a meat cleaver to hack through the raw emotion cloaking Katie DeLuca. Maybe she'd be up to talking later, maybe not. That was more important for Parker's human interest piece than it was for my accident coverage, anyway.

Katie's eyes lit on the wreckage, and sorrow overran her silent stare. She pulled in ragged breaths that issued back anguished sobs I wouldn't soon forget.

"Nate!" she screamed, then crumpled to the ground, reaching toward the flames that still danced on the water.

Parker and Coach Bill tried to pull her up, and I was sure the rocks were slicing into her bare knees, but she just sagged when they tried to lift her and they let go. My hand clapped over my mouth and I felt tears well up in my own eyes as a lump blocked off my throat. I had never seen anyone in such agony.

"No," she moaned between sobs, her head tossing back and forth hard enough to shake her whole torso. "Not Nate. No. We were going to spend our whole lives together. He's not dead. He's not."

All right, dammit. I couldn't lift her, but Parker's hours in the gym ought to be good for something besides making the interns giggle and blush.

Elbowing him none-too-gently in the ribs, I swallowed my tears and balanced—or tried to—on my tiptoes to get my lips close to his ear. "Do something. She's not in any shape for any of this. Get her out of here."

Parker nodded, concern plain on his face as he watched Katie drop her blond head to her knees. He knelt next to her and laid a hand on her back. "Katie? You can't do anything out here, honey, and you're hurting yourself on the rocks. Let me take you to your car and Bill will drive you home."

"Nate," she dissolved into a fresh round of sobs.

"I know. I'm so sorry." Parker scooped her into his arms and looked at Bill for direction.

I gasped when Parker stood up. The blood streaming down Katie's shins testified her legs had indeed been mangled. She didn't seem to notice.

The coach pointed in the general direction of the gravel road, and Parker walked that way, Nate DeLuca's widow cradled against his chest.

Jenna pulled on my arm and I turned. She looked like someone had backhanded her. So much for Mr. Cuervo.

"That was horrible," she said.

I sighed. "She didn't ask to be newsworthy tonight. She'd much rather have her husband walking in their front door right now telling her about his boys' night. And no matter what kind of story we're doing about the victim, I can never quite get past feeling like an ass when I ask the family to talk to me."

"That's officially the uncool part of your job. I couldn't do it."

"You think you've seen enough now?" I slung my arm around her shoulders. "I'm not going to get much more tonight. I can take you home and call Aaron for an update in the morning when I get to the office."

She nodded, and we turned toward my car and ran into Parker. His face was pained. This was pretty far from the kind of story he usually worked on.

"Bill's taking her to her mother's house after the fire department finishes patching up her legs," he told us, gesturing behind him to a red BMW coupe where Katie was slumped in the passenger seat, a crouching paramedic tending to her wounds. "Thank God her parents live around here. I didn't really want to think about her going home alone tonight."

"You're a good man, Charlie Brown." I nodded sympathetically. "That was nice, what you did for her."

"What I am is out of my element. And I have to say I much prefer talking to my players and covering my games and writing my column to moving in your world. This shit is depressing."

I laughed. "I guess to most people it would seem that way. There are accidents and murders and people dying every day. Is it terrible that I'm pretty happy most of the time?"

"On the contrary, I'd say it's admirable," he said.

"I'm going to take Jenna home now. Her girls' night out has become a little more than she bargained for, I think."

"I think I'm gonna go home and try not to have nightmares," he said. "I want that column in on Sunday, though, so I guess I'll see you at the office tomorrow?"

"You'll like it," I said. "It's quiet on Saturday."

He moved off through the still-bustling crime scene with the unconscious grace of the professional athlete he should have been. I watched him go, impressed by the way he'd dealt with Katie and wondering for a second if it was sad for him, writing about people who did what he'd always dreamed of doing.

I helped Jenna into the car and then climbed in myself and started the engine.

"Sorry about all that," I said.

"Don't apologize. I got to go to work with you. And I got to meet Grant Parker. He's so gorgeous. And he seems nice. Do you think you should—"

"Don't start," I interrupted. "What would I even talk to Grant Parker about? I like baseball enough, but that will only take a relationship so far."

"But —"

"Jenna, seriously. I never said a dozen words to the man before today, and I'm sure I won't say a dozen words to him in the next five years, either. I'm glad you thought it was fun to meet him, but leave it alone. I'm not some twit who's going to go chasing off after biceps and a killer smile."

She opened her mouth and sat there for a split second, then closed it again. "Whatever."

I stayed quiet, running back through the interviews I'd gotten at the accident scene and focusing on the long list of phone calls I needed to make the next morning. The silence wasn't uncomfortable, lingering until I slowed the car to a stop in front of a lovely white colonial nestled in a wooded suburban neighborhood with great schools.

"We'll do it better next time," I said as she hopped out of the car.

"I had fun," she called over her shoulder as she walked a pretty straight line up her sidewalk. "At dinner, anyway. Really. Thanks for a great girls' night. Chad will be disappointed I'm not still blitzed, but he'll live."

"Next time," I repeated, inching the car away from the curb. "I promise to return you suitably intoxicated."

The porch light flickered on automatically when I pulled into my driveway. Drained, I dropped my keys on the counter and grabbed a tall glass from the overhead cabinet, pushing the door shut with enough force to make it stick even though several layers of paint made it difficult.

I gulped the lukewarm tap water and set the glass in the farmhouse sink. Yawning, I untied the bow on my hip and tugged my wrap shirt off as I walked through the house, pausing at the archway to the living room.

"Sorry, girl," I told my tiny Pomeranian, patting her head. "It looks like you're going to be a bachelorette again this weekend." Unless Jenna wanted a playmate for the little ones. I brightened at the possibility.

"You want to see Gabby?" Darcy hopped in a circle and barked. Jenna's daughter was a tireless fetch partner.

I shuffled to the bathroom and scrubbed my face, pulling on boxer shorts and a tank before I shut off the lights. The imposing cherry four-poster that dominated the floor space in my bedroom beckoned with mounds of down pillows wrapped in lilac silk and a sage green duvet so soft it could make a cloud jealous.

It was coming up on three, according to the glowing numbers on my alarm clock. Good Lord. I bet the White House Press Corps gets to go to bed at a decent hour.

I flipped onto my stomach and snuggled deeper into my pillows, the backs of my eyelids playing a montage of Darryl Wright's blown-out baseball cap, Katie's grief-stricken stare, and the burning river. It had been a long day, and I had a feeling there was a longer one coming. I slowed my breathing, dreading the nightmares that often came with covering tragedies. But I was so tired, I didn't even dream.

4.

Curiouser

By the time I made it to the office Saturday, I'd nearly mowed down an unfortunate cyclist who'd thought better of crossing the street just as I'd careened around a corner with my passenger side tires off the ground. Minutes later, I barreled through the half-open elevator doors to the newsroom, and some surprisingly sharp reflexes were the only thing that saved Bob from getting better acquainted with the tacky seventies carpet.

I stopped so suddenly I dropped my bag, and he dodged to one side and waited until I had collected everything before he looked pointedly at the big silver and glass clock on the wall between the elevators.

"Good morning, sunshine," he said. "Sleep well?"

"Chief! I didn't think anything short of another Kennedy getting shot would get you in here on a Saturday." Shit. If memory served, I'd heard the last time my boss came to work on a Saturday was when the space shuttle Columbia came apart in the skies over Texas in 2003. "I'm sorry I'm late. I didn't set the alarm. I can't believe I overslept."

"You're behind on the biggest story of the year," he said, his eyes disappointed. "You've got five dead people, two cops and a ballplayer among them, and an explosion half the city either heard or saw last night. Charlie had four and a half minutes on the early show, and she's done two newsbreaks since. The last one said something about the FBI being out there this morning."

Damn, damn, damndamndamn. And after all the nice things he said to me the day before. Bob was undeniably the father figure in my little pseudo-family in Virginia—the closest thing I ever had to a father, period, when you got right down to it—and I didn't want to let him down.

"I really am sorry, chief. I'll get it. They can put it on the web as soon as I'm done, and I'll find you something she hasn't had for tomorrow. Everyone was gone by the time I got Aaron's message last night or I'd have sent something in from the scene. You'll have it by four, I swear."

"Really?" Shelby's drawl came from behind my left shoulder.

And the hits just keep on coming.

"This is huge, from what I've been watching on Channel Four this morning. Charlie's got a good head start on us." Shelby kept her eyes on Bob as she talked. "Are you really going to have it ready in just a few hours? Maybe I could help you. I've been here since before eight, and today is my day off."

"I think I can handle it, but, wow, it's so nice of you to come by on your day off." I fixed my best attempt at a put-upon smile on Shelby and imitated her syrupy tone. "I would have been here early, too, but I was working until three o'clock this morning, covering an accident. Those unpredictable hours are the most inconvenient thing about reporting. Though I don't suppose the garden club ever had a midnight meeting."

Bob cleared his throat. "Don't go home, Shelby," he said, cutting a glance at me. "If Nichelle can't get it together in time, we may need you to pitch in. Nice of you to offer."

I stared at him. Over. My. Cold. Corpse.

Shelby assured Bob she'd be available and tossed a smirk at me before she sashayed off.

"Nothing personal, kid. Just the wrong day for you to sleep in," Bob said. "We have to have it nailed down. It's leading page one."

"A lesser reporter might feel pressured by that," I said. "I was just on my way to pester Aaron."

"Don't let me keep you," he said. "I'm looking forward to reading."

"You're staying all day?"

"This is a big story. Call me a micro-manager, but I'm going to see it before it goes. The TV has been all over it since early this morning, and I want to make sure that between your piece and Parker's piece, we have them outdone." Bob winked. "He has a good start on that. There have been reporters camped out at the pitcher's family's houses all day today, but no one's said a word to any of them. Somehow, he's on his way to interview both the guy's parents and his in-laws. I love it."

Scooped on a news story by Mr. Baseball? And Shelby Taylor on standby to help me get my story out? Oh, yeah. This was shaping up to be a helluva day.

"Find me something great, Nicey. Anything Charlie hasn't had," Bob patted my shoulder as he walked back toward his office. "You outdid yourself all week. But Ken and Barbie have gone out with the recycling."

"Twenty column inches of greatness, coming up." I spun on my heel and hurried to my desk, grabbing a pen and the phone before I even sat down.

Aaron's uncharacteristic grouchiness told me his day wasn't going any better than mine was.

"I'm tired of talking to reporters about the accident last night," he said when I asked how he was. "I wish I was out on my boat with a beer and a fishing pole. No offense."

"None taken. I don't exactly want to be here, either. Has the daylight given you guys anything new? I saw you told Charlie they sent a unit from Quantico." My inner Lois Lane did like the sound of that.

"I told Charlie no such thing," Aaron said. "She saw them in their damned logo-emblazoned hats and windbreakers and probably frigging boxers, out there picking through every black rock lining the shore of the James."

Damn. She'd been back to the scene. The only thing keeping me from pulling my hair out was the knowledge that FBI agents are about as welcoming of TV cameras as a PETA convention would be of Michael Vick.

"Why are they here?"

"Something about the police vessel that was involved." He sounded huffy. "Like they think we did something wrong. Not that they've turned up anything. Their official report won't be ready for weeks, probably, but they're sticking with the scenario I gave you last night. Man, those guys are a pain in the ass, but don't you dare quote me on that!"

"I wouldn't." I laughed. "But why don't you tell me how you really feel, detective?"

"You have no idea."

"Do you have an official statement on their involvement?"

"You'd have to call their field office to get that. All I can tell you is they have people working at the scene."

"Is there any chance the driver of DeLuca's boat was under the influence?"

"Unfortunately, we won't ever know that." Aaron's tone turned somber. "There wasn't enough left of any of the victims to check."

I swallowed hard, closing my eyes. "Oh," was all I said.

"Anything else?" he asked.

"I need the service records and background on the officers who were killed," I said. "Also contact information for the next of kin, and who will tell me what they were doing out there."

"If you check your fax machine, you will find you already have what I can give you from their personnel files and the families' contact information," he said. "You're welcome. And call Commander Owen Jones over at the river unit. When I talked to him this morning, he was pretty shaken up, but he should be able to give you what you need."

"Thanks, Aaron. What would I do without you?"

"Have a lot less fun at work? I hope you at least get tomorrow off."

"I may. You going fishing?"

"Absolutely. I've had as much of this place as I can stand for one week."

I grabbed the faxes and dialed Commander Jones as I stared at the grainy photos of the dead officers, Alex Roberts and Brian Freeman. I wondered what they had been doing when the other boat hit them. Did they see it coming?

I introduced myself when Jones picked up. "Is this a good time to ask you about the accident on the river last night?"

"As good a time as any," he said. "I think I'm going to be busy with this mess for a while."

"Let's start with the obvious: what were they doing?"

"That's the first question I've gotten from everyone today, and it's one I don't have an answer for. I didn't give those orders, so I don't know."

"Oh." I hadn't seen that coming. "Where did their orders come from, then? Is there someone else I can talk to?"

"I'm not really sure, to tell you the truth. I can't find anything in the system about why they were out there. Orders for use of the aquatic fleet would go through me or someone above me. If it came from over my head, you need to talk to the big brass downtown, but I would be very surprised to find any of them in the office today, and I haven't even had time to turn around twice because of all the media calls this morning."

Nothing like another story with more holes than the back nine at Jefferson Country Club. Especially when Bob was hanging around just to read my stuff. Dammit. I scribbled down Jones' comments, such that they were.

I asked Jones about date of the last fatality accident in his unit. He told me there hadn't ever been another one, and the only other accident of any kind involving a police boat had been in 1967.

"How long had Roberts and Freeman been with your unit?" I asked.

"They weren't part of my unit, strictly speaking. They both went through the training for this unit, but neither requested a transfer over here. I can't tell you how much wish I had more answers, Miss Clarke, but I'm figuring this out as I go."

Thanking him, I tried to piece it together in my head as I put the phone down. What the hell? I stared at the photo of Jenna's kids that sat on my desk without really seeing it. Did they take the boat for a joyride?

With a new picture of the rookie cops out fishing, maybe even drinking, I reached for the phone again. Charlie hadn't come anywhere close to that, but someone else—someone important—had to say it. How could I get ahold of the command staff on a Saturday?

I drummed my fingers on the handset, one of the little pink message slips that covered the surface of my banged-up desk catching my eye.

Yes!

I dug first through the pile closest to me, then two others, before I hit pay dirt. Three weeks before, I'd interviewed the deputy chief of police about the success of the anti-bullying program he started in the city's public schools. And he'd left me a message to call him. On his cell phone.

That'd teach Bob to pick on me for having a desk that looked like an episode of *Hoarders.* If I succeeded in doing anything but pissing Dave Lowe off by calling him on a Saturday, of course.

I turned back to the file Aaron had faxed me before I picked up the phone to call Lowe.

According to their service records, Roberts and Freeman had been exemplary officers. No reprimands, no poor reviews, no trouble. Was it possible these two guys stole a city-owned boat?

I grabbed a pen and settled the handset on my shoulder, determined to find out.

Lowe sounded mildly irritated when I identified myself, but he didn't hang up on me, so I plunged into my questions before he could think to. My sails depleted as quickly as they'd filled when he explained he wasn't sure how much help he could be if I'd already talked to Jones.

"Commander Jones said he hadn't ordered the officers to be out on the boat," I told him. "He also said any orders that didn't come from him would have to come from a member of the command staff. Do you know who sent them out there and what they were supposed to be doing?"

He was silent for so long, I wondered if he had hung up.

I waited.

Still nothing.

"Chief, are you there?" I asked finally.

"I'm here." There was something in his tone I couldn't read. "I'm not in Richmond at the moment, and I've mostly been following Channel Four's coverage on my cell phone, to tell you the truth."

My jaw clenched so abruptly my teeth clacked. The deputy chief of police was getting his news about dead officers from Charlie? Ouch.

"I assumed the orders had been given by Commander Jones," he said slowly. "I can't fathom who or what put those boys on the river if they weren't doing something for Jones."

Scooping Charlie looked more improbable with each phone call, but the thought of Bob sending Shelby in as reinforcement was enough to make me nauseous, and I refused to let Parker best me on an accident story. I opened my mouth to thank Lowe and go back to the drawing board, but he spoke again before I could.

"You know, Miss Clarke, I've been meaning to call and tell you how much I appreciated the piece you did on my program," he said. "That project is very dear to my heart. I'll tell you what, I'm going to make a couple of calls and see if I can figure out what the hell's going on up there. If I hit on anything, I'll give you a call back. What's the best number to reach you?"

The heavens might as well have opened to a choir of angels.

I thanked him and cradled the phone in a daze. My weekend just kept getting more curious. First, it was matching drug dealer slayings that likely had nothing to do with fat stacks of drug money. Then, two dead cops on a boat they'd ostensibly had no reason to have out.

I threw my pen down and stomped in the direction of the break room, mulling over the scant facts I had.

"I thought you were out of here until Monday?" Eunice, our grandmotherly features editor, called from behind me.

I turned, waiting for her to catch up. A helicopter crash in Iraq during the first Bush administration had left our former war correspondent with a bad hip, a new job at the features desk, and plenty of time for cooking.

"I thought I was, too." My eyes flicked to the clock between the elevators, which practically chuckled at me that it was five after one.

"Unfortunately, tragedies don't care about weekends." I waved a hand toward the TV, where Charlie clucked about Nate DeLuca's boat and its maximum speed capability "I was late this morning, and it's already after one o'clock. I'm never going to make deadline. Especially without caffeine."

"You better grab some and get moving." Eunice patted my shoulder and stepped into the elevator. "Good luck, sugar."

Walking back to my desk with a half-empty Coke bottle, I found renewed determination. There was someone, somewhere, who knew what the hell was going on. I just needed to find them. In the next two hours and ten minutes.

"Damn." My eyes fell on the pink message slip on my laptop. Of course, I'd missed the call from Lowe. Under it, I found a post-it from which I learned two things: the first was that Parker had God-awful handwriting, which I had to decipher to get to the second: he was back and would email me his story when it was done in case he had info I wanted.

Well, at least he hadn't screwed up. The *Telegraph* would have something on Sunday no one else did, and in the age of digital information, that was damned hard to do. But my ego was getting more bruised by the second.

I snatched a blue Bic out of my pen cup and dialed Lowe.

"I'm not sure how much good my gratitude is going to do you today," he said. "I can't find anyone who knows diddly about Roberts and Freeman being on that boat last night. But I can tell you I ordered internal affairs to open a file. No one knows that but myself and the captain I spoke to."

An internal affairs investigation? I could work with that.

I scribbled. "What does that mean? Do you think they were joyriding?"

Lowe's voice made a low, rumbling sound through the phone, like a murmur or a fading cell signal, but then came through loud and clear again.

"We're looking at this case from every angle. The theory the officers took the boat without orders certainly is among the scenarios under review, but it's not the only one. We'll know more as the investigation progresses."

From doing me a favor to doubletalk in less than a minute. Welcome to covering cops.

After we hung up, I dialed the next number on my list. I read Charlie's stories on the Channel Four website and hummed along with two Aerosmith covers and a Rolling Stones song as I waited for the FBI agent assigned to avoid questions from the press. Experience told me this call was probably an exercise in futility. Special Agent Starnes said nothing to disprove my theory.

"What I can tell you is limited by the constraints of an ongoing investigation." Her words were clipped.

Charlie had footage of FBI agents, logo caps and all, squatting and peering at blackened bits of something on the riverbank, but no quotes from anyone at the FBI, including Starnes. Which meant I was more determined than usual to get something I could use.

"I understand that," I said. "I also understand this is the first police boating accident in Richmond in more than forty years. Does the FBI always investigate water accidents involving police vessels?"

"Not always."

"Then why this one?"

"Miss Clarke, I really can't discuss an ongoing investigation," she said. "It's bureau policy."

I sighed. Her wall was well-fortified against badgering, so hammering at it with quick questions was unlikely to produce the information doorway I needed.

"Agent Starnes, I appreciate that. I know you're just doing your job. I know the police detective who blew off the FBI's involvement this morning is just doing his." I didn't think I threw Aaron too far under the bus, and I hoped the idea of the locals dismissing the feds might annoy her. "But I have a job to do, too. I have readers who want to know why these men are dead. Clearly you're investigating for a reason. Give me something, anything. Why is the FBI involved?"

She paused. "We got a tip."

I added another line of chicken scratch to my notes, hoping she might elaborate but knowing she probably wouldn't.

She didn't.

"A tip that there might be foul play? That the boat was stolen?"

"That this might be…more than it seems."

"Have you found anything to support that?" I asked.

"I'm sorry," she said. "Ongoing investigation."

I wondered if there was a daily budget for frustrated sighs when another one escaped my chest as I laid the phone down, partly because her cryptic answers weren't hugely helpful, and partly because it was time to call the families. Last on my list.

Valerie Roberts sounded spent, her voice scratchy and hollow when she answered the phone. I stumbled over my words as I apologized for bothering her and asked if she felt like talking about her husband.

There was a heavy, hitching sigh on the other end of the line. "Maybe," she said. "I can try, I guess."

"Thank you. I won't keep you long. How long were you and—" I glanced at the file again. "—Alex married?"

"Two years." Her voice broke. "We just started talking about trying to have a baby."

I bit my lip and forged ahead. "Your husband was with the police department a little under a year. Did he ever tell you why he wanted to be a police officer?"

"He talked about it all the time. We dated for three years before we got married, and the whole time we were in college, all he could talk about was being a cop. He got his degree in criminal justice and he went straight to the academy after graduation. He wanted to help people. And he thought the guns were cool." Her tone lightened as she told me about him.

"I was nervous about him doing this for a living. I didn't know if I would be able to handle him putting himself in danger every time he went to work. He reassured me constantly, and he showed me all his safety gear. I was always afraid he was going to get shot. Something like this never even crossed my mind."

The tears returned then, making her voice thick again. She took a deep breath before she continued. "Alex was a good man. Caring and thoughtful and generous, and honest to a fault. He was my soul mate. I truly believe that. He would have been an amazing father."

She dissolved into sobs at the last sentence, and I waited as she collected herself. I tried to think of something to say, but "I'm sorry" seemed woefully inadequate, so I stayed quiet.

I asked her if there was a phone number where his parents could be reached, and she told me they both died in an accident when Alex was young. He'd been raised by his grandparents, who also died in recent years.

"I see," I said. "Just one more question. Did Alex mention anything about why he went out on the river last night?"

"No. He said he had to go to work. Didn't the department tell you what he was doing?"

"They can't find anyone who ordered the boat out last night. They're investigating the possibility it was taken without orders."

She sucked in a sharp breath and when she spoke, her tone was a peculiar mix of incredulous and hurt. "Wait. They're saying Alex and Brian were what? Fishing? Partying on the department's boat?" There was a long pause, and I didn't even chance breathing too loud.

"Miss Clarke," she finally said, her words deliberate. "My husband was not the kind of man who did anything even remotely against the rules. Alex was the straightest of straight arrows. Eagle Scout, honor society, the cleanest record in the department. I may not know why he was out on that boat last night, but I sure as hell know him. He did not take it without orders. If someone suggested he did, they're lying. I'd stake my life on it."

5.

Deep background

There's nothing more frustrating for a reporter than a heap of unanswered questions. Facing a blank computer screen with only a sketchy idea of what killed five people, each of whom had been the center of someone else's universe, had me zipping past frustrated and aiming straight for pissed off. Talking to Brian Freeman's mother had only made me feel worse. She lost her husband in January, and Brian had been her only child.

I slammed my hands down on my desk and jumped to my feet. What the hell was so hard about "Why was the boat out there?" I paced behind my cubicle as my mind tried to force this puzzle into some logical order. There were way too many holes to see a clear picture. I finally asked myself what I'd tell Jenna first. Which, of course, was what Charlie hadn't already told the greater Richmond metro area. That worked, and I resumed my seat and quickly lost myself in the rhythm of the keystrokes.

After receiving information regarding Friday night's fatal boating crash on the James River, FBI agents joined Richmond po-

lice in combing the riverbank for clues Saturday.

"We got a tip," Special Agent Denise Starnes said Saturday, "that this might be more than it seems."

I quoted Lowe about the internal affairs investigation next, and wrote about the victims, including notes Parker emailed me about the pitcher, DeLuca, and his two friends. Describing the scene at the river, I used Aaron's estimation of how the accident happened. I put the accident history for the unit I'd gotten from Jones toward the end, and finished with Valerie Roberts' emotional assertion of her husband's innocence.

I added Parker's name to the bottom of the article as a contributor and copied him when I emailed my story to Bob.

While I waited for a reply from my boss, I skimmed through the twenty-seven emails in my inbox, saving three replies from defense attorneys about other cases I was following, and deleting the rest.

Bob's edits arrived as I finished reading the last junk press release. He asked me to clarify a couple of things and said he hadn't heard about the FBI's tip-off or the internal investigation. His equivalent of a thumbs-up, which was especially gratifying when a story had actually given me a headache. I fished two Advil out of my purse.

I was halfway through my second Coke of the afternoon when Parker found me loitering in the break room. Once it was time to leave, I'd discovered I didn't want to go home.

"Thanks for the stuff you sent me." I leaned back in my chair and smiled when he stopped in the doorway. "It was good. Nicely done, scoring an exclusive with the families."

"Thanks. And anytime." He walked into the room with his hands in the pockets of his navy blue slacks. "What are you going to do tonight?"

"I have no plans," I said. "After the day I've had, I should go home and go to bed. But I'm starving. So I need to eat first."

"That sounds suspiciously like a plan. I could eat. Mind if I join you?"

Really? I opened my mouth to make an excuse, and realized I didn't have a good one. I eyed him for a second. Oh, what the hell? I'd been to dinner with people from work before, and he'd certainly been a lot of help.

"Why not?" I stood up. "Let me grab my purse."

"Anyplace in particular you were planning to go?"

I grinned as my stomach growled. "Do you like barbecue?"

Pop-Tarts were never intended to provide an entire day's nutrition, and the hickory-and-meat smell in the air reminded me of that as I climbed out of my car in the restaurant's postage stamp of a parking lot a few minutes later.

Parker strapped a shiny red helmet to the seat of a still-dealer-tagged BMW motorcycle in the space next to me and I raised one eyebrow. It was a nice bike for a reporter's salary. Maybe he had family money or something.

I followed him through the picnic tables on the covered porch. He held the door as I stepped inside, the fantastic aromas coming from the kitchen momentarily overpowered by a clean, summery cologne when I ducked under his arm.

"I have an ulterior motive for inviting myself to dinner," he said as we joined about ten other people waiting in line in the cramped entryway. "Did you read my column today?" His eyes dropped to the floor and I laughed.

I wasn't sure what I'd expected to hear, but that wasn't it.

"I wasn't going to ask," he said. "But I can't stand it anymore. If it sucked, you can tell me."

"I have not," I said, wondering why he cared what I

thought. "Though not because I don't want to. I will, I promise. And you know, I meant it when I said your stuff was good today. So I'm sure it doesn't suck."

"I hope not. Sometimes I wonder if people are just nice to me because I used to be a decent ballplayer, you know? But you've never seemed impressed by my slider." He cocked his head to one side, and I surmised he wasn't too used to people who didn't fall all over him. "You're the real deal. Syracuse, right? I hear their j-school is the best. How'd you end up here, Texas girl in Virginia by way of New York? There has to be a story there."

I stepped up to the counter and ordered a chopped barbecue sandwich and a double helping of sweet potato fries, glancing at Parker as I signed my credit card slip. "There's a story. I'm not sure it's very interesting, but everyone has one, don't they?"

He ordered ribs and spoon bread and dropped a few bills from his change into the tip jar, stuffing a thick wallet back into his hip pocket and turning from the counter.

"Something tells me yours is more interesting than most."

We found a booth in the back of the tiny dining room, talking about how the place should really be bigger. It boasted what was easily the best barbecue I'd ever eaten, and given my Texas roots, that was saying something. With less than a dozen tables inside, standing room only was a common state of affairs.

I left Parker at the table with his bottle of Corona and went to fill my glass with the best sweet iced tea in town, glancing at the flat screens on the far wall as I waited in line. One offered a cooking show, the other a Red Sox game. His and hers entertainment. What ever happened to talking to each other over dinner?

Parker flashed me a grin when I sat down across from him again.

"So? What brings you to this neck of the woods, Miss Clarke?" He leaned forward on the wide walnut bench, resting his forearms on the scarred wooden table and looking genuinely interested.

"You really want to hear this?" I laughed.

"Shoot."

"Well, I did grow up in Dallas, and I did go to Syracuse," I said. "I thought I was hot stuff when I graduated, too. I was the editor of the *Daily Orange*. I was a University Scholar, which is a big deal award given to twelve people in the graduating class every year. I even got to go to a dinner at the Chancellor's house for that one. I carried a double major in print journalism and political science, and I just knew the *Washington Post* was going to fall down and beg me to come take their seat in the White House press corps."

"Ah. But they didn't so much commence with the begging?"

"They did not." I shook my head. "They all but dismissed me. The politics editor wouldn't even see me, and the metro editor said he didn't need the headache of training a green reporter. Told me to come back when I was seasoned."

"Ouch."

I nodded. The memory stung a little, even half a decade later.

"That's about it. Confidence shot to hell, I figured I wasn't going to get hired anywhere. My mom let me whine for a while and then told me to apply in a medium market close to D.C. and get to work making the guy sorry. Bob took a shot and gave me the police beat. I saw a way into the courthouse when they started slashing personnel two years ago, and I took it. I'm just waiting for the story that's going to make the *Post* notice me. I thought Ken and Barbie might get it, but so far…crickets.

"The FBI interest in this one makes it sexier than your average accident. Maybe if there's really something to this and I can stay ahead of Charlie this week, I might blip up on their radar."

He nodded. "See? Interesting. And good luck. Though it could be hard for Bob to fill those heels of yours if they stole you from us."

They called our order and he stood up before I could.

"You hold the table," he said. "They're a precious commodity in this place on a Saturday night."

He disappeared into the growing crowd.

A pulled pork sandwich, sitting tall in the plastic basket next to a huge pile of cinnamon-sugared sweet potato fries, appeared in front of me with a flourish.

"Dinner is served, ma'am." Parker's Virginia drawl didn't quite lend itself to the Texas accent he tried to affect.

"Why thank you, kind sir." I grinned, not even waiting for him to sit down before I popped a fry into my mouth. I devoured half the pile in the ensuing three minutes, ignoring the fresh-from-the-fryer temperature. I moved to get up as I gulped the last of the tea that was soothing my blistered tongue and Parker raised one hand.

"Iced tea?" he asked, already on his feet. "You eat. I've seen starving linebackers who couldn't plow through fries like that. Something tells me you're hungrier than I am."

I thanked him when he came back with my refill, and tried not to laugh when he dripped barbecue sauce down the front of his pumpkin-orange polo before he'd taken two bites of his food.

"Blot it, don't swipe at it," I said when he made the stain twice as big trying to get it off.

"Oops. Oh well. I see shirt shopping in my future."

"Spray some hairspray on it and let it sit," I said. "It's my mom's cure-all for stains and it's never failed me."

He raised a skeptical eyebrow, then shrugged.

"Who am I to argue with mom?" He washed the beef ribs down with a swig of Corona. "Speaking of your mom, you said yesterday she had breast cancer. Is she okay now?"

I nodded. "She's been in remission for almost four years. Five is the benchmark. She's pretty amazing."

The conversation drifted into a natural lull as we ate, and my thoughts strayed to my mother, and how proud I was of her. Not many women would have been able to do the things she'd done, leaving California the day after she graduated high school with her seven-month-old in the backseat of the car that held all her worldly possessions, and stopping in Texas because the bluebonnets were the prettiest thing she'd ever seen. She'd raised me by herself after my grandparents disowned her. Her pregnancy, and subsequent refusal to marry her boyfriend, embarrassed them at their Hollywood cocktail parties.

She fussed over me and I tried to make her proud. We had danced around our cozy living room like Publisher's Clearinghouse had arrived with a giant cardboard check the day my acceptance from Syracuse came.

I'd been determined to go, thousands of dollars in student loan debt be damned. Then the week before I'd turned eighteen, my absentee grandparents dropped the bombshell of all bombshells. A courier arrived with a fat yellow envelope full of legal papers from a firm in Malibu telling me I had a college fund.

The smaller envelope that fell out of the paperwork had "Lila" written in intricate calligraphy, and my mom had tears in her eyes by the time she finished reading the letter.

Her mother wrote an apology, explaining there were no strings attached to the gift and they hoped I'd use it well. I'd read it so many times in the last ten years, I had to tape it back together when the paper gave from being folded and unfolded over and over. I'd often picked up the phone and started to dial the number in the letter, always hanging up before I pushed the last button. Ten years and a free education later, and I still wasn't sure if I could forgive them for not wanting me. Or for punishing my mother for so many years just because I existed.

"Did you find out anything more about what happened to your drug dealers from yesterday?" Parker's voice snapped me out of my reverie and I tore a paper towel from the roll on the table and wiped my mouth.

"I didn't even have time to ask," I said. "But the good news is, neither did anyone else. I'll check Monday, though."

"Your job is never dull, huh?" He spun his empty beer bottle back and forth between sure hands.

"Very rarely. Though it's usually not quite this insane, either. I miss my happy medium."

We chatted about nothing in particular for another half hour. As the sun sank in the western sky, I told him goodnight and slid behind the wheel of my car, flipping my scanner on and sighing in relief when I heard nothing but normal Saturday night traffic cop chatter. Thank God. I wanted nothing more than to sleep until Monday.

By the time I tended to my Pomeranian, Darcy, and crawled under the duvet, my thoughts were tangling again, my headache threatening to return. Charlie. Shelby. Dead people in a boat accident nobody could explain. Dead drug dealers nobody robbed. They all fell together in a hopeless jumble, making my brain hurt. I wondered, as I closed my eyes, if the odd cast of characters heaped together in my head would create weird dreams. If they did, I didn't remember them by morning.

My phone was ringing when I got to my desk on Monday. I stared at it for half a second, my innate inability to ignore a ringing telephone battling with the certainty that answering it would make me later for the meeting.

"Clarke," I sighed, picking it up. "Can I help you?"

"Nichelle?" The voice that came through the line was so hesitant I almost didn't recognize it as belonging to my narcotics sergeant.

"Mike? Is that you?" Maybe Sorrel had something on the dope dealers. I dug in my bag for a pen, flipping over a press release and scribbling Mike's name and the date across the top. "What can I do for you?"

"I, uh, I need to talk to you. There's some stuff I think, well, you might be interested in." He sighed. "Not might. Will. It's big. Can you meet me for coffee?"

"Sure." Curiosity made it difficult to keep my voice even. I knew Sorrel fairly well, and he didn't sound like himself. "Meet me at Thompson's in twenty minutes?"

"NO!" I moved the phone away from my head, but it was too late. His Greek heritage came with a booming voice that left my ear ringing. "I'd rather go someplace out of the way. Can you meet me at the Starbucks in Colonial Heights in forty-five minutes?"

Agreeing, I cradled the phone wondering what was all the way out in Colonial Heights.

I hitched my bag back onto my shoulder, the desire to avoid snapping a heel on my newish, strappy red Manolos the only thing keeping me from breaking into a sprint on my way to find out.

6.

And curiouser

I sipped my white chocolate mocha while I waited for Sorrel, recalling my first meeting with him. After I'd managed to get past my rookie jitters and through the interview about the biggest drug bust in department history, my first crack at covering cops had come out pretty good. Good enough, at least, to earn Sorrel's respect and trust. And leave my mind racing, a half-dozen years and hundreds of stories later, through possible explanations for his peculiar call.

Just as I was digging in my bag for my Blackberry, I saw his unmarked cruiser turn into the lot. He pulled a briefcase out of the passenger seat and ambled toward the door. Mike was about as tall as I was, and twenty years of chasing bad guys kept him in good shape. He had broad shoulders, but a wiry build, and with his dark coloring and clean-shaven face, he cut a striking figure in his pressed chinos and camel-colored blazer.

I waved unobtrusively from my post in the corner. He picked up his coffee and sat down in the simple wooden chair across from me, pulling a file folder out of the handsome black leather case and pushing it across the shiny round table.

"We have missing evidence," he said.

"Missing evidence?" I echoed as I reached for the file. "From where?"

I scanned the page on top and gasped, casting a quick glance around and ducking my head even though no one was paying attention to us. I looked at Mike, my eyes wide.

"The drugs and the money? How the hell does that even happen?"

He shrugged. "I wish I could tell you."

I turned back to the file. Between my two murdered drug dealers, the police department had confiscated nearly four hundred thousand dollars in cash and a veritable truckload of various narcotics, the last of which had been cataloged on Friday afternoon. It should've stayed in the PD's evidence lock-up until after the killer's trial, when the drugs would have been incinerated in a sealed steel drum, and the cash given to the city to subsidize the cost of the narcotics unit. But that morning when Mike went down to look at one of the prescription bottles from the second murder scene, he'd discovered it was all gone.

"Did someone break into the evidence locker over the weekend?" I asked the obvious question first, but I knew I would've already heard about it if that were true.

Mike shook his head. "No. This thief had clearance. A cop, or someone from the CA's office, maybe."

In Virginia, prosecutors are known as commonwealth's attorneys instead of district attorneys, a quirk I'd finally gotten used to.

I nodded as I scribbled, and he continued.

"There was no sign of forced entry."

My mind colored some of those blank pieces in my drug dealer puzzle with stolen evidence and the possibility of crooked cops. Hot damn. Talk about a sexy news story.

"Are you sure, Mike?" I exploded in a loud whisper. "That's…wow."

He just nodded.

"How much can I have on the record?"

"That depends on how you feel about using unnamed sources. I don't want it attributed to me, at least not now. If it's someone in the department, it could get ugly."

I flipped through the file and nodded. "This corroborates what you said. I have no problem citing it as 'a police department source.' "

I paused and studied him for a minute, taking a longer drink of my cooling latte.

"This is huge. And it's not going to make the department look so good," I said. Mike was nothing if not loyal. "I'm grateful to be sitting here, but why bring me this? Why not keep it quiet?"

He exhaled slowly and toyed with his keys. "Because this is just flat-ass wrong, any way you look at it," he said finally. "You're my insurance it's not going to disappear. While I don't relish the idea of the department being dragged through the mud, I also know if I don't say something, this may never go anywhere. It happens. Shit like this goes on and it just gets swept under the rug. I love my job, Nichelle, but I hate how I've felt about it the past couple of hours. I've known some of the guys I work with for more than twenty years, and now I'm looking at everyone like they're a suspect."

"Maybe it wasn't a cop," I offered. "Didn't you say something about the CA's office?"

"If they can tie it to a lawyer, they will. Keeping the department's collective halo shiny is priority one." He tapped the file. "The only prosecutor who signed in this weekend came in yesterday afternoon. The major crimes unit is picking him up for questioning, but if someone's going to steal evidence, they probably wouldn't sign the log at the desk."

"Doesn't everyone have to do that?"

"I don't," Mike said. "Anyone my rank or better can go in and out at will. Since we go in the most, it simplifies the record keeping."

"Was there anything else missing?"

"I don't know. The inventory will take a while. A few days at least."

I nodded. "Did you talk to internal affairs?"

"Yeah, right before I called you. I've never done that before. I feel like I'm tattling to the teacher on the playground."

I jotted a note to call the captain of internal affairs, wondering if he'd tell me anything. A lock of hair escaped the clip at the nape of my neck, and I pushed it behind my ear as I looked back up at Mike and reached for the file folder. "Can I take this with me?"

"What the hell?" He pushed it toward me. "If I'm going to risk my badge to get a story in the newspaper, I might as well not half-ass it."

"What's the use in that?" I winked. "I'll keep it safe."

"Make sure you keep you safe, too." Mike drummed his fingers on the table. "You read about this happening in other places, but you never think it will happen in your own backyard. I want you guys to blast this all over the front page. I wouldn't be here if I didn't. It'll force the brass to figure out who did it and fire their sorry ass. But be careful. If this was a cop, they're into something very serious. Something they could go to prison for. And going to prison is pretty much every cop's worst nightmare."

The solemn look in his dark eyes sent such a chill through me, I actually shivered.

"I'm not trying to scare you. But you should know what you're getting into."

"I'll be careful," I promised, shoving the folder and my notebook into my bag and hooking it over my shoulder as I stood. "Thanks, Mike. I appreciate the call. I definitely owe you one."

"I guess that depends on how you look at it," he said, picking up his briefcase and moving toward the door. "You get a headline, I get to sleep at night. Win-win. But remember this next time you're bugging me about something I don't want to tell you, huh?"

"I'm sure I won't," I said as I walked through the door he held open. "But you'll remind me."

The thought of an exclusive put a bounce in my step as I crossed the parking lot, already stringing my lead together in my head. Mike had his pick of reporters to meet with that morning, but he called me. Boy, was Charlie going to be pissed. The rush of warmth at the thought wasn't even iced over by the memory of his parting words.

Kicking the door of the car open before I'd even put it in park when I got back to work, I made a beeline for Bob's office, stopping short and grumbling when his door was closed. Bob's door was never closed, and this was a hell of an irritating time for it to be that way. I went to my desk to wait, figuring maybe I could get more information before I talked to him.

My only experience with Captain Simmons at internal affairs had been pleasant enough, but it had also been a relatively minor case of an officer being arrested for drunk driving, so I wasn't sure what kind of reception I'd get when I dialed police headquarters and asked for him.

Voicemail. I rattled off a quick message with my deadline time and a plea for him to return my call, which I wasn't at all sure he'd do. But I'd tried. If he didn't call back, I could stick a "didn't return a call seeking comment" into my story.

I blew a raspberry at nothing in particular as I put the phone down and picked up my pen, tapping it on the desk. So many questions. And answers had been hard to come by lately. I was beginning to miss the simplicity of Barbie and Ken and the gruesome homicide trial.

Popping halfway to my feet, I looked at Bob's door. Open. I grabbed my folders, half-running to his office.

"Chief? Did you get my message? Wait 'til you hear what I've got!"

"I didn't have time to check my messages this morning," he said, his bushy brows knit together in a glare that would've been scary any other day. "I had a meeting. That you didn't bother to show up for. The staff meeting is mandatory for the crime reporter, Nichelle. You know that."

"But I did call," I protested. "I had an interview, and you're going to be glad I went. I've got an honest-to-God exclusive. And it's fabulous." I took a deep breath and launched into the story. I may not have inhaled again before I finished.

Bob leaned forward in his seat. The more I talked, the faster he nodded, and though his brow furrowed when I got to the part where "my source" warned me to be careful, he certainly didn't look pissed anymore by the time I sat back in my chair and grinned.

"So, what do you think? It's great, right? And no one else will have it."

"Holy shit, kid. Nice work. But slow down. How much do you trust your source?"

"Implicitly. I have a copy of the file on the missing evidence right here, and I already called internal affairs. Maybe they'll give me confirmation."

"Don't bet on it," Bob said, opening the file as soon as I handed it to him. "But this looks pretty solid. And it's damned fabulous, all right. You're sure no one else has it?"

"No one," I said. "My source assured me I was the only reporter he talked to."

"Then we'll hold the web version for morning and release it when the papers hit the racks," he said, his face wrinkling up in a grin. "I need it by three. Legal will want to check it, I'm sure."

I nodded and started to get to my feet.

"One more thing," he said.

I stared at him blankly. What? I had solid information. It was a huge story. I eyed the Pulitzer on his wall again. Most of the time I wasn't terribly interested in contests or awards for my work. But that one was different.

"Nicey," Bob spoke slowly and his expression was serious. "You're a good reporter, but you're young. I know the only way for you to get experience is to go get the story, but watch yourself. If you're dealing with crooked cops, then everyone you talk to at the PD is a suspect. I want the story. It's a great story. But you just mind how you handle yourself."

"There's no reason for you to worry." I smiled my most reassuring smile. "Really. My guy was being a little dramatic."

"I'm not convinced of that." Bob gave me an age-begets-wisdom look. "There are dangerous people out there, kid. You might not want to think about the things they're capable of doing, but they can be pretty horrible."

I held his gaze. He wanted the exclusive, and I didn't want some misguided concern for me to trump that desire.

I looked back at the Pulitzer. I knew he had won enough awards in his career to fill a good-sized closet, which was where I suspected the rest of them lived.

"Why do you keep that on the wall in here?" I asked him, gesturing to the frame.

"The Pulitzer?" He looked confused. "Well, because it's the one I'm the most proud of. I think I actually did something special to earn it."

"Why?"

"Because that series was great," he said softly. "There were civil rights activists who said my stories helped heal wounds that festered here for more than a century. I'm still quite proud of that."

"Didn't you tell me the KKK threatened you while you worked on that series?"

Bob's mouth tightened into a thin line.

"Nicey." He sighed. "This is different."

"Why? Because you don't mind putting yourself in danger, or because I'm a woman?"

He flinched.

"That's not fair," he said. "It was a different situation. The crackpots I dealt with weren't armed public officials who stood to lose everything because of what I was writing."

"But they threatened your life," I pressed. "No one has done that to me, and besides, I've already called internal affairs, so it's not like my source is the only person at the PD who knows I know about this."

Bob was quiet for a long moment, bending his head and massaging both temples. He took a deep breath before he looked up.

"It is one hell of a sexy lead, isn't it? Go get it. Just be careful. And get it to me by three in case it needs shoring up."

I leaped out of my chair and managed to resist the impulse to pump my fist in the air. Grinning instead, I pushed Mike's warning to the back of my mind and locked it there.

"You'll have it," I said. "This is going to be huge, Bob. I can feel it."

"Three o'clock," he repeated.

"Not a second past," I promised over my shoulder, already on my way back to my desk to see if Captain Simmons returned my call.

Sprinting the last few steps, I grabbed the ringing phone, my breathlessness more from excitement than exertion.

"Hi, sweetie, I'm sorry to call you at work." My mom's voice deflated my enthusiasm. "You didn't call me this weekend. Is everything all right?"

"Mom?" I hastened to cover up the disappointment in my tone. "Hey! How are you?"

"I'm fine. Tired. But fine. You don't sound happy to hear from me. Are you very busy today?"

"I am, but I have a minute. I'm waiting for a call, though, so if I hang up on you, don't take it personally."

"Noted," she said with a laugh. "What are you working on? There was something yesterday about a boating accident over the weekend? I didn't read it yet, but it looked like a sad story."

"It is. The guys who died were all my age or younger. Not a fun weekend. I'm sorry I didn't call you yesterday. I was at the accident scene until ridiculous-thirty on Friday night, and then back here all day Saturday, and I stayed home with Darcy and tried to relax yesterday."

"I see." Her tone brightened. "Speaking of relaxing, I went to the pool for the first time in years yesterday, and guess who I bumped into?"

"A handsome doctor who swept you off your flip flops?"

"Not quite." I could hear the smile in her voice. "But I did have a nice chat with Rhonda Miller."

"Aw, really?" It was entirely possible that I missed Kyle's family more than I actually missed him. His parents were among the sweetest people I'd ever met. "How is she?"

"She's doing really well. And so is Kyle. He's somewhere up there, actually. She said he followed his dad into law enforcement and he's in Virginia working on a case."

"I'll be damned," I said, tapping a pen on the desk and wondering how to steer the conversation away from my old boyfriend before she asked me to look him up. There were a variety of reasons why I had no interest in doing that, none of which I wanted to discuss right then. "Small world. Hey, Jenna says to tell you hello."

"Wow, that might be the worst segue ever," she said. "But all right. I won't push it. Just wanted you to know. Give Jenna my love. How is she?"

"She's great. Carson isn't nursing anymore, so she had her first margaritas in two years at girls' night Friday. Then she went with me to the accident scene at the river, which she was very excited about until we got there and she got an eyeful of why reporting isn't always as much fun as it looks in the movies."

"Ah." My mother fell silent for a minute. "I can sympathize with that. I'm happy you love your job, but I don't think I would care to see it for myself. I read your stories and I can't imagine how you stand dealing with that day after day and stay off medication…"

She trailed off and when she spoke again she sounded slightly alarmed.

"Nicey, you're not on medication, are you?" she asked.

"Not unless you count vitamins." I laughed. "Contrary to popular belief, my job does not generally depress me. It's usually pretty exciting. I have a story going out today I'm very excited about, in fact."

"About what?"

"All sorts of intrigue at the police department this morning," I said, refusing to elaborate any further. "You'll have to read it like everyone else."

"I gave you life, and you won't even tell me what you're working on," she lamented. She sounded so convincingly pitiful, I almost felt bad, but then she laughed and I could picture the mischief flashing in her blue eyes.

"I love you, mom," I said, my voice thickening slightly. Growing up the only child of an "I was an attachment parent before attachment parenting was cool" single mom made for a different dynamic. I missed her. And I lived in constant fear of her cancer returning. "Are you okay? Why are you tired?"

"I love you, too, kid. I'm fine. You stop worrying about me. I'm a pretty tough chick. I've just been busy at the shop, that's all." She'd expanded her flower shop into a one-stop wedding boutique after she'd recovered from the mastectomy. She loved it, which I found hilarious given that my mother's opinion of marriage echoed the regard most women hold for sandals worn over socks: almost always good for a laugh and almost never a good idea. No wonder I had issues with my love life. "Have a better week. And call your mother more often."

"Yes, ma'am."

I hung up the phone and shoved the stray lock of hair behind my ear again before I unfastened the clip and twisted all of my hair back up into it, my thoughts still on my mom.

The ringing phone jerked me back to the present. I picked it up and tilted my head to brace the receiver against my shoulder as I reached for a pen and paper with both hands.

"Miss Clarke, this is Don Simmons at the Richmond PD." A smooth, deep voice came through the line and my pulse quickened.

"Captain! I won't take up too much of your time today," I said. "I'm working on a story about the missing evidence from the Southside dealer murders."

"So you said in your message," Simmons said. "Do you mind if I ask you how you know about that?"

"I do, actually." So that's why he'd returned my call. "I can't reveal my source on this story. But I am wondering if you have any comment on your investigation."

"The situation is being investigated by internal affairs for possible officer involvement, but we don't know anything definitive yet," he said a little stiffly.

Strike one.

"Captain, I know you're frustrated. I can imagine your job is pretty stressful, and I'm really not trying to make it worse." If the sympathy plea had worked on Agent Starnes, it could work on anyone. "I'm just trying to do mine, that's all."

Silence. I held my tongue, knowing this game well: he who speaks first loses.

Simmons hauled in a deep breath. "I can appreciate that, ma'am, but I need you to understand this is a very sensitive matter."

Strike two. I had one tactic left.

"Yes, but the taxpayers who pay your salary have a right to know what's going on. I'm not the only person in town who thinks so, or I wouldn't know about it in the first place."

More crickets. Another long breath.

"Look, lady," he said. "This has everybody upstairs convinced the four horsemen are on their way or some shit, pardon my French. I'm sorry—no comment."

A swing and a miss, and the two most dreaded words in the English language for the out. I thanked Simmons for his time and hung up, tapping the nail of my index finger on the handset. He confirmed the theft, but I wanted more than that. Though given his position, I supposed I should be thankful he'd even called back.

I glanced at the file Mike gave me. Gavin Neal. The attorney who'd been in the evidence room on Sunday. Assuming he wasn't busy stashing four hundred thousand dollars in drug money, maybe he'd talk to me. Lawyers were generally easier to pump for quotes than cops.

I dialed the CA's office and found Neal in the robot-voiced directory. And got his voicemail. Reeling off my name and phone number, I wondered if my aversion to checking messages stemmed from having to leave so many of them.

I cradled the phone and stared at the log from the evidence locker. The longer I stared, the fuzzier the lines became, until something finally jumped out at me. Neal's signature was scribbled hastily. So hastily, someone went back and printed his name next to the scrawl. If I were planning to make off with half a million dollars, I'd be in a hurry, too.

I wondered if my friend DonnaJo, who was also a prosecutor, might be able to help me track down Neal before deadline. I called her cell and dispensed with the pleasantries quickly, asking if she knew him.

"He's one of our best attorneys, Nichelle," she said. "A great guy, and a damn smart lawyer. Very charismatic—juries love him. I just cannot believe this rumor that he's a crook. Anyone who knows this man knows he's not a thief."

My eyebrows went up.

"Jump to conclusions much, counselor?" Not that I hadn't, but she seemed pretty defensive. "I think they just wanted to question him."

"Which would be no big deal, if he were around to question. The grapevine has it the cops went to pick him up and his wife reported him missing. He never went home after he went to the PD yesterday. I hear she's pretty freaked. Their kid has some sort of medical condition, so Gavin never misses her calls."

My thoughts careened in several directions at once. Part of what I loved about covering crime were the puzzles embedded in the stories, but this one was getting more complicated than the three-dimensional Capitol Building my mom sent for my last birthday. It had frustrated me to the brink of throwing it out half-finished, and I never attempted another.

Now the lawyer was missing? Did a family man with a successful career really take off with hundreds of thousands of dollars in evidence and not even tell his wife? Or was the wife lying?

Medical condition meant medical bills. And prosecuting isn't where the big bucks are in the legal game. Sounded like a motive to me.

I cleared my throat.

"Hey, DonnaJo," I said, running a finger over the evidence locker sign-in. "Do you have any idea why Neal would have been at the PD on a Sunday?"

"I go up there sometimes, if there's evidence I want to look at again when I'm prepping for court," she said.

"How long would it take you to get me a list of the cases he's working on?" I asked. "The PD isn't talking, and I want this for my piece today."

"About an hour. I have a hearing."

"Can you also see if there's anyone he put in prison who's gotten out recently?"

"Sure. It might take a bit longer, but I'll send you both. If you're going to run them, they didn't come from me, though."

"No worries. The courthouse fairy brought them to me."

I thanked her and hung up.

Glancing toward Bob's door, I got up to go ask if he wanted a separate piece on the attorney by way of the soda machine. I decided as I ambled along, the condensation from my Coke bottle mingling with the sweat breaking out on my hands, that my best bet was to lay out the facts for him as lightly as I could, and ask him if he thought the attorney's disappearance warranted its own headline. Writing about a lawyer, I didn't want to get in hot water with legal for tying him to the missing evidence if there was a reason I shouldn't.

I kept my eyes on the mottled brown carpet as I walked through Bob's door, my nerves overriding my manners and making the knock more cursory than usual. Perching on the edge of my seat, I began listing the latest developments in my story before I looked at my editor, who was slumped over in his chair, barely breathing.

7.

In a heartbeat

"Bob!" I knocked over the wastebasket and pushed a tape dispenser and a bottle of white-out off the desk dragging Bob's heft from the chair, which crashed into the wall when I kicked at the casters under it to get it out of the way.

Once he was on his back on the floor, I knelt and popped his cheek with my palm, rapid-fire style.

"Bob!" I shouted, my nose inches from his. My hand left a red mark on his otherwise bloodless skin.

He didn't move, his breathing still shallow.

"Help!" I turned my head in the general direction of the door I couldn't really see from behind the desk.

"HEY!" I bellowed in my best press conference voice. "In Bob's office. Someone help! We need an ambulance!" Damn. Mid-morning on a Monday was not the best time to find newsroom staff in the office.

"Nichelle?" Shelby's voice came from near the doorway.

"Shelby, thank God." I'd have been glad to see Adolf Hitler himself right then if he knew how to call the paramedics. "Over here, behind the desk.

"Call 9-1-1. Then go get someone who can help with CPR, just in case he stops breathing." I barked the orders automatically, having been through this more than once when my mom was weak from her chemo.

For the first time ever, Shelby didn't argue with me or offer a smartass retort. She gaped at Bob for a split second and then snatched up the phone, giving the operator the building's address before she sprinted out into the newsroom.

She returned shortly, hauling Eunice behind her.

"Christ on a cracker, what's going on in here?" Eunice's golden brown eyes widened as they studied Bob, and she laid a hand on my shoulder. "Shelby said you needed help with CPR, but he's breathing."

"I just want to make sure it stays that way," I said, stroking Bob's hand and meeting Eunice's gaze as she gripped the edge of Bob's desk and eased herself onto the floor next to his legs. "His pulse is thready. His breathing is getting worse. Shelby called an ambulance. This looks like a cardiac something-or-other. Or maybe a stroke."

I pinched my eyes shut, praying for the heart attack. People survived them every day. A stroke...well, what that might do to my quick-witted editor was too horrible to contemplate.

"Don't you worry, sugar. The Good Lord don't want Bob up there giving Him orders. It'll be just fine." Eunice reached out and patted my knee as I laid my fingers over Bob's carotid artery and stared at my Timex.

"Hang on, chief," I whispered. "The cavalry's on its way."

Just then, shouting from the newsroom heralded the paramedics' arrival. They brought a small gang of onlookers from our floor, comprised of section editors and copy desk folks. Most of the people in the building continued about their Monday with no idea that our resident journalistic legend needed medical attention, sprawled on carpet that still stank faintly of cigarettes from the days when chain-smoking and reporting went together like champagne and strawberries.

I took two steps backward, willing away the pricking in the backs of my eyes that meant tears were coming.

"He'll be fine," I said, my nails digging into my palm. "He'll be just fine." A couple of deep breaths dispelled the waterworks.

Shelby whimpered, and I looked around to thank her for her help and found her burying her face in the managing editor's shirtfront, sniffling as he patted her back.

"Are you all right, sugar?" Eunice asked me, watching the medics lift our boss onto a gurney.

"He was slumped in the chair when I came in." I cleared my throat. "I got him onto the floor so his airway would be less constricted."

"Great land of plenty." She folded her arms over her soft chest and shook her head. "I just saw him at the meeting. He was fine."

"Obviously not," I said. "But he will be. He has to be."

The medics started for the door.

"What do you think?" I asked the one closest to me.

"Looks like a heart attack. I can't say anything for sure, though," she said, not looking up from her watch on Bob's heart rate and oxygen level. "We're taking him to St. Vincent's. Has anyone called his family?"

"He doesn't really have one," Eunice said. "His wife's been gone three years now, and he doesn't have any children."

Both medics nodded as they rolled Bob, still unconscious, through the onlookers.

I closed my eyes and took a deep breath. He did, too, have a family. Just like me, the *Telegraph* was his family. And I'd be damned if he was going to wake up in the hospital alone. I stepped toward the door and Eunice put a hand on my back.

"You going to watch after him, sugar?"

I turned slightly and smiled, blinking at the threatening tears again.

"We're his family." I said simply.

She wrapped my left hand in her arthritis-twisted fingers and nodded. "You're damned right we are. Give him our love when he comes to. And let me know if you need me to do anything."

I packed up my things and turned into the hospital parking lot less than ten minutes later.

I had grown up without a father or a grandfather, and I'd always thought I didn't need either in my life. Then I came to Richmond with no job and no friends, and Bob hired me. After his wife died, he found himself as orphaned and out of place as I sometimes still felt. That kinship, coupled with our fondness for each other, had forged a bond as strong as one shared by any blood relatives. Sure, he gave me hell about deadlines and scoops, but that was his job. I knew he liked me, and there wasn't much I wouldn't do for him.

I left the car at the curb, tow away zone signs be damned, and rushed through the sliding glass doors, accosting the first white coat I saw.

"You have to check in with the front desk before you can see him," the doctor said, raising an eyebrow in the direction of the fingers I'd curled around his arm. I ignored the look, but thanked him over my shoulder as I bolted for the desk.

I tried my best to be patient with the harried clerk, but it seemed to take hours before she glanced in my direction, and when she finally did, she flashed a halfhearted smile that looked out of place on her perky face. "I'll be right with you."

I fidgeted as I waited, my thoughts running to the weeks I'd spent at Parkland Memorial with my mom. But she was fine now. Making bridal dreams come true every day. Bob would be back to glaring at my tardiness soon enough. I refused to entertain another option.

By the time the clerk began typing information into the computer for the fifth person who'd walked up after me, I was over polite waiting. Glancing around at a roomful of people who were caught up in their own problems and paying me absolutely no mind, I edged to the end of the long counter and slid a black clipboard off the edge of it, then turned toward the doors to the treatment area.

Bob shared a theory with me once that clipboards are the most commanding of office supplies, instantly lending an air of authority to anyone carrying them.

"I hope you're right, chief," I muttered, flattening myself against the wall outside the secured double doors.

When a tiny redheaded woman carrying a sleepy toddler came out, I slipped inside. Straightening my shoulders and ramrodding my spine, I kept my eyes on the clipboard and walked to the back edge of the nurse's station. A dozen or so women and men in scrubs milled about, talking. Hanging near the corner, mostly out of sight, I scanned the whiteboard of patients' last names, doctors, and room numbers. Jeffers, no doctor name, room twelve.

White-knuckling the clipboard, I strode down the hallway, not making eye contact with anyone. And it worked. Either Bob was right about the power of the clipboard, or everyone was too busy to notice me, but I rounded the corner into his room without so much as an eyelash batted in my direction.

Once inside, I stopped so suddenly I teetered forward on my stilettos. Bob looked frail, half-reclined in the narrow bed, a myriad of tubes and wires tethering him to four different machines. So much like my mom had after her mastectomy, it knocked the wind out of me.

I pulled in a long breath and looked closer. The heart monitor's beeping was reassuringly steady, and Bob's chest rose and fell in a much deeper, more even pattern than it had before.

I stepped to the side of the bed, grasping his big hand in both of mine, and Bob opened his eyes.

"Nicey?" He blinked and looked around, the confusion obvious on his face. But that face was symmetrical, his words clear. "What the hell?"

"They think it was a heart attack," I pasted a smile on my face and tried my best to sound breezy, thanking God silently for the lack of stroke markers. "We tried to tell the paramedics that we give you those every day around deadline, but they insisted you come see a doctor."

Bob laughed and then winced.

"Shit. That hurts. No more wisecracks," he said.

"Yes, sir." I saluted and clicked my heels together and he smiled.

"A heart attack, huh?" Bob surveyed the equipment in the room. "Well, hell. You want to fill me in?"

"I went to tell you about my latest hot scoop and found you passed out in your office," I said. "I pulled you out of the chair, screamed for help, the paramedics came. And here we are."

"Thanks, kid." Bob half-smiled at me. "I owe you one."

"Eh. Just keep ignoring my tardiness so I can keep up with my workouts, and we'll call it even."

"Done." His color was coming back, at least a little. The monitor kept up its steady rhythm, and I smiled.

"Speaking of tardiness, my story's going to be late if I don't start typing soon," I said. "What time is it?"

Bob pointed to the clock on the wall before he read it to me. "When the big hand is on the six and the little one is just past the one like that, it's one-thirty. You find out anything from the internal affairs guy?"

I poked my tongue out at him.

"Smartass comments mean you must be feeling better." I planted myself in a chair in the corner where I could keep an eye on him before I reached for my laptop. "Internal affairs was less than forthcoming. Lucky for me, I have a girlfriend at the CA's office. Guess what? That prosecutor who signed in to the evidence locker yesterday didn't go home last night."

Bob grunted. When I looked at him, his brows were knitted together over his closed eyes.

"Really?" He sounded a little less tired. One of the machines next to the bed beeped, and I jumped.

"Don't go getting too excited about that, chief." I smiled. "I wouldn't want to have to cut you out of the loop."

Bob smiled, his eyes still closed. "I wouldn't know what to do if I was ever out of the loop," he said. "I am the loop."

"Truer words may have never been spoken." I opened a blank document. "And we're glad to still have you around."

"I'm too stubborn to die," Bob said, and his tone was so genial that I burst out laughing.

"I stand corrected," I said. "I think that might be the truest thing ever said."

"Get back to work." He tried his hardest to sound gruff. "Your copy isn't going to write itself, is it?"

"No, but I'm going to write it from this lovely little beige room where I can keep an eye on you," I said. "I'm not leaving until I talk to a doctor."

"You don't have to stay here," Bob began, and I raised a palm in his direction.

"Don't even try it, chief. Have laptop and Blackberry, will travel. Eunice and everyone else send their love."

He eyeballed me for a long minute and then seemed to give in, muttering something about overreacting as he closed his eyes.

I turned my attention back to the blinking cursor on my screen and decided for myself to mention the missing CA in my evidence piece, and try to get more information before I devoted a whole story to his whereabouts. If I watched the wording, I probably wouldn't get an ass-chewing from legal. As far as I knew, I was the only reporter in town who knew the evidence was gone, and I might be the only one who knew the lawyer was gone, too.

I grabbed my Blackberry and checked my email. The courthouse fairy had landed, and though the recent parole rosters didn't show any of Neal's bad guys, he did have a murder case scheduled to open Wednesday. It was just a simple domestic dispute gone very wrong, but the weapon was probably in the evidence room, assuming they'd found it.

The question became, then, was the trial the reason for his presence at police headquarters on Sunday, or was it a good excuse?

"Hell if I know," I mumbled, thinking about what Mike said about the department's halo. "But I'm going to find out."

Bob began to snore softly as I started to type.

A search for suspects turned inward Monday for Richmond police after more than $600,000 in cash and street-valued narcotics disappeared from police headquarters over the weekend.

Documents show the last of the evidence in question was cataloged Friday afternoon. Monday morning, it was nowhere to be found, a confidential police department source said.

Also missing on Monday was Assistant Commonwealth Attorney Gavin Neal, who, with a murder trial scheduled to open Wednesday, was one of the last people to sign into the police evidence locker. An official who asked to remain unnamed said Neal was being sought for questioning about the theft.

I stopped there and picked up my Blackberry again. As soon as I was outside, I dialed the PD and launched into a preemptive apology when I heard Aaron's voice. "I'm working on a story about the missing evidence in the drug dealer murders, and I have an unnamed source. It just occurred to me the internal affairs guys probably think it's you."

He chuckled. "Why yes, as a matter of fact they did. I'm not sure why they give two shits. The report is public information. I guess they figure they could have kept it out of the news if no one had tipped you off, since this wouldn't make the list of routine report subjects you people request. They're pissed about someone telling you. They checked the records on every phone line I have readily accessible, but they seemed satisfied when they saw I hadn't talked to you since Saturday."

I caught a movement out of the corner of my eye and was surprised to find a young, good-looking guy with cocoa skin and serious brown eyes staring at me from a bench on the other side of the sidewalk. He didn't look familiar. I smiled at him.

He didn't return the smile, just kept staring.

I shifted my attention back to my phone call and repeated the apology.

"Good luck with that mess you're working on today," Aaron replied. "And don't worry about IAD. I can handle them, especially when I didn't actually tell you anything they don't want you to know. Though I'm dying to know who did. I've started a list."

"Police department sources." I clicked my tongue. "I know you understand. That's why you're my favorite detective."

"And here I thought it was my boyish grin."

"Well, that goes without saying." I laughed. "Hey, speaking of 'us people,' has anyone else asked you about the missing prosecutor today? And what can you tell me about him?"

"How the hell do you know about that? I'm beginning to suspect I'm not as great an information gateway as I thought." Aaron made a tsk-tsk noise, but he didn't sound even a little bothered. "They want to question him. His wife says he's disappeared. Missing persons is on it. That's all I got. And no, Charlie doesn't have it. Or at least, if she does, she didn't get it from me. But apparently you people have other ways into this place, so take it for what it's worth."

I looked back at the bench across from me as I thanked him and hung up, but the kid was gone. Shrugging off my curiosity, I dug my keys out of my pocket and walked down the short brick path to my car, which was still ticketless. Thank Heaven for small favors.

I parked it in the ER lot and hurried back inside, the sharp sound of my heels on the tile increasing in tempo when I saw Bob's door closed.

I had been booted from enough hospital rooms to know that meant the doctor had arrived, which meant my computer was captive for however long it took to examine my boss. I leaned against the wall and closed my eyes.

I didn't have to wait long.

"How is he?" I blurted, righting myself when the door swung open.

"He's going to be fine." The soft brown eyes behind the doctor's wire-rimmed glasses were just as kind as her smile. "I'm Doctor Schaefer. And you're...?"

"His daughter," I smiled, feeling no remorse about the lie. I knew she wouldn't talk to me if I wasn't family, and I was pretty sure I'd find myself tossed back out to the waiting room.

Dr. Schaefer didn't look much older than me, if she was older at all. About a head shorter and a little softer, she had a tidy chestnut bob and wore a pretty batik skirt and a violet top beneath her lab coat.

She flipped a page in Bob's chart. "I didn't see a mention of the family being here."

I kept the smile in place and offered a little shrug, holding her gaze until she returned the smile and let the page fall back into place. She shook my free hand and told me Bob had indeed had a heart attack, but a fairly mild one.

"He should make a full recovery," she said. "We'll keep him until tomorrow, or possibly Wednesday, but then he'll be able to go home and ease back into his regular routine. We have a few more tests yet to determine the exact cause of his episode and how to treat it best, but I'm confident he'll be fine."

"Is OD'ing on burgers and hot wings an actual diagnosis?" I grinned, her reassurance the happiest thing I'd heard in weeks. "I don't think he eats at home—well, since his wife died."

"I see," she nodded. "So, your mother was the cook in the family?"

"My—" damn. I flinched. Not visibly, I hoped. "My stepmother. Yes, she was."

"Well, if you're in town, and you can, maybe you cook for him sometimes," she said. "If he keeps eating that much junk, he'll end up right back here, and we don't want that. He seems like a nice man, but I'd rather not see him again."

I thanked her and she flipped his chart closed and nodded. "I'm sure I'll see you around. Just have them page me if you have any questions."

I peeked into the room when she walked away and found it dark, my boss snoring again. Slipping my Manolos off, I tip-toed to the chair and picked up my laptop and my bag, then snuck back out. I'd just pulled the door closed and put my shoes back on when my stomach made one of the rudest noises I'd ever heard.

My nose wrinkled at the prospect of hospital cafeteria food, but I decided there had to be something prepackaged I could scarf down before I finished my story. I turned, intending to ask someone at the nurse's station how to get to the cafeteria, but my eyes locked on a still figure maybe twenty yards down the hallway.

Hunger forgotten, I stared at the same teenager I had seen outside. Because he was staring at me. Again.

Taking in the dingy jeans, over-washed wifebeater, and backwards Generals cap, I stood up straight and started walking, the click of my shoes on the tile echoing in the quiet corridor.

"Hi," I said when I reached Mr. Sullen Stare, extending my hand and smiling. "I'm Nichelle."

"You work at the newspaper." His voice was flat, his baby face made older by the somber expression and serious brown eyes.

I blanched, surprised he knew that. "I do. Have we met?"

"No, but I heard you give your name to someone when you were talking on the phone outside, and I remember it because you wrote that story about my brother," he said. "Darryl. Somebody shot him. And it wasn't a random gangbanger like the cops want folks to think. Darryl knew something he wasn't supposed to know."

8.

Rabbit holes

Darryl Wright's little brother scuffed the toe of his worn sneaker over the marble floor in the waiting room, tracing the outline of the diamond-shaped inlay and staring past me at the coral-colored blooms on the azalea outside the picture window.

"Troy?" I leaned forward in my dusty blue armchair. "Do you want to tell me what you think happened to your brother?"

He nodded, and when he raised his head I saw tears in his eyes.

"His friend Noah was bad news. That's what happened to him. They worked for the same pusher. They knew something. Darryl said he had a big payday coming and Noah was helping him with it. And now they're both dead."

I inhaled sharply at the mention of the first victim, but I stayed quiet.

"I didn't pay any attention to him," Troy said, his voice dropping. "To be really honest, I was embarrassed I had a brother who was dealing, you know? I'm trying so hard to get a scholarship for college, and there's Darryl, looking for the easy way out of everything. Sitting on his butt waiting for the junkies to roll up. He liked to talk big, so when he started jawing about all this money he was getting because of some big secret he and Noah knew, I just blew it off. But it looks like he was telling the truth."

The borders on the puzzle in my head shifted to make room for the new pieces.

"You know he didn't even take drugs?"

"Isn't that unusual for a drug dealer?" I asked.

"Yeah." Troy sighed. "But that was Darryl. He didn't mind taking the money from the junkies, but he said the stuff did bad things to people. He saw it with the addicts he sold to. So he didn't ever get into it."

"And the other victim, Noah?" I asked. "How did Darryl know him?"

"I'm not sure. That guy moved up here from Florida about six or seven years ago, I guess. I don't remember how they met, I just remember him being around. I was in elementary school the first time I remember him being at our house.

"He was into drugs, and he thought it was really funny Darryl sold them when he didn't use them. He was always telling Darryl he sold more because he had more faith in his product. Then he got busted, and it was only a few weeks after that that Darryl got busted, too. They both ended up in the same prison, and then they got out within a few months of each other, too.

"It was like this guy Noah was Darryl's personal bad luck." His fingers flew to a gold cross that hung from a thick chain around his neck. "I won't ever know if my brother would have had a decent life if Noah hadn't been there. I'm not sorry he's dead."

Troy's chin dropped to his chest and the tears made little wet spots on his jeans as they fell. They came faster for a few minutes, and I sat with him as he grieved. When he looked up, he drug the back of his hand across his face and took a deep, slow breath.

"Anyway, do you think there will be anything else in the paper about Darryl?"

"Yes, Troy, I do." I looked straight into his earnest eyes. "This story keeps getting curiouser, and I'm not about to let it go. I appreciate you talking to me. If I need to talk to you again, or if my guys at the police department have any questions for you, how do we get in touch with you?"

Troy jotted his phone number on the back of an old receipt he pulled out of his pocket and handed it to me. The vulnerability in his eyes when they met mine hadn't been there before, and it tugged at my heart.

"I miss him," he said. "I didn't know I would, but I do."

I patted his hand.

"I'm not a cop, Troy, but it seems to me like there's a lot more to what happened to your brother than anyone's saying. Let me nose around and see what I can find out."

He nodded and excused himself to check on the friend he'd brought in with a broken ankle. I settled back in the chair and pulled out my laptop, my quest for food lost in the abyss of weirdness that had invaded my world since Friday.

The dealers had been friends. And not just any friends, but conspirator friends. I drew a blank when I tried to figure why their pusher would've left the drugs and money, though. A drug pusher would know the cops would confiscate that stuff.

Unless the pusher knew he'd get it back.

Oh, shit.

My little puzzle was suddenly a lot more interesting.

I dug out Mike's file on the missing evidence and scanned the sign-in sheet a fifth time.

Just cops. And Gavin Neal.

DonnaJo sounded pretty sure her friend Neal was innocent. Just like Mike sounded sure the cops he worked with couldn't be crooks. Everyone was a good guy, yet it looked more and more like someone was in bed with a drug pusher. Curiouser and curiouser indeed.

The clock caught my eye, and I grabbed for my notebook. I had a story to get out, and if Les Simpson was pinch hitting for Bob, I'd better not be late. Crooked cops and shady lawyers would just have to wait.

I flipped through my notes for the quotes I wanted as I added the rest of the information about the internal affairs investigation and the vanished prosecutor, throwing in Aaron's confirmation of Neal's disappearance.

I leaned my head back after I sent my story to Les, closing my eyes and letting my mind meander through everything that had happened since that morning. Bob, Mike, Parker, Aaron, and Troy whirled on the backs of my eyelids as if riding a souped-up carousel. I listened to the whisper of the doors sliding next to me as people came and went, punctuated by the occasional siren from the ambulance bay. It was nice to just sit still.

I jerked myself awake, disoriented as I rubbed my eyes with my fists and looked for a clock. Whoever decided twenty minutes of sleep was a "power nap" must've been recharging a pretty dim bulb, but it would have to do.

I found my phone and called Les to make sure he had my story.

"I wish you could've cited your source on the evidence thing. I haven't seen it anywhere else, and it'd be nice to have it from someone credible," he said. "And that bit about the lawyer was interesting, but kind of thin. I got a green light from legal, but I didn't see where you mentioned the family refused to comment. You did call his wife, didn't you?"

Wow. Les was usually hard to impress, but I figured the exclusive would make him happy since the paper's bottom line was his chief concern.

"First, my source is quite credible, I assure you. Second, I didn't see the point in calling his wife." I clenched the phone too hard and tried to keep the frustration out of my tone. I'm not sure I did a very good job. "If she knew where he was, wouldn't she have told the police?"

"If he's really the prime suspect in a robbery of the police department, do you think the police are going to be completely honest with you?"

I opened my mouth to fire back a reply and instead just sat there, realizing I didn't have a quippy answer for him. To tell the truth, I hadn't considered the possibility of anyone outright lying to me. I knew how to dig information out of the PD better than anyone in town, except sometimes Charlie, but Les was right. I assumed they told me the truth.

"I've worked with some of these guys for better than twenty years, and now I'm looking at everyone like they're a suspect," Mike had said.

What if he was right?

Shit, shit, shit.

"You know what, Les? I didn't think about it that way," I tugged at a strand of hair. Missing something on Bob's watch was bad enough, but at least Bob forgives the mistake so long as you learn from it. "You're right. This isn't exactly a typical burglary. Let me see if I can get ahold of her."

"You do that," he said. "For tomorrow."

"But— "

He cut the objection off before I even got going.

"But nothing. It's almost six o'clock, the front is already down in the pressroom, and I'm not spending tens of thousands of dollars we don't have because you fucked up, Clarke. Do it better tomorrow."

The clatter in my ear as he slammed down the phone told me he was done talking to me.

"Well, you have yourself a nice evening, too, jackass." I muttered, dropping the phone back into my bag. Dammit.

I found no trace of Bob in the room where I'd left him, but a nurse with too-bright lipstick and a severe blond bun scrawled the number of his room in the cardiac unit on a purple post-it and pointed me to the elevators.

I heard the familiar arguing voices from CNN and scattered laughter from the hallway as I approached the open door to room three-two-three.

"I'm sorry, I thought I was in the cardiac ward," I teased as I peeked around the corner, "not the newsroom."

My grin widened when I saw Bob sitting up in the bed eating dinner, surrounded by half of our editorial staff. "You look like that nap did you a world of good."

He nodded, smiling back at me and looking much more like himself than I had seen him look all day.

"I think the drugs helped a little, too," he said, and my smile widened. Yep. He was going to be fine.

I leaned against the wall next to the door and sighed.

"I heard you found him." Parker separated himself from the crowd and gave me a worried once-over, running a hand through his hair. "I wish I'd been there. What happened?"

I recounted the story for the third time.

"Damn." He leaned a shoulder on the open door next to me, throwing an affectionate smile at Bob. "My dad had a heart attack three years ago. I'm glad you went in when you did. He looks great, all things considered, and this is the best cardiac unit in Virginia."

"The doctor said he should make a full recovery." I smiled. "Thank God. It scared the hell out of me. He's going to have to change his diet, but he can do that."

"If my dad can learn to like vegetables, anyone can." Parker grinned and stuck his hands in his pockets before his eyes went skipping between the people and the monitors. "What did you need to talk to him about it the middle of the morning, anyway? You didn't show for the staff meeting today."

"A story." I stepped to one side as the nurse poked her head in and shot the crowd of well-wishers the stink eye. "I had an interview that pre-empted the meeting. Though I wasn't aware you were keeping tabs on my attendance." I waved as people trickled out, leaving me, Parker, and Bob.

Smiling at Bob, I dropped into a chair and cast a glance around what resembled a fairly-tastefully-decorated bedroom, with soft blue walls accented with handsome navy and emerald borders. The bed was one of those hospital numbers I'd seen on TV shows. The kind with a headboard and footboard that tries to impersonate a real bed.

"You're really not going to tell me what you're working on?" Parker asked.

Bob opened his mouth and I shot him a look that clearly said "shut up."

"You can read all about it in the morning," I grinned at Parker. "And you don't even have to cough up the seventy-five cents."

Bob did the chuckle/wince thing again.

"I thought I said no more wisecracks."

"No wisecracks? Why don't you take away her shoes while you're at it, boss?" Parker shook his head, his eyes on me as he addressed Bob. "Good to have you talking to us again. You gave everyone a nice little jolt of adrenaline."

"Sorry." Bob grinned. "No game tonight?"

"Nope. I was at the ballpark trying to hunt up a story when all the excitement actually was in your office today. And you always say nothing newsworthy happens in there." Parker glanced at the heavy, stainless Tag Heuer on his wrist. "I have to run, though. Rest. Feel better. We'll miss you, but we'd like for you to, you know, not die."

Bob snorted. "Thanks."

Parker nodded as he backed out the door. "And holler if you need anything. I'm usually around somewhere, and I have certifiable experience. I made sure my mom got downtime when my dad was recovering."

Well, check you out, Captain Ego. I felt a grudging wave of respect for the second time since Friday as he disappeared with a wave. First he'd been gentle with Katie DeLuca down at the riverfront. Now Bob. I remembered the days after my mom's mastectomy all too well. Caring for an ailing parent was a damned sight harder than chasing crime stories or interviewing ballplayers.

Bob turned his attention to me. "I take it you got your story done?" he asked between bites of what appeared to be instant mashed potatoes.

"I did. Les wasn't happy with it, though. He's sort of a prick, you know that? Get better."

Bob chuckled. "He means well. I like to think, at least. He is completely unforgiving with the budget, though, and he doesn't miss much. What'd you do?"

"What'd I fail to do, actually. I didn't call the lawyer's wife."

"You trust your cops."

"And you think I shouldn't, either?" Damn. If they both thought I should've called her, then Charlie might have actually done it, if she knew Neal was missing. I reminded myself she hadn't called Aaron about it, and hoped she didn't have another source on the force. I'd seen nothing on the station's website at five-thirty, but there was always a chance they could be holding it for the eleven.

Bob shrugged. "Most of the time? I think you're okay. It's hard to cover a beat and not grow fond of the people, and I know you have your favorites down there. But on something like this, you have to question everything. No sense in losing sleep over it, but get it tomorrow."

"Consider it done."

"Anything new?" He sipped milk out of a carton so small I wondered if they'd swiped it from an elementary school cafeteria.

"Don't you need to be eating more than that?"

"This is what they brought." He shrugged. "What else did you find out?"

"Good stuff. Not on the lawyer, but on the drug dealer murders and the missing evidence. You'll never believe who I happened across this afternoon."

I talked while he finished what passed for dinner. He murmured or looked surprised occasionally, but didn't interrupt. When I sat back and sighed a few minutes later, he stared at me for a long moment and then cleared his throat.

"Damn, kiddo," he said. "This really is like chasing the white rabbit down the hole, isn't it? Things keep popping up, and one is more spectacular than the last. But you listen to an old man and take some advice. You're getting into investigative territory, here. These are the stories that make careers, and the kind of thing that might get you noticed by the guys up at the *Post*."

My mouth popped into a little "o" at that and he smiled.

"I might be old, but I'm still pretty sharp. I know that's your brass ring, and I'm glad you want it. Makes you work harder. It's my job to talk you into passing it by if the time comes—and that could be sooner than later if you've got something here. But I'd be an asshole if I didn't warn you to watch yourself. Investigative reporting is a whole different beast. You'll be in as much real danger as a cop working a case would be. Drug pushers, crooked cops. These are not people you want to piss off."

"I am careful. I promise. But you wouldn't give that speech to one of the guys." I hated being treated like I wasn't as capable as a man, but it wasn't worth arguing with him about. I like it when guys open doors for me and kill bugs so I don't have to, and I figure the chivalrous impulse that makes them do those things also compels the good ones to be protective.

"I'm a big girl. And you know all those meetings you bitch about me being late for? I take body combat four days a week. So maybe it's them you should worry about."

"Judging from your stories, they have guns. And experience using them." He leaned back against the pillows and I noticed his coloring had faded a bit. "But remind me not to piss you off."

I changed the subject. He had no business being preoccupied with dangers lurking in my story.

"So, I was thinking today, after I met Troy," I began, trying to sound flippant. "And no matter what happens with this case, I might do a feature story on his family. A sort of 'growing up in the city' piece."

Bob didn't open his eyes as he shook his head. "A feature? Do you even remember how to write one?"

"Of course I do."

"I didn't say you couldn't. I am shocked you want to. That kid must've made quite an impression. I don't see why not, though you might not want to start until you finish this. You can only do so much at once."

I agreed and told him goodnight as the sun faded into half-light outside his window. "I'll check on you tomorrow. Have to make sure you don't, you know, die." I stretched my face into my best exaggeration of Parker's wide smile, and Bob did the chuckle/wince thing again.

"Dammit, Nichelle, that's three." His smile didn't fade. "Knock it off."

"Yes, sir."

"Go find your story," he said. "And don't get too cross-ways with Les, either. They say I'm on house arrest for a while, and I don't want you on his shit list when I get back. He never forgets anything, and he's a pain in my ass when there's someone in the newsroom he doesn't like."

"I'll do my best to fly under his radar."

"You'll have to fly under Shelby's, too," he said. "He's suddenly become her biggest fan the last few weeks, which makes me think I don't want to know exactly what's going on there."

"Are you fucking kidding me?" I rolled my eyes, thinking of her sniffling into Les' chest in Bob's office earlier. From Parker to a snappish, balding bean counter? There was no figuring Shelby out on any front. "No pun intended. And ick."

"It's none of my business, so long as it doesn't affect my newspaper. But just watch it. I know you two ladies don't get along, and I know why." His words began to slur sleepily. "She's not as good as you are, kid, but she could get there. She's a hell of a writer. She just lacks your personality and experience. But if she's got Les' ear, you might have a rough stretch coming. So don't screw up."

"You got it." I backed out of the room as he drifted off.

A bike with a red helmet was in the space next to my car, but it was a Honda, not a BMW like Parker's. I considered our resident jock for half a second, a little ashamed of myself for stereotyping him as a talentless, shallow ass. He seemed like a decent guy, really. The kind I wouldn't mind having as a friend. When I had time for friends again, anyway. I hadn't even spoken to Jenna since Friday.

I rolled the windows down and turned the music up as I tried to make sense of what might be going on at the PD. What if it was a cop? What if it was the lawyer, and he took off because he didn't want to share with the drug pusher? What if said drug pusher had someone on the inside?

I tried to ignore Bob's allusion to "investigative reporting," but the words pulsed through my head in time to the music. It was what I'd always wanted. And it might be right in front of me, if I could just figure out how to get to the answer first. And who I could trust to help me.

I grabbed my phone and dialed Aaron's cell number. Everyone might be a suspect to Mike, but Aaron couldn't be in on this. I'd heard enough of his war stories to know he'd been a damned fine detective, back when he'd worked in homicide.

"Nichelle?" he said when he picked up after the third ring. "What'd I miss now?"

"Don't get me started," I said. I gave him the short version of Bob's medical situation and continued into how I'd met Troy and what he'd told me about his brother and Noah.

"Look, Aaron, there's something really bizarre here. Something that could be huge. I want this story more than I've ever wanted anything, and I need to know what you know. On the record, off the record, whatever. No bullshit. I'm calling in my favor."

He let out a short, sharp breath.

"How do I get myself into this shit?" He paused, and I waited. Finally, he said, "off the record, you promise? You cannot put my name on this. Internal affairs hauled in everyone and their brother for questioning today. They've got this case locked down tighter than a nun's panties, and even I don't know everything. I can tell you where to look, but that's about it."

"What have you got?"

"Someone really wants the lawyer to go up for the stolen evidence," he said. "His wife reported him missing, and she and his buddies at the CA's office suspect foul play. But I'm getting a lot of pressure to put out a story listing him as our prime suspect in the robbery. They know you're going to have that in the morning anyway, so they're throwing this guy under the bus solely on the strength of a signature on the log, best I can tell."

"But you don't think he did it?"

"I don't know what I think. This is all really fucked up, if I'm being honest. And I don't like being asked to put my name on something that's trumped up. Especially when all accounts paint this guy as a decent one, as lawyers go."

"What if the kid's right, and the drug pusher is your murderer?"

"You're thinking he left his stuff at the scenes to throw us off because he was going to steal it back?" Aaron sounded doubtful. "Except this wasn't a breaking and entering situation. They've searched every inch of that locker. There's no sign of anything wrong. Except the shit that's gone, that is." He paused, them asked, "You think this kid will talk to me?"

"I told him you guys might have a few questions for him. He seemed fine with it."

"This might be the break we need. Jerry's gotten little or nothing out of anyone he's talked to. I suppose it's too much for me to hope the kid knows who his brother worked for?"

"If he did, he didn't tell me. But I didn't get the idea he knew." I fished the receipt out of my bag and read Troy's phone number aloud.

"Thanks. And off the record, remember?" Aaron said.

"All access, remember?" I countered. "If you come up with anything, you call me. You promised."

"I suppose I did," he said. "All for keeping a vigilante out of the paper. I think I'm getting screwed on this one. Just don't get me fired."

"I wouldn't have anyone to call for information if I did," I said, my mind already chasing Bob's rabbit down the next hole. "Hey, Aaron? Did you happen to hear anything new on the boat crash? I didn't get around to calling Jones."

"As far as I know, they're still trying to figure out what Freeman and Roberts were doing on the river, and they haven't had much luck. Your story was good. What'd you make of Roberts' wife? I saw that she told you her husband absolutely would not have been out there without orders. You think she's telling the truth?"

"I think she believes that, at the very least."

Aaron murmured something I didn't catch and then he was quiet for a minute.

"What?" My inner Lois perked up.

"I don't know," Aaron said. "I have a hunch. I used to be good at following them. Let's see what I can manage to stir up if I poke this hornet's nest."

"Don't stir up more than you can handle. I recently got a lecture about these particular hornets being nasty business."

"Could be," he said. "I'll call you if there's anything here. If I'm right, I may need your help as much as you need mine."

"If you're right, you're going to need a week out on your boat when this is over. You going on vacation this summer?"

"I'm good." He laughed. "I'll have two kids in college come September. No vacations for a while. I'll take the extra paycheck for my time off. I can always go out to the boat on the weekends, when I don't have a media shitstorm at work."

Passing the *Telegraph* office as I hung up, I glanced at the trucks lined up to transport the papers coming off the presses in the basement, resisting the urge to hop out and grab an early copy to see what Les did to my story. But it'd be there waiting to stress me out in the morning. I wanted a hot bath, a decent meal, maybe a glass of wine—and my bed. And to not ever have another day like this one.

I shoved the kitchen door open and bent to greet Darcy out of habit, but she wasn't there. And she wasn't barking.

I turned and looked over the low wooden fence, but she wasn't in the backyard, either.

"Darcy?" I dropped my keys on the counter and walked through the kitchen into the living room. The last of the evening light was just enough to illuminate the shadowy shape that didn't belong. I froze, wondering if I should scream as my heart rate shot into the stratosphere.

"Is that her name?" the broad-shouldered man who was sitting on my sofa holding my shedding, long-haired dog with complete disregard for the Armani suit he wore asked in an Italian-by-way-of-Jersey accent. "Nice dog you got here, Miss Clarke."

9.

Interview

"Who the hell are you and what are you doing in my house?" I started to step forward and thought better of it, trying to remember if I had anything handy to use as a weapon. Save for a tennis racquet in the back of my little SUV, I didn't think I did. I made a mental note to remedy that situation immediately.

I trained my eyes on the dog, swallowing a wave of nausea and trying to control my breathing. Darcy wasn't barking. She wasn't even whimpering. She was licking his hands. Darcy didn't lick anyone. Ever. Either he had cheddar-flavored fingers, or he wasn't a terrible threat—my dog was an excellent judge of character.

I raised my eyes slowly to his face.

Mr. Breaking and Entering smiled at me and held his hands up, letting go of Darcy. She flopped over on his knee. I shot her a you-little-traitor look. Throwing a sad glance back at her new friend, she hopped down, scurried to my feet, and laid across the right one. Her belly was smooth and warm on my toes, which peeked out of the Manolos I hadn't had time to kick off.

"Please, sit down," Mystery Man said, gesturing to my tufted red chaise as though I were the guest. "I'm not here to hurt you. I'm here to help you, as a matter of fact."

"I'm good." I folded my arms over my chest, hoping I looked braver than I felt. "Easier to get back to the door from here."

Knowing my Blackberry was in the car, I slid a hand into my pocket anyway. No dice. Damn. I scooted the foot Darcy hadn't occupied back into a punching stance slowly, trying to make it look like I was getting comfortable in the doorway.

"I'm not here to hurt you," he repeated.

Because large men break into the homes of single women with benign intentions so often. I was scared. In my own house. And that pissed me off.

"Then why don't we get to why you are here." My hands clenched at my sides and my breathing sped again, from anger instead of fear. "And why the hell are you sitting on my couch when the house was empty and the doors were locked?"

He stared for a long minute.

"You're not afraid of me." It was more a statement than a question. A statement that was a hundred and eighty degrees wrong, but maybe my bravado was working. A glint of what looked like appreciation shone in his amused brown eyes. "You got some guts, Miss Clarke. I respect that. And I like people I respect. That spirit of yours will come in handy."

I bit my tongue to keep from telling him it was about to come in handy kicking his ass out of my house, returning his silent stare instead. I wondered just how afraid I should be.

He met my gaze head-on, and I could read nothing menacing in his eyes or on his face. In another setting, I'd call that face attractive, all dark eyes and strong jaw, and the cut of the suit showed off a nice physique. But there was definitely something about him that put my asshole radar—perfected by years of regular exposure to murderers, rapists, and assorted other lowlifes—on a low hum. His body language was relaxed and open, though. He didn't appear to be an immediate threat. My pulse slowed to near-normal and I relaxed into the doorjamb.

He flashed a sardonic little grin. "We okay?"

"Look, I've had one hell of a day, so could we just get on with this, Mr.…?"

"Call me Joey." Again with the grin. He cleared his throat and continued. "I know something. A few things, really, that I think you'd like to know, but I need your help finding out more."

I cocked my head to one side. Come again, Captain Cryptic?

"Let me lay it out for you," he said. "You've had quite a weekend, even for someone in your line of work. First, a second drug dealer complicates an open-and-shut murder case, then a boat blows up and kills a handful of people, two of them cops. Now you have a conspicuous vacancy in the police department's evidence room and a missing attorney. What I came to tell you is that all of those things are related. The evidence was on the boat. And the lawyer is in on it, but I'm not sure which side."

Well, then. While I wasn't sure of much of anything right then, that was pretty far down the list of things I'd suspected Mr. Hair Gel might want with me. He leaned forward, resting his elbows on his knees, and waited for me to answer him.

"I guess it's possible," I said slowly. "The last time anyone knew the evidence was in the locker was Friday afternoon. So if someone took it after that, and before the boat went out…"

I trailed off, shaking my head. "I saw the logs from the evidence room. Roberts and Freeman were nowhere on the list. Patrolmen have to sign in. So they couldn't have taken it."

"Unless someone else loaded the boat and sent them out on it."

Well, hell. I opened my mouth to ask him another question when it dawned on me we were talking about the missing evidence. Shit.

"Wait, how do you know about the evidence and the lawyer? That's in tomorrow's newspaper." Suddenly way more interested in whether or not someone else had my story than in the man who'd broken into my house, I stood up straight. "Did one of the TV stations have that at six?" I had checked Charlie's stuff, but what if someone else had gotten wind of it somehow?

He shook his head and smiled. "Your scoop is safe, Miss Clarke. And it's a good one, too. But I'm offering you a chance at something so much better. I have friends everywhere. They tell me things. I came here to ask you for a favor, in return for this information."

I raised one eyebrow and waited for him to get on with it.

"I know what's going on, or most of it, anyway. What I don't know is who's doing it. I'm working on finding out, but I've been following your stories closely, and you can help me. You have access to people I might not be comfortable talking with. Interested?"

"I'm interested in everything. It's an occupational hazard." Holy shit.

His gaze was level, his expression unguarded. I'd interviewed so many criminals I could spot a lie at twenty paces. And this guy was not lying. The puzzles in my head shifted and melded together as I studied my uninvited guest. Who the hell was he?

The suit was Italian. And expensive. I was pretty sure it was authentic Armani. The men's department at Saks was adjacent to women's shoes, where I tried on things I couldn't afford, making a list for eBay. He had big rings on three of the long fingers of each hand, and a chunky gold watch on his wrist. His nails were neat and shiny, probably recently manicured; his black hair slicked back from his oval face. The features and accent smacked of an Italian heritage. He wasn't much older than me, and exuded a throwback debonair quality that belonged in a black and white movie. Sort of like DeNiro's portrayal of Monroe Stahr from Fitzgerald's *The Last Tycoon*. But taller, with a better smile.

"Are you a cop?" He was too well dressed, really, but I wouldn't know most of the internal affairs or undercover guys if I tripped over them, and I couldn't figure out how he'd come by his information.

He shook his head and laughed, a deep, rich sound I found pleasant in spite of myself.

"I think that's the first time I've ever been asked that." He winked.

Bob's comments about Washington popped into my head and I tried to match his face with one from C-SPAN. I had a nagging feeling I'd seen him somewhere. "A politician?"

"Not the kind you mean."

"There's more than one kind?"

"Politics is making people think what you think," he said and leaned back, casually draping one arm over the sofa cushion. "It wouldn't be unreasonable to say that's one of the things I do."

"But you're not going to tell me who you are, or what it is you actually do?"

"It's not important."

The hell it wasn't.

"Why should I believe anything you say if you won't tell me how you know it?"

He sat up and adjusted his suit jacket, holding my gaze without blinking. "Because I'm right," he said. "And when you have time to think about it, you'll know it. Tell me something, what happens to evidence after a trial ends?"

I shrugged. "They destroy most of it. Once they're pretty sure the case won't go to appeal."

He nodded. "Anything noteworthy they should have destroyed recently?"

Noteworthy? There was a ridiculous variety of stuff in the police evidence lock up on any given day. People could turn some crazy things into weapons when they were mad enough or drunk enough or any combination of the two.

Evidence was destroyed depending on the court calendar. The drugs and the money from the two dealer murders shouldn't have gone anywhere for at least a year. There hadn't even been an arrest made in the case.

So what had cleared the courtrooms by enough to be trashed lately? If he was right and everything was connected, Neal's cases made the most sense. I ran mentally through the list DonnaJo sent me, trying to tie the missing lawyer to whatever Joey was talking about.

"Oh, shit." I clapped a hand over my mouth. "The guns. That trucker from New York." I could picture it, Gavin Neal waving a gun over his head during his closing argument and dropping it back into a sizable trough of semi-automatic and automatic weapons seized off of a truck on its way from New York to North Carolina over a year before.

Neal got the truck driver convicted of transporting the stolen weapons across state lines with intent to sell. There had been a lot of guns in that box in the courtroom that day, and I'd watched the bailiffs carry them out to a police van after the verdict came back.

I shoved the pesky lock of hair that wouldn't stay in my clip behind my ear again. I didn't know a lot about guns, but I'd bet a whole shitload of them with unregistered serial numbers would be worth a pretty penny on the black market.

"The guns." Joey nodded. "Along with the drugs and cash from your murder cases, were on the boat. That baseball player and his buddies cost someone a lot of money Friday night."

"And you really don't know who? Or you just don't want to tell me?"

He smiled again. "I don't know. Truly. I do think this could work out well for us both if you handle it right, and I'll help you as much as I can, but I'm not what you would call a quotable source." He rose smoothly and walked toward me. "So you'll have to find some things out for yourself. See what you can dig up, and if I come across anything I think might help, I'll be in touch. I hear you're a very determined lady, and I have a hunch you'll get to the bottom of this. You'll have the story of the decade when you do, I promise you."

I held my ground and kept my eyes on his face. His movements were easy. His lips turned up slightly as he slid sideways through the door, brushing closer to me than he needed to. I caught my breath at the unwanted shiver that skated up my spine. He smelled good, too.

"What if you're wrong?" I turned and walked with him to the front door, noting it wasn't damaged. Just like the evidence lock up. "Why would anyone steal evidence from the police and put it on their own boat?"

"I suggest you think about that, because I am not wrong." He turned his head so his face was inches from mine, then stepped out onto the porch. "I like you. You're smart. You're determined. I'm going to be your friend, Miss Clarke—and I'm a very good friend to have."

I waited while he walked to the end of the sidewalk, where a black Town Car idled at the curb. What a day. I couldn't even come home and go to bed like a normal person. No, I had to have James Bond's better-looking Italian cousin giving the dog Stockholm Syndrome. I closed the door and turned the deadbolt, slid the chain home, then tugged on the knob to make sure it was secure.

Moving through the house with Darcy on my heels, I checked every door and window and closet; even peering under my bed. When I was sure I was alone, and likely to stay that way for the rest of the night, I freshened the dog's water and filled her bowl with kibble before I went to the cafe-style kitchen table with a legal pad and a pen, recording every detail of what was very possibly the strangest conversation of my life. The mental puzzles I'd been juggling all weekend suddenly melted neatly together, a chunk of the picture clear, if I believed Joey. And I did.

Still mulling it over, I stirred the contents of a can of chicken noodle soup around in a pan on my aging GE stove and then took the pad with me to the couch. I pulled my legs up onto the cushion beneath me while I ate, picking my notes back up when I put the bowl down.

"What'd you think?" I asked Darcy, who had retreated to her pink bed in the corner after her own dinner, curled up so she resembled a furry russet pom-pom. "He's telling the truth, or at least, he thinks he is. But before I get in too deep, I need to find out who our visitor was and why he doesn't want me to know."

Remembering Joey's comment about not being a quotable source, I flipped back through my notes. An undercover cop couldn't be quoted or it would blow his case. But he'd thought it was funny when I'd asked about him being a cop.

He said he was like a politician, but "not the kind you mean."

"Oh, shit, Darcy," I whispered. "What if he's more Vito Corleone than Monroe Stahr?"

I flipped faster between the pages, my eyes lighting on certain words. "I have lots of friends. They tell me things… Politics is making people think what you think." He expected me to be afraid of him. He wore an expensive suit, he left in a chauffeured sedan, the accent…"I'm a good friend to have."

Of course. The cherry on top of my crazy Monday sundae. The first sexy guy I'd met in months, and he was probably an honest-to-God mobster. Why the hell not?

I leaned my head back against the damask-covered sofa cushion. "Stolen evidence. Missing lawyers. And the fucking Mafia in my living room," I laughed, mostly because it was better than screaming. The dog whimpered. "Well, Tuesday, you have a heck of a lot to live up to. Monday set the bar high this week."

Darcy looked downright indignant when I ordered her through the runt-sized doggie door on my way to bed, but I didn't want to unlock the door to let her go pee, never mind step out for her customary game of fetch. She took less than a minute to do her business and bounce back in, turning her head away from me as she trotted to the bedroom. I double-checked the locks and turned off the lights, peering out the window into the still darkness, not even really sure what I was looking for.

As a peace offering, I lifted Darcy out of her bed and onto mine when I crawled under the covers. Drifting off to sleep with *Goodfellas* and *Donnie Brasco* playing in my head, I felt her snuggle behind the crook of my knees and knew I'd been forgiven.

By the time I got out of the shower the next morning, I had convinced myself the Mafia was the only logical explanation for "call me Joey," altogether dismissing the idea that the guy was a cop. My inner Lois was sure of it, and going with my gut had never failed me. I also couldn't shake the feeling that I'd seen him somewhere before.

I brushed my teeth and tried to place Joey's angular features in a courtroom, focusing on the handful of times I had heard rumors of Mafia activity along the Atlantic coast and trying to remember things I'd once made a concerted effort to forget.

My initiation into the courthouse fraternity had been a formidable one, and among the first trials I'd covered was a particularly grisly murder case that sanity and sound sleep had demanded I repress in the nearly two years since. I tried to call up the details. The guy was an accountant, and he had been beheaded. His girlfriend found his head on his desk atop a stack of files that detailed a little side action. He'd been skimming cash from several local business owners who trusted him with their books, and he'd built an offshore nest egg that would've supported a family of four comfortably for at least a decade. The crime scene photos fueled my nightmares for weeks.

The prosecutor walked into the trial almost cocky. He had a gruesome murder that was pulling huge ratings for the TV news, and consequently getting him a lot of face time with the cameras, and he had a confession from the defendant. The accountant had stolen money from the guy's construction company. A slam dunk. The prosecutor didn't mind that he didn't have a murder weapon or DNA or any witnesses putting the accused at the scene of the crime. He had it sewn up, he'd told us at his self-organized ego-fest of a pretrial press conference on the courthouse steps. I hadn't seen that lawyer in court since, but it wouldn't occur to me to miss him.

Ultimately, the New York legal celebrity who'd argued for the defense got the charges dismissed. It had been quite a show.

No fancy loopholes or backroom deals, just outright dismissal by the judge on the most ridiculous of technicalities. The defense attorney, in his shiny wingtips and Hugo Boss, reminded me of a hunter stalking his prey as he'd led the arresting cop into admitting on the stand that he hadn't read the guy his rights when he picked him up. Simple as that: no Miranda rights, no conviction. But thanks for playing.

Before that little revelation swept the courtroom into chaos, however, I'd been eavesdropping on two prosecutors who were sitting in the cheap seats with the rest of us between court appointments of their own.

"You don't tend to live long when the Mafia catches you skimming money off the top," one of them had said, chuckling. The other lawyer had agreed, and I'd rolled my eyes, tuning out their conversation and thinking they had seen too many movies.

Suddenly sure I'd been mistaken, I shook off the memory of Joey's eyes moving over me on his way out. It didn't matter if he liked what he'd seen, because I didn't find organized crime attractive, shivers or no. I gave myself a stern glare in the mirror to punctuate that thought.

"I'm going to be your friend, Miss Clarke, and I am a very good friend to have."

I spit out the toothpaste and grabbed my hair dryer.

So I just had to figure out if he was the kind of friend I wanted. I threw on a five-minute face and decided to skip body combat in favor of learning exactly what I was dealing with. Filling a travel mug with Green Mountain Colombian Fair Trade, I added a shot of white chocolate syrup and headed out.

Halfway to the office, I thought about Bob.

The worry of Monday afternoon eclipsed the evening's interview with the young Godfather, and I laughed at the absurdity of such a convergence of drama.

"Was there some kind of planetary alignment?" I asked out loud, raising my face to the heavens. "Have I angered somebody up there? How the hell does that much happen to one person on one day?"

Somehow, ranting—even if it was just at my sunroof—made me feel better. When I noticed I was parked in the garage at the office, I shut off the engine and crossed the space between the car and the elevator quickly, looking over my shoulder twice in no more than two dozen steps. I figured I'd be paranoid for life because of that one interview.

It was quiet in the newsroom in the early morning. I didn't usually arrive before eight a.m. It was eerie for it to be so still with light outside the windows.

I reached for my headphones and turned on a pulsing dance number before I opened my browser and clicked the Google tab on my favorites bar. I stared at the screen for a long moment before I typed "Mafia" into the box and hit the search button. I got more than forty-seven-million results.

Scrolling down, I chose a Wikipedia article that turned out to be a complete history of organized crime in Sicily. It was fascinating, even if it wasn't particularly relevant, and I read through half the page before I saw a link to something more promising. I waited for the article on the American Mafia to load and became engrossed in the information on the screen. It could've been lifted from any one of a hundred novels.

"Yeah, I never would have believed any of this yesterday morning," I said to the empty room, my eyes getting big as I read the long list of American cities with known Mafia families. Some of them were an easy day's drive from Richmond. And the fine print said the list was a partial one.

"Holy shit." I exhaled forcefully, sat back in the chair, and dropped the headphones to my desk. Looking at a chart of how

Mafia families are organized, I surmised Joey must be up there. I didn't figure foot soldiers wore three-thousand-dollar suits and rode around in chauffeur-driven cars.

There was a whole section on initiation and how it usually involved murder. I remembered the sardonic smile that played around Joey's lips for most of the time I had talked to him, and shivered. Had someone, or more than one someone, taken their last breath looking at that smile?

"A good friend to have," he'd said.

I guess if my choice was limited by him being in my living room, I'd certainly rather he like me than not.

Bob was right. Missing lawyers, stolen evidence, and organized crime. It was a bona-fide investigative story. But I needed to know more about what I was dealing with. I clicked over to the *Telegraph* archives, searching old courthouse photos for Joey's face. I found it in a shot from the decapitated accountant trial. Joey was part of a crowd of onlookers, leaning on a column behind the bigheaded prosecutor. I couldn't zoom in too much without making the image fuzzy, but I'd recognize that little half-grin anywhere.

"What the hell am I getting myself into?" I wondered aloud. Even as I said the words, I had a feeling it was too late to back out. And I wasn't at all sure I wanted to.

10.

Missing links

"No telling, where you're concerned," Shelby's voice came from behind my shoulder and I jumped, whacking my knee on the underside of my desk. That would leave a mark. "Anything interesting?"

Seriously, universe? I searched the memories of my college religion class for the words to the Hail Mary. Not that I was Catholic. I was just trying to cover my penance bases as Shelby stared at me with her ping-pong-ball eyes, making a tsk-tsk sound with her tongue.

"Nothing you'd be up for," I stretched my lips into a tight smile and cocked my head to one side. "Though, you know, I've read your stuff. It's not bad."

She smiled, her eyes getting impossibly bigger. "I know."

I shrugged. "Like I said, not bad. But covering cops and covering garden parties are about as similar as the Oscars red carpet and a kid playing dress up. You wouldn't last a day in my shoes. Bob's not giving you my job, so give it up."

"Bob's not here, is he? Les wasn't happy with you last night. Not to kiss and tell, but I'd watch my step if I were you."

"Are you serious? Is there anyone in this building you haven't boinked trying to get a promotion? Do you have, like, any self-respect?"

"Sure. I respect my ability to find ways to get what I want," she smiled. "You're a good writer, Nichelle. And you're a good reporter. Bob thinks you're the next Helen Thomas, and it's totally obvious to everyone how much you love that. But I'm a good writer, too. I just got hired for a beat that was expendable. Cops is not, and once I get away from the copy desk, I have no intention of going back."

I narrowed my eyes and started to say something, but she kept talking.

"So do me a favor. Go get your story. I don't even have to know what it is right now. Les said you were into something big he didn't think you could handle. I, ever selfless, offered to help, which he thought was very sweet of me." She smirked. "And as long as we're talking about what everyone knows, we all know you've got your eye on the *Post.* And we all know if you were really good enough, you'd already be working there. Look, Nichelle, at the end of the day, it makes me no difference how you go. Ride off into the sunset to be a politics superstar, screw up and get yourself fired. All I care is that right now, Les is in charge, and I'm next in line for a byline as the crime reporter. So you have yourself a nice day. Just remember, I'll be around."

She shot me one last smug grin, turned on her heel, and started to walk off.

"Hey Shelby?" I called.

She turned back.

"If you were so great at what you do, Bob wouldn't have hired me in the first place. You were already here, remember? Too bad you're not his type. You may be leading Les around by his dick right now, but Bob still makes the staffing decisions.

And just because you were a convenient threat on Saturday, doesn't mean you're next in line for jack shit." I sounded way more confident than I felt, and her smile faltered, which made mine widen. "So you have yourself a nice day at the copy desk, okay?"

Tuesday, mercifully, did not live up to Monday in terms of drama. I didn't see Shelby again, and my day passed in a blur of phone calls and faxes. I called Gavin Neal's wife (who had no comment, thank you, Les, but at least I had it in my day-two story), and looked through Neal's recent cases again. The case I had remembered while I was talking to Joey, with the stolen guns, was the only notable one. A search of public records revealed a bankruptcy filing, mostly for medical collections, that hadn't been granted, but I couldn't access more than the final judgment, which held that Neal's bills must be paid because of tougher standards in the bankruptcy code.

Money was always good motive.

But then Joey's words rang in my head, and no matter how I turned them over, I couldn't fit Neal into a scenario where the money blew up on the river. First, he went to evidence on Sunday, not Friday. Second, why would he put it on a PD boat if he was stealing it from the PD?

If Joey was right about the boat, then Neal wasn't the logical suspect in the evidence theft. Yet Charlie had blasted Neal's face, superimposed over images of the evidence room, all over Channel Four beginning with the early show. Aaron was right—the PD cast Neal as the bad guy. Charlie had nothing on his financial troubles, but I knew she would soon, and that only strengthened the case against him.

After a good deal of back-and-forth, my desire to not lose to Charlie beat out my doubts about Neal and I went with it, bankruptcy and all. I threw in comments from DonnaJo and other prosecutors who proclaimed Neal's innocence to balance my story, but it still didn't look too good.

If he didn't take it, who did? I wondered about Aaron and his hornet's nest, but I didn't hear anything from him and he didn't answer when I called.

I went to see Bob on my way home and found him holding court in a hospital room that looked like it had been attacked by a florist on speed. I nodded to the mayor, three guys in suits I didn't recognize, and the *Telegraph*'s advertising director, who all rose to leave when the phone rang just after I walked in.

Bob talked to Les about the next day's newspaper for a few minutes, picking at a tray of overcooked chicken, limp broccoli, and orange Jell-O. He looked almost like himself. He was even wearing pajamas Parker dropped off that morning instead of the hospital gown.

Dr. Schaefer stopped in before I left, and she said she planned to send Bob home the next day. I grumbled about insurance companies and told Bob I'd be happy to help with whatever he needed. He said Parker had already volunteered for that job.

"It sounded like he has some experience." I smiled. "Something tells me he'll take good care of you."

Bob muttered something about a babysitter and I laughed, wishing him a good night.

Darcy streaked to the door in a little furry blur, barking her head off like always, when I got home. I scooped her up and kissed her fuzzy head, scratching her chest while I inspected the house. After a third check of all the locks, I relaxed a little.

I spooned a can of beef and carrots Pedigree into Darcy's bowl and ate a sandwich at the counter while she snarfed it down, then took her out for the shortest game of fetch in history, checked the locks again, and fell into bed, comforted by the soft feel of the sheets on my skin and the heft of the duvet as I settled back into the pillows.

I dreamed of Joey.

We were in a long room, like a conference room minus the table, and he was at the other end trying to tell me something. I couldn't hear him for the god-awful buzzing noise, like honey-bees in hyper-drive, and no matter how I waved or beckoned, I couldn't get him to come closer. He reached into his jacket pocket and produced a fat brass ring. He held it out to me, then pulled it away when I reached for it, holding it up and thumping the outside of it instead of tossing it over.

I woke up Wednesday with the covers twisted around my legs as if I'd been fighting them in my sleep, my hair damp with sweat in the air-conditioned room. I stretched, grumbling as I climbed out of bed, still craving sleep. The unsettling dream had kept me from resting.

I went to the gym anyway, and as I threw jabs, angled, and perfected my *ap chagi* (I was fairly certain the instructor was butchering the Korean when he called for the front kick by shouting "ap shaggy," but no one seemed to mind), I thought about Joey. Freud probably wouldn't see anything deeply hidden in my dream. Bob called the *Post* my brass ring. I was pretty sure Joey had the key, but he wouldn't give it to me. Fair enough. Except I couldn't get past the feeling I was missing something.

Jab, jab, bouncebouncebounce, uppercut. Brass. What else was brass?

Gallop, gallop, *ap chagi*! Old chandeliers. Saddle fittings. Military officers.

Oh, shit.

I stopped suddenly, and the guy behind me *ap chagi*-ed me in the ass. I think he apologized, but I was already halfway to the door.

The police command staff. Brass. Dammit, I hated feeling slow.

I tried Aaron again on my way into the newsroom, wondering if his hornet's nest was on the top floor of police headquarters.

When I got to my desk, I called Captain Jones and asked him if the destroyed patrol boat had been taken out recently, besides the night of the accident.

"I pulled that on Saturday, and there was only one other outing in the past month, a training." I heard him typing in the background. "Here it is. Looks like two weeks prior to the accident." More keystrokes. "Huh. I didn't check the notes on this the other day, the damned phone was ringing off the hook and I got sidetracked. This is a little odd, actually. It was a Saturday, and Deputy Chief Lowe ordered it out on a training exercise. I wonder what kind of training he was doing?"

"Lowe?" I asked. My breath sped. "I take it you didn't know anything about a scheduled training that day?"

"I don't do training on the weekends, and I know I wasn't here that Saturday, because it was my wife's birthday and we were at the beach."

"Was Lowe the only officer on the boat that day?" I asked.

"It doesn't say," Jones said.

I couldn't tell from his tone if he was talking to me, or to himself. He sounded far away, as if thinking out loud. Then more clicking. I scribbled furiously.

"There's another notes screen. Says one of my sergeants went to the boathouse, found Chief Lowe there on the boat. At which time Sergeant Mayer reminded Lowe he had to log the boat out, even for training. Mayer was heading out to search for a missing swimmer and noticed that the patrol vessel hadn't been checked out."

I stopped writing, distracted as I ran through the memory of my conversation with Lowe the day after the accident. Had the odd inflection I'd heard in his voice and dismissed as sorrow been something else? Like guilt? "You would think the deputy chief would be familiar with standard operating procedures."

"I certainly would," Jones said.

I stared into space after I put the phone down. Lowe? Joey's hints would fit: someone with enough clearance to sign the boat out, and avoid signing into the evidence locker. Was the deputy chief stealing evidence and selling drugs and guns right out of police headquarters? Joey's face was replaced in my head by Troy's as I considered that: if Darryl and Noah knew they were working for the deputy chief of police, then it gave them ready ammunition for blackmail. And made them expendable.

I grabbed the phone and drummed my fingers on the desk while I waited for Mike to pick up. Before I went wholesale with Joey's version of events, I wanted to know if anyone saw the evidence on Saturday.

"Narcotics, this is Stevens." A low, unfamiliar voice came through the handset.

"I'm sorry. I think I ended up at the wrong extension. I was looking for Mike Sorrel."

"The sergeant isn't here today. Can I help you?"

"No, thanks, I'll try his cell phone," I said. "I need to talk to him today."

"He's not picking up his cell, miss," Stevens said, his tone a mixture of patient and concerned. "Can I ask who's calling?"

"This is Nichelle Clarke at the *Richmond Telegraph*. What do you mean 'he's not picking up his cell?' Is he sick?"

"I wish I knew, Miss. No one has heard from him for a couple of days now. His wife says he didn't go home from work Monday, and he wasn't here yesterday, either."

My stomach flip-flopped, my insides going cold. "He's…he's gone? Like, missing? I…" I couldn't finish that sentence.

"Every spare detective we have is searching," Stevens said. "We'll figure it out. Myself, I'm hoping he just needed to get away for a few days. Maybe a fight with his wife she doesn't want to tell us about. Wanted some distance from her. That's usually how these things end up."

"Sure," I said.

I closed my eyes and dropped my head into my hands when I cradled the receiver. Mike is missing. The words looped through my mind, speeding until they ran together. Mikeismissing. I pictured his grave expression as he cautioned me about the information he gave me Monday morning. And he didn't go home that night. For all I knew, I was the last person who saw him. But no one knew he'd talked to me.

Torn between keeping his confidence and worrying, I grabbed the phone and pushed redial, trying to keep the frantic note out of my voice as I asked for Aaron.

"Davis."

My stomach knotted again when Jerry Davis, the detective working the drug dealer case, answered Aaron's phone.

"Hello?" Jerry said, drawing the word out.

I struggled to make my lips work.

"Jerry? It's Nichelle Clarke at the *Telegraph*. Please tell me Aaron's in a meeting and you just happen to be hanging out waiting for him."

Jerry laughed. "You have some sort of hot scoop today?" he asked, misinterpreting the desperation clear in my tone. "Sorry, Nichelle, he's on vacation this week. He emailed yesterday morning that he was taking the boat out and he'd be out of cell range for a week or ten days, so I'm trying to cover for him. I gotta hand it to him. You people are pretty time-consuming. His job is harder than I thought."

"Vacation." I repeated, my voice hollow.

I heard Aaron in my head: "I'm going to have two kids in college, come September. No vacations around here for a while. I'll take the extra paycheck for my time off....Let's see what I can manage to stir up if I poke this hornet's nest."

What if Aaron stirred up more than he bargained for?

"You're sure the email was from Aaron?" My voice was too high.

"I didn't see him typing it, or anything, but it was sent from his RPD account. Hey, are you okay?"

"Yes. No. I don't know, Jerry. There's some weird stuff going on this morning."

"Anything I can help with?"

I bit my lip and tried to think of something. Was there anything he might not ask too many questions about?

"I don't think so," I said finally.

"Let me know if there's anything I can do for you while Aaron's gone."

"Thanks, Jerry. If you do happen to hear from Aaron, ask him to give me a call."

Twisting the top off a Diet Coke bottle in the break room a couple of minutes later, I remembered that Bob was supposed to be getting his walking papers from Dr. Schaefer.

I went back to my cube and called my boss' house. He picked up on the second ring, and if I hadn't seen him looking so frail two days before, I would never have believed the man had a heart condition.

"Hey, chief," I said. "How are you feeling?"

"Nicey," Bob said, more cheerful than I was used to. "I'm fantastic. I'm home! It's nice to be in my own clothes and watching my own TV. I have two news channels on, but Warden Parker here won't let me talk to Les for more than seven minutes an hour, which is driving me insane."

He didn't sound the least bit annoyed.

"You're not fooling anyone. And he's trying to make sure you get well quickly," I said. "He's done this before. You listen to him and you'll be back in here hollering at us in no time."

I could hear the smile in his voice. "Yes, ma'am."

"I'm glad to hear you sounding like yourself. I want to come by and see you."

"Sure," Bob said, his grouching about babysitters apparently forgotten, at least for the moment. "I think Parker said he has to run up there at three to get his column filed because he forgot his laptop."

"Tell him no rush," I said. "I'll come hang out with you while he gets his piece taken care of. Do you need me to pick up anything on my way?"

"I don't think so. He got groceries already." His voice dropped to an exaggerated conspiratorial whisper. "He's making some kind of soup. Do you figure whatever he comes up with will be edible?"

Parker's good-natured laugh rang in the background.

"I'm sure he's not going to kill you," I said. "It's good to have you back, Chief. Get some rest."

As far as actual printable copy was concerned, my day was pretty light. There were a couple of follow-ups on small trials I had been waiting for verdicts on, but nothing worthy of sitting at the courthouse. One was a hit-and-run (minor injuries, acquitted), the other an animal cruelty case (puppy mill, convicted). I interviewed the prosecutors and defense attorneys for both cases, pounded out the stories, and sent them to Les. Two hours early. That ought to shut Shelby up for a while.

Parker's bike was still in the driveway when I pulled up outside Bob's stately brick-front colonial that afternoon. I sat in my car, listening to the radio and rehearsing what I was planning to tell my editor. I needed to keep it light so I wouldn't give him another heart attack, but I also wanted to know what he really thought. I wondered if there was a punch line to a mob boss being in my living room. Knock, knock. Who's there? The Mafia. Except he didn't knock. Yeah, there's not much funny about that.

Parker left before I had a good plan, waving as he settled the helmet on his head. Damn. I stepped out of the car. Short of a sudden flash of brilliance, I could just watch my tone, lay it out straight, and hope for the best.

"Nicey?" Bob called when I opened the front door. "I'm in the living room."

I walked down the long entry hall, past the parlor and the dining room, and found Bob, looking normal save for the plaid pajamas and blanket, stretched out on his brown leather sofa watching CNN. MSNBC was running in a small box in the corner of the screen.

I grinned. "Glad to see you up and around, sir," I said.

"Not up and around," he scowled. Being at home evidently lost its novelty quickly. "If someone would let me up and around, I'd go to the office. Instead, I'm here with another babysitter, and Parker ordered me to stay on this couch unless I have to use the bathroom. I feel like I'm in first grade. I should have eaten a few more salads, I guess."

"It's not too late to remedy that, you know." I tried not to sound too reproachful. "We need to introduce you to the farmer's market."

"So I've been told," he said, gesturing to the big brown leather recliner. "Sit. Tell me what's going on with your story."

I took a deep breath, surprised it had taken him more than two minutes to ask.

Still lacking a better idea, I tried to keep my voice light as I told him about my uninvited guest. It didn't work.

"Jesus, kid." Bob blew out a slow, controlled breath. "I'm out for three days and this is what you come up with? The god-damned Mafia? Are you sure?"

"It's not like he gave me a business card that said 'Good-fellas, we deliver.' But the story fits. And I found him in that photo from the embezzler murder trial, too. I heard a couple of the ACAs down there talking about the guy stealing from the mob. What do you think? You're the first person I've told about this."

"As much as I don't want to, I think you're right. I've heard rumors. Once you get involved with these people, you don't get uninvolved until they get what they want. But why haven't you asked your guys at the PD about this Joey?"

"Because they're not there. Either of them." My voice caught a little on the last word. "Mike didn't go home Monday night and they're saying Aaron is on vacation. I guess that might be true, but he just told me he wasn't taking vacation this year."

"Did either of them take the money?"

"I don't want to think so." I sighed. I needed his opinion, and for him to give it to me, he needed to know what was going on. "Here's the thing: Mike's the one who brought me the story on the missing evidence. He went down there to check something out and it was gone, and he called IAD and then he called me. So, part of me wonders if Mike stole it, but why would he bring me the story if he was the one who did it?"

"To make it look like he's not?"

I dropped my head into one hand. And Mike had been at the river on Friday night, too. As much as I hated the idea, if

Joey was right and the evidence was on the boat, what if Mike wasn't just being helpful?

"Yeah, that's kind of where I landed, too." I peeked through splayed fingers at Bob's furrowed brow before I raised my head. "Shit, Chief. I don't know. I don't know who to trust. I don't know what to think. I do have another theory, though. I think there's a decent chance the deputy police chief is running this whole thing, no matter who's involved in it." I forged ahead, talking so fast I wasn't sure he could keep up.

"I think he stole the evidence and sent those rookies to take it somewhere," I said when I finally sat back in the chair. "But if that's it, what I don't know is whether or not Roberts and Freeman knew there was anything illegal on the boat. Or who else might be in on it."

"It's a hell of a sexy story, isn't it?" Bob asked. "I can't say I'm quite as excited about it as I was Monday, but…good God, you can't not go after it. I know you, and I remember what it's like. But you can't imagine how shitty I'm going to feel if you get yourself hurt chasing a headline."

"Well, no worries, because I have no intention of doing anything but cracking the case and saving the day. Step aside, Lois Lane."

He laughed in spite of the crease in his forehead. "Work fast, huh, Lois? The sooner you're out from under this one, the better I'll feel. Plus, Charlie won't be far behind you. You don't want to end up second chair after all this mess." He smiled at me and changed the subject. "Let's talk about something a little less stressful before we both have a heart condition. Tell me everything else that's going on. I'm going through withdrawals."

Two hours later, I had him fully back in the loop and we had just moved on to politics when Parker walked in the front door.

"Just checking in before I head out for the night." He nodded a hello at me and focused on Bob. "You need anything, boss? That minestrone should be done by now, and I have a date. Did y'all know there's a new reporter at Channel Ten? She was at the DeLucas' house the other day. Said she likes my column."

He glanced at me. "Speaking of, at the risk of being a pain in the ass, did you ever read my piece from Saturday?"

I shook my head, unable to keep a rueful smile off my face.

"I'm going to, I swear," I said. "I've just been busy. Nothing personal."

"Sure it's not. What could possibly have you so busy you don't have time for a fifteen hundred word story?"

Bob's eyes flicked between us as I paused for half a beat too long.

"Mostly personal stuff," I said, not wanting my lead offered up as a way to get the new girl at Channel Ten into the sack. "Nothing that would interest you. But I really will get to it. I don't break promises, even when I have to delay them."

Parker pinched his lips together and studied me for a second before he flashed the trademark grin and told us goodnight.

We heard the door click as he let himself out.

I moved to follow suit and my boss shot me another warning glare.

"Quick and clean. Don't piss Les off, don't get us sued, and for fuck's sake, don't get yourself killed," he said.

"Yessir," I said.

My thoughts tangled up in my story as I drove home to the gravelly twang of Janis Joplin, and I pondered what Bob had said, wondering if Aaron and Mike really could be knee deep in this and unable to think of a single person who could tell me the answer to that.

But what if I could find out for myself?

Cranking up the music, I cut across two lanes and hung a sharp left on Thompson, heading for the freeway. The often-annoying ability to remember anything I read, which tended to leave my mind cluttered and hard to shut off at night, produced a perfect image of the map on Aaron's office wall—and the big black circle around the marina on the Appomattox River where he docked his boat.

11.

Move over, Lois

The Appomattox is nearly an hour south of Richmond, and the sun was low in the sky by the time I got close enough to check my maps app for the exact location of the marina. There were two in the vicinity of Aaron's black circle, and I pulled into the nearly-deserted gravel parking lot at the first and hopped out, not sure if I was excited or nervous.

I wanted the boat to be gone—though I wouldn't know for sure until I'd checked both locations. But the wringing in my gut told me I would find something. True, he didn't answer to me, but it didn't seem like Aaron to tell me he wasn't going on vacation and then take off the very next day. Especially not in the middle of such a big case.

"Alyssa Lynne," I muttered, strolling down the dock trying to look like I belonged as I checked the names of the vessels tethered there. He'd told me once that the boat was his other baby, so he'd named it after his daughters.

I counted thirty-four boats on one side of the slip and turned to start up the other, still alone with the sun sinking fast in the distance. A breeze ruffled my hair and I closed my eyes and took a deep breath, unable to relax even in such a peaceful place.

Still no dice on the other side. Slightly buoyed by that, I went back to my car and sat with the windows down for a minute, listening to the water.

My phone binged the arrival of a text just as I started the engine and I glanced at it, only the top half of the message visible over the edge of the cup holder.

It was from Les.

"What now?" I sighed, talking to my Blackberry. "All my stuff was done early today, in case you didn't notice."

"Charlie has the missing lawyer's wife on camera," it read. "If you can't handle this, there are other people here who can."

Shit. I'd called the woman and she'd refused to comment. What did he want me to do, stalk her?

My mobile browser was lousy with streaming video, but I clicked onto Channel Four's site and tried anyway. Charlie's story was the second from the top, and a scan of the text didn't reveal anything Earth-shattering. I didn't even see the wife's name, which was Grace, according to the court papers I'd found the day before.

I tried the video, and after several minutes managed to put together enough patchy footage to see it was close to the same story they'd run the night before, save for the addition of the bankruptcy filing, some information on a few of Neal's old cases, and about five seconds of a puffy-eyed Grace Neal telling Charlie "no comment" and shutting the door in her face.

"I'm getting threats over a 'no comment?'" I tossed the phone back into the cup holder and banged my head against the back of the seat. "Is he kidding me?"

I slammed my foot down on the accelerator and spun the tires on the gravel, not wanting to lose the sunlight completely before I got to the other marina. What I did want to do was text my makeshift boss a very polite "please bite my ass," but I knew Bob would frown on that, so I focused on the road, taking the unfamiliar turns too fast, Janis wailing loud enough to rattle the windows.

Twilight had fallen by the time I parked at the second marina, which had roughly three times as many slips, though about half of them were empty.

I hurried down the closest dock, the bait shop closed and not another soul in sight, cursing my lack of a flashlight and scanning the names on the boats as I went.

I found nothing on either of the first two docks and was almost at the end of the third, ready to decide he'd changed his mind and I was losing mine to paranoia and conspiracy theories, when I saw it.

My stomach twisted as I stared at the RPD shield painted on the hull next to his daughters' names. Damn.

So he wasn't on vacation. One question answered, but five new ones in its place.

Had he lied to Jerry? Had Jerry lied to me? Aaron knew all about boats and rivers. Was it really him the whole time? Had he taken off after the crash because he was afraid he'd get caught? Or had his hornet's nest been nastier than he'd anticipated?

I stepped closer to the boat, which was a nice one—with a small cabin and everything—especially for a guy with two kids and what I knew about cops' and teachers' salaries. Dammit. I hated feeling like everyone was a suspect, and I had no idea what to think.

If it was him, and he had taken off, why would he say he was going on the boat and then leave it here? And in that same vein, if they were moving the goods over the waterways, what if there was something on there?

I took another step toward the boat and stopped, biting my lip. It wasn't exactly a house, but still private property. And a cop's private property at that.

But what if it wasn't him? What if something was wrong, or something happened to him, and there was a clue on there somewhere?

I looked around, the first of the evening stars twinkling overhead. Nothing out here but me and the fish and the man in the moon. It wouldn't hurt to take a quick peek. If he was guilty, I wouldn't care if he minded, and if he wasn't, I was nearly sure he wouldn't mind.

I stepped onboard shakily, looking around the deck and wondering what my chances were of finding anything interesting.

There was a console near the captain's chair, which looked like as good a hiding place as any, but held only a box of fish hooks, a flashlight, and a package of batteries.

Maybe down in the belly, then. I crossed the deck to the galley door, jerked it open, and slipped inside before I could change my mind, telling myself I wanted as much to know what had happened to my friend as I wanted to know anything else about this case.

It was a tight space, with sleeping berths stacked up the walls on both sides, then a kitchen, bathroom, and booth-style table in the back. At first glance, there didn't look to be much in the way of storage, but when I lifted on the lowest bed, it came up easily to reveal a bin full of life jackets. I dug through them, but the only thing sharing the space with them was a dead spider that might have made me shriek under different circumstances—the thing was almost as big as my thumb not counting the legs.

"Jesus, they do grow things bigger out here." I shuddered and closed the lid, then crossed to the other bed and lifted it.

Empty. As were the kitchen drawers, the toilet tank, and the refrigerator.

So maybe he wasn't a bad guy. Or if he was, he kept it to police department boats. But he wasn't on vacation on this boat, that was for sure.

Where was he, then?

I sighed and kicked the door open a little too hard, looking for any other visible storage on Aaron's sportfisher, but there was none.

So much for my first attempt at trespassing.

I'd just turned back toward the dock when I heard footsteps.

I glanced around, but there wasn't much in the way of places to hide. I dove behind the end of a long bench seat and curled myself up as small as I could, listening for more steps and cursing the water, which was suddenly deafening as it slapped the hulls of the boats.

The steps grew louder, pausing just outside, from the sound of it, and I held my breath.

I heard a low voice, but I couldn't make out what it was saying, let alone who it belonged to or who it might be addressing, and I was afraid to look.

Then the voice stopped and the footsteps retreated as quickly as they'd come.

I stayed in my ball, in case whoever it was decided to come back. When it seemed reasonable I was alone again, I unrolled myself and crept back onto the dock, looking in every direction and listening hard for company. I only heard the water and cicadas.

I stared at the name on the hull for a long minute. Aaron's family was his whole world. His face always lit up like a frat boy on Friday night when he talked about his daughters. His youngest had just been accepted to Princeton—he'd about popped a button off his shirt relaying that news, and I'd passed it on to Eunice and the features team, where it begat a very flattering profile of his little girl in our "Senior Class" section.

But was money for college really enough motivation to risk the job that put food on the table and paid the mortgage? To risk prison?

I didn't think so. Especially not when that boat itself was probably worth about a hundred grand. Assuming dirty money hadn't paid for it in the first place, selling it would buy her four semesters, at least.

I picked my way carefully back to my car by the moonlight, not wanting to lose a heel off my slingback Jimmy Choos to the spaces between the boards on the dock. Climbing behind the wheel and starting the engine, I wasn't sure the trip had been worth it.

Pulling out of the lot, I turned the puzzle around in my head.

Someone was lying about Aaron being on vacation. The boat at the dock said that much. But whether it was Jerry, or someone lying to Jerry (Aaron or Lowe, maybe), I had no idea.

The road was narrow, with tight curves that looked much different by the light of my high beams than they had in the fading sunshine. I tried to push the story to one side of my brain so that the other could focus on not running the car into a tree, and thought I'd made good progress when a wide sedan roared up behind me, headlights either off or broken, careening to the left and attempting to pass me while straddling the center line.

I slammed the brake and turned the wheel hard, depositing my mini SUV into a ditch full of wild grasses and chiggers. Breathing like I'd been to the gym, I turned my head in the direction of the road. I didn't even have time to honk.

"You can't take your half out of the middle, Bubba," I hollered at the stillness, my heart still pounding.

It took twenty minutes, every swearword I knew, and about a dozen chigger bites to push/maneuver the car back onto the road, and even by moonlight, I could see the dent in the fender. At least it was drivable.

It wasn't until I was back on northbound 95 that I realized the only place the sedan could have come from was the marina, because it was the only thing between me and the water. The idea that my adventure in the ditch had been anything but a random bit of bad luck courtesy of a drunk redneck verged on terrifying when I considered it for more than thirty seconds, so I turned my attention back to Aaron. Or tried to. But if someone had tried to send me careening into the woods in the boondocks at forty miles an hour over the little info I knew, how far might they have gone to shut Aaron up if he'd actually found something?

I needed more background on Deputy Chief Lowe. And there was still the pesky issue of not knowing who I could believe. Tuesday, I'd have called Jerry without hesitation. By Wednesday night, I wasn't sure I trusted another soul save for my mom, Jenna, and Bob, none of whom could be much help to me right then.

As if delivered by the muses, the police chief's all-American face popped into my head as I exited at Grove, and I resolved to call him for an interview early the next day before I'd even finished wondering if he was suspicious of Lowe. Or anyone else.

Someone had to have the answers I needed, and Donovan Nash seemed like an excellent place to start.

12.

Old news

Sweating my frustrations out at the gym took a backseat to getting ahold of Nash's assistant, and by the time I walked into Bob's office for the staff meeting Thursday, I had an appointment with the police chief the following morning.

"What are you looking so chipper about this morning, Clarke?" Les leaned his big frame back in Bob's chair, not bothering to veil his sarcasm. "Given that Charlie didn't have anything breaking this morning, I assume it has nothing to do with your job?"

I ignored the dig. I'd scooped Charlie three times that week by my count, and numbers were supposed to be his forte.

"As a matter of fact, I have an interview with the police chief tomorrow. And if I'm right, by next week, I'll have all of Richmond going 'Charlie who?' for at least a month."

I thought for a split second about keeping my suspicions to myself, but Bob had warned me against making Les mad, and I figured even he'd be impressed with the possibility of a drug ring running out of police headquarters. Since no one else had arrived for the meeting, I went ahead and told him.

He listened to the whole story and studied me in silence for a full minute before he spoke.

"Why would he rat out his deputy to a reporter?" he asked. "You're assuming you're right about Lowe, but are you also assuming Nash suspects his right hand of being a crook? If he does, he's not going to tell you anything. And if he doesn't, there's no point in asking. You can't seriously be thinking about telling him what you think. His loyalty will lie with his man, I promise you."

So much for impressed. "I know it will, and no, I'm not stupid enough to accuse the deputy chief of being a crook. I'm counting on the chief being unaware of Lowe's involvement. I'm working on a list of very specific, yet routine questions, like 'Is Lowe responsible for training the officers in the river unit?' I don't know that I can get everything I need out of him, but I'll be closer by the time I get through talking to him."

"That might actually work." He laced his fingers together and rested his chin on them, his elbows on Bob's desk. "Make sure you have questions about a lot of different things: the boats, his role in an investigation like this, the FBI. As long as you don't only ask about Lowe, you're okay. Maybe."

He sat back in the chair again and spun it toward the computer.

"You just make damned sure you have it dead to rights," he said. "Libeling the deputy chief of police will not be good for your career, no matter how much Bob likes you. We cannot afford a lawsuit."

"You got it." I pulled out a notepad, jotting random questions for Nash around the important ones I'd already listed. As the rest of the staff began filing in, I wondered if there was any way to get on Les' good side, or if I should just try to stay out of his way.

Chatter about politics and sports swirled around me, but it was difficult to keep my attention on the meeting. My eyes must have strayed to the clock forty times in as many minutes, and as soon as Les pushed the chair back to stand up, I jumped to my feet and bolted for the door.

"Where's the fire, Lois?"

Parker. And I still hadn't read his column from Saturday. I mildly regretted talking to him about it in the first place as I stopped outside the door and turned around, apologetic smile already in place.

"I have about eleventy billion things to do today, but I swear I'll read your breast cancer piece tonight. Really."

"You know, someone with less confidence might be bothered by the fact you haven't made time yet." He grinned. "I can take it, though. But hey, I wanted to talk to you about Bob when you have a minute. I'll be around."

He started to turn away and I sighed, leaning against a long row of filing cabinets.

"You have ninety seconds. Go."

He glanced at his watch, feigning alarm. "What'd you make of how he looked yesterday?"

"He seemed fine to me, but he's Bob. He doesn't tend to let on when he's not fine, obviously."

"That's what I thought. He actually tried to talk the doctor into clearing him to come in for today's morning meeting when they were discharging him yesterday."

I laughed. "Only Bob would have a heart attack Monday and try to come to work Thursday. She told him he was crazy, right?"

"She told him the first week he was permitted five minutes of walking, five times a day. She said he could progress to short trips out of the house next week as long as he feels up to it. He argues he feels fine and this place is going to implode without him."

"Well, if Les doesn't get off my ass, I may implode. But I think we'll be all right long enough for Bob to recover."

"Why is Les giving you a hard time?"

"You mean besides Shelby whispering in his ear about how happy it would make her to have my job when she's not blowing him?"

Parker's eyes widened and he pinched his lips together. Oops. Les wasn't anywhere near Parker on a physical scale of one to ten, but he did outrank him in terms of pull with the powers that be. Still, that had to sting a little.

"Sorry," I said hastily. "I figured if Bob knew that, everyone did. I'm usually the only person around here who pays so little attention to office gossip."

"It is a newsroom," he said. "But I must have missed that bulletin. She really is something else."

He shifted his feet and stuck his hands in his pockets.

"So, have you found out any more about the missing lawyer or those dead drug dealers? See? I read your stuff."

I wondered why he wanted to know. "Nothing definitive," I waved a hand. "It's there somewhere, though. I'll get it."

"Good luck. Let me know if you ever get around to reading my column."

"Today. I swear."

He gave me an exaggerated nod and disappeared into the maze of cubicles. My thoughts turned to Aaron and Mike, and I went to call Jerry for an update.

"Nothing new on the Sorrel case," he said.

Except that it was now a "case." Damn.

"Aaron hasn't called in to check for messages?" I asked, but finding the boat had somehow cemented Mike and Aaron together in my head. If one of them was still gone, the other wouldn't have turned up, either.

"No, but he didn't say he was going to. Are you sure I can't help you with whatever it is you want to talk to him about?"

"I don't think you can, Jerry," I said. "Thanks, though."

I started to hang up.

"Hey, Nichelle?" His voice dropped in pitch and volume. "You can tell me to go to hell if I'm overstepping, but what's wrong? We've had some strange shit around town this week, and now you're worrying so much about Aaron calling in from his trip. I'm a detective, and a pretty good one. If you think something's up, I could help. I could meet you after work, if you like. I don't have plans to do anything tonight but watch the Seminoles in the College World Series, and I can DVR the game."

I tapped a pen on my desk blotter, wishing I knew who to trust.

"Thanks, Jerry, but I have a lot going on right now. I appreciate the offer, though."

"Just let me know if you change your mind."

I hung up and turned to the day's police reports. The lone interesting one had me giggling as I dialed the complainant for an interview, a junkyard owner who called 9-1-1 the day before when he got to work and found the driveway blocked by an abandoned casket.

"Turned out the damned thing was full of rusty hubcaps, of all things, but I made the cops come open it." He spit audibly as he spoke and I swallowed a laugh, picturing a beer-bellied Bubba, complete with overalls, staring at a coffin someone dumped in his driveway.

He filled me in on the details of his call for help, clearly still annoyed at the amused response he'd gotten. "They asked me what was in there. Can you believe that?" he said. "I told 'em I wasn't opening the damned thing. I didn't want to be looking at rotted old bones first thing in the morning. That's what my tax dollars pay them for!"

No rotted old bones before coffee. I could go with him on that.

Why anyone had the thing in the first place was a mystery, but Jerry said when I talked to him again there was no forensic evidence it had ever been used for its intended purpose. I laughed as I typed. It wasn't a front-page exclusive, but the "news of the weird" vibe made it an interesting read—the kind of story likely to get a ton of Facebook shares, which usually made bean counters like Les very happy. So score one for the crime reporter.

After I filed the story, I opened my Neal folder and stared at the documents inside, trying to wedge him into my scenario with Lowe as the drug pusher. My brain sparred between DonnaJo's praise of Neal and the idea that a failed bankruptcy filing and his kid's mounting medical bills might make it pretty hard to walk past several hundred thousand dollars in cash.

No matter which way I turned my puzzle piece, I couldn't make Neal fit with Lowe. But if he wasn't guilty, where the hell was he?

What if he's the victim? I listened to my instincts as I thought again about Mike's parting words. *"If this was a cop, they're into something very serious, something they could go to prison for. And going to prison is pretty much every cop's worst nightmare."*

An assistant CA could certainly help put a crooked cop in prison. What if Neal suspected something? Or someone, and they decided their secret was worth killing Neal?

The skin on my arm pricked up into goosebumps. From everything I'd seen, if there was a way to make the lawyer the villain, the police department was determined to take it. Which made me wonder who would prove Neal's innocence if he hadn't done it. My short list consisted of DonnaJo and myself. A story that kept an innocent man out of prison and locked up a dirty cop as a bonus? There was no way the *Post* could ignore that. The goosebumps didn't go anywhere.

You're so far ahead of yourself, you're going to lose sight of your own ass, I thought, trying to couch the excitement. One thing at a time. I snatched up my phone and dialed DonnaJo's cell.

"I have about three minutes. I'm in recess," she said when she picked up.

I talked fast, not mentioning anyone specifically, but giving her a broad overview of what I suspected.

"I'm still in the middle of this," I said. "But I have a pretty good hunch the cops want to send Neal up for it if they can."

"What do you need?" There was no hint of reservation in her tone. "Those assholes at the PD aren't going to set Gavin up. No way. He didn't do it, Nichelle. I'd bet my license on that."

"Hopefully I won't need you to. But I do need to know about Neal. If he's made any enemies, maybe? Assuming he didn't take off with the evidence, our most viable option is foul play."

DonnaJo was quiet, the background chatter from the courthouse the only sign I hadn't lost her.

"Jesus, I guess it is, isn't it? Makes you think," she said finally. "I love my job, but I'm not willing to die for it. I really don't know what Gavin has going on, but something's had him in a foul mood for the past few weeks."

I'd bet it had. And I had a sudden idea for how I might find out what that something was.

"Can we grab a drink tonight?" I asked. "I'll come by there to get you about six?"

"Sounds good. I can meet you, if you'd rather."

"Nope. I'll come get you."

She was quiet for a long minute, and I held my breath. DonnaJo was smart.

"I don't think I want to know, so I'll just see you when you get here."

Very smart.

"See you then."

I hung up and flipped open my computer, typing Lowe's name into my Google toolbar.

Facebook and LinkedIn were the top two hits, but his accounts were locked down to exclude everyone but friends or connections. I went back to the search results and kept scrolling. A ton of stuff from the *Telegraph*, most of it written by me, and a good many city council meeting minutes and agendas. TV news stories. A magazine article.

I was on page seven by the time I saw it.

The current command staff at the PD had been in place when I'd come to Richmond, and I'd never done any backgrounding on any of them. So until Google provided me with an old team photo, I had no way of knowing that Dave Lowe had been a trainer for the 1998 UVA baseball team.

And grinning his perfect grin from the back row of the photo on my screen was Grant Parker.

"Fuck me," I whispered, sitting back in my chair, my eyes locked on the photo. No way.

And yet, there it was. Full color. Undeniable.

"Could I be any dumber?" I said, muffled by the fingers that had flown up to my lips. Parker had hardly ever spoken to me before I'd mentioned the drug dealers in that staff meeting, yet in a week, he'd managed to become something like a friend. At least, I was beginning to think he might.

I ran back through every conversation, ticking off questions about my story he'd tossed into each one. He'd even shown up at the river Friday night.

Covering cops for six years taught me true coincidences are few and far between.

Closing my eyes, I called up the crime scene shots of drug dealers Noah Smith and Darryl Wright from my memory, their eyes open, blood and gore splattering the walls behind them.

Jesus. What if our sports columnist had been responsible for that?

I dropped my forehead into one hand and pulled in a deep breath, my head swimming.

Think, Nichelle.

With an enshrined jersey number at UVA and a popular sports column, Grant Parker was a local hero, beloved by thousands of people. Apart from his occasional ego Tourette's, he seemed like a nice enough guy, too. Why would he be in on a massive murder and drug trafficking scheme?

I had only one answer, and I'd never wanted so badly to be wrong.

The fancy new motorcycle. The thick stack of fifties he'd pulled out at the restaurant. I'd seen a lot in my tenure at the crime desk, and money was second only to sex on the list of motives for murder.

I thought about Parker carrying Katie DeLuca to her car and wondered if the kindness was motivated by guilt. What if Parker knew about the boat all along? Hell, what if he'd set up some sort of rendezvous between the cops and the ballplayers, then shown up to check it out when it went bad? Suddenly nothing seemed too crazy to consider.

I bookmarked the team photo on my computer and sat back in my chair, unsure of what to do with that information. I couldn't tell Les, and I sure as hell couldn't tell Bob. They'd laugh me out of the building—possibly the city. I had no one I trusted at the police department, even assuming that Mike and Aaron weren't part of my growing conspiracy theory, and staring at a photo of Parker and Lowe, that no longer seemed a safe assumption.

I glanced back down at my desk and saw DonnaJo's email about Neal and his active cases.

His wife had refused to comment on Tuesday, but she was just going to have to get over that. She had to know something, even if she didn't know she knew it. And I needed to know it, too.

Scribbling down their address in Henrico, I stuffed the files into my bag and took a drive to the suburbs.

Grace Neal looked positively haggard when she opened her front door, her flat brown eyes not even registering surprise to see me standing there.

"Could you please just leave me alone?" she said, her voice raspy. "I know everyone thinks my husband is a felon, but I just want to take care of my little boy and have my husband back at home. I told Charlie Lewis yesterday when she came by poking a camera in my face: I'm not giving interviews. Go away."

She moved to shut the door. Desperate, I stuck my foot in the crack, wincing at the pressure. She was strong for a petite little thing.

"Are you serious?" Her eyes widened and she pushed harder.

I gritted my teeth and stood my ground.

"Mrs. Neal, I know you don't want to talk to me, and frankly, I don't blame you," I said. "I can't believe I'm actually doing this, but I sort of don't have a choice. There's something wrong at the police department, and I think your husband might know what it is. I thought he might be part of it, but now I'm not so sure. So I'm going to need you to open that door and let some blood back into my foot, and then I'm going to need your help to figure this out."

She stared a good thirty seconds, my foot still pinched in the heavy oak door, before she swung it wide and waved me inside.

"Just be quiet, please," she said. "It's so hard to get him to sleep sometimes."

I hobbled through the bright foyer into her family room, wide and sunny with butter-colored walls and cushy, overstuffed furniture. It looked like a spread from Better Homes and Gardens, save for an end table that held a small lamp and a very large piece of medical equipment with a mask attached to it.

"My son has Cystic Fibrosis," she said, following my gaze. "It means he has a buildup of thick mucus in a lot of his organs, including his lungs. That helps him breathe a little easier."

"I'm sorry to hear that." I was, but the words sounded lame. I didn't really know what else to say.

"It is what it is." She flashed a tired half-smile. "He's a wonderful little boy, and I wouldn't trade him for anything. But sometimes it's hard. I've never had to take care of him by myself for so long before."

"And you haven't heard from your husband at all?" I watched her for signs of dishonesty.

"Not since he left here on Sunday." Grace Neal held my gaze as she spoke, not fidgeting or wavering. "I know he didn't steal that evidence, but why do you think my Gavin's innocent?"

"I have a theory, and I'm wondering if your husband may think the same thing."

"He's suspicious of something." She nodded. "He got his nose all out of joint a few months ago over the guns from that case he worked last year. The trucker from New York?"

I nodded as I reached into my bag and pulled out a notebook.

"Tell me why he was mad." I clicked out a pen.

"Gavin has a thing about guns," she said. "A sort of personal vendetta. He had a good friend when he was a little boy who was in the wrong place at the wrong time and caught a stray bullet from an unregistered gun. He became a prosecutor to keep them off the streets. I've never seen him work so hard on a case. He triple checked every detail, staying at the office until midnight for a week before his opening argument. He was ecstatic at the thought of so many guns being destroyed after he won, and he spent months after the trial counting the days until they were sent off to be scrapped."

I guessed where her story was going from what Joey had said about the guns being on the boat.

"About two months ago, he went down to the police department to ride along while the guns were taken out of the evidence lock-up over to be chomped—they put them in this big shredding machine and the city sells the scrap metal. Gavin thinks it's the greatest invention of the twentieth century." She half-smiled, then sighed.

"But then he got to the evidence room and they told him he wasn't allowed to go. They kept saying it was against regulations. He put up a fuss because he knows the rules inside and out, but they wouldn't budge. The guy in the evidence room said he had orders from the command staff."

"Of course he did," I muttered.

"Excuse me?" Grace paused and gave me a quizzical smile.

"Sorry. Thinking out loud. Please, go on."

She sighed again. "So Gavin called the command office, and someone gave him some bullshit about how they couldn't be liable for putting Gavin in a dangerous situation in case someone tried to hijack the truck or something. Gavin argued, but the guy refused to give in. I felt so bad for him. Not that I wanted him to be in danger, but he was so excited about this. They finally said they'd send the deputy chief. That's the second-in-command, right?"

I nodded.

"He said he'd go along and then call Gavin as soon as they got back from dropping the guns off at the shredder.

"And he did. Called Gavin a couple of hours later, said everything went smoothly. Gavin was so excited. He brought home champagne."

"But then something went wrong?"

She nodded.

"The next day, he called his friend at the plant to see how much scrap they got out of them, and the guy said the guns never arrived."

I sucked in a sharp breath even though I had suspected the words were coming.

"Yeah," she said. "Gavin was pissed. We've been married for twelve years and I've never seen him so mad. He drove straight to the police department and demanded to see this deputy guy, but of course, the cop didn't have time to talk. Gavin filed a complaint with the civil service commission. It got bogged down in red tape, but he kept after it.

"Finally, the commission told Gavin the guy at the scrap plant swore under oath he destroyed the guns. Apparently he was 'mistaken' when he told Gavin the guns never arrived. Gavin didn't believe any of it, swore to me something fishy was going on at the police department, and from that point on, he made weekly random checks of the evidence room. Then Sunday, he never made it home." Her voice faded on the last word.

Bingo. I nodded my head as I scribbled.

"Did he tell you what he suspected?" I asked.

"He did not." She brushed at her eye and shook her head. "He said I didn't need to be part of it, and I didn't press him, to be honest with you. There were things he had to see at work that I didn't care to know about. When he comes home after this nightmare, he'll join a private firm with a fat salary and a corner office and a lot of tax law or something equally boring, if I have anything to say about it. He turns down half a dozen offers every single year. My husband is a brilliant lawyer, and he has a good heart. But I'm through with the crusading if this is how it's going to end up."

"Can't say I blame you," I said.

"Why are you asking, anyway?" she asked. "Do you think something happened to him? Something bad?"

"You don't?" I didn't mean to blurt it quite so bluntly, but I couldn't believe she didn't think the worst after what she just told me.

Grace bit her lip, her effort to control her breathing not really working. "I don't want to," she said, a small sob escaping with the words. "I just want him to come home."

"I hope he does," I said. "Thank you for talking to me, Grace. This is a big help. Can I ask one last favor?"

She sniffled and drug the back of one hand across her face. "Sure."

"Does your husband have a home office, and may I check it out?"

She stood up and moved toward the back of the house.

"In here," she said. "He likes to work in the sunroom where he can see the trees."

I looked over the desk, but all of the files were labeled with one of two things: the names of medical companies and doctor's offices, or defendants. I rifled through two drawers and a cabinet, but came up empty-handed. Damn. I had just turned back to the doorway to thank Grace for her time when an ear-splitting trill split the silence in the house.

"Shit," the word slid between clenched teeth as Grace lunged for the cordless phone on the desk. "I keep the ringer up so I can hear it over Alex's breathing machine." She hit a button on the white handset and raised it to her ear.

"Neal residence."

I looked back at my notes, but a small, strangled sound from my hostess snapped my head back up.

"Thank you." The words were automatic, little more than a whisper, her eyes wide and staring at nothing. The phone clattered to the tile floor and I jumped to my feet, dumping the notebook under the desk.

"Grace?"

"He's gone." She said it so softly I almost didn't hear, tears falling fast. "My Gavin. He's dead. That...they...the police pulled him out of the river an hour ago. They said his body was dumped there. Weighted down."

Her face crumpled into a mask of grief and she would've fallen if I hadn't caught her, leading her back to the sofa in the buttery-bright family room and holding her while she sobbed.

There are times when being right really sucks.

13.

The weight of the world

By the time I found a phone number for Grace Neal's mother scrawled across the babysitter pad on their fridge and waited for her to arrive, my Blackberry had rung itself into a nearly-dead battery.

"Where the fuck have you been?" Les screamed in my ear when I called him back as I pointed the car down West Broad toward the city. "Don't you own a goddamn scanner anymore? Your missing prosecutor just turned up in the river, dumped like something out of an old gangster movie, according to Channel Four. Of course, I have to get my information from Charlie Lewis, because my cops reporter is nowhere to be found when the biggest crime story of the year breaks. They're having a press conference at police headquarters at five-thirty."

I checked my clock. It was already five-fifteen, and I was all the way out in the west end. Damn.

"I know about the lawyer. I was interviewing his wife when the cops called. I stayed with her until her mother arrived."

"You what? Since when are we in the business of babysitting strangers?"

Since I'm a decent human being, you prick. I clenched my jaw. He totally would have left the poor woman sitting there in shock. Of course, Charlie probably would have, too.

I gulped a deep breath. Don't piss him off, Bob said. And I didn't want to give Shelby any more ammunition.

"I'm sorry," I said, fighting to keep my tone even. "I did talk to the widow, and she told me her husband was suspicious that something wasn't right in the police evidence room."

I paused, waiting for an "attagirl." He was quiet. I gave up.

"I have my laptop, and I'm on my way to the PD," I said. "They never start press conferences on time, anyway. Watch your email for my write-up and tell Ryan to be ready to get it on the web. Has Charlie been out at the recovery site? Did you send photo?"

"Yes, I sent photo. I know how to do my job. And of course Charlie's been out there. Even the new girl from Channel Ten has been out there. Everyone has kicked our ass on this, thanks to you. Don't bother going to the PD. Shelby's already there. We can take it from here."

I slammed my foot on the brake just in time to keep from rear-ending the corvette in front of me, no retort at the ready for that. And the beeping in my ear told me he'd hung up, anyway. I threw the phone across the car and it clattered against the passenger window before it bounced into the floor.

"Dammit!" I slammed my hands down on the steering wheel. "This is really what I get for not being a heartless bitch? Hey, karma, I think I'm getting screwed, here."

The light changed and I drove aimlessly, the urge to kick something (namely Les) pretty strong as I replayed the conversation in my head.

Coasting up Monument Avenue, I passed the stunning collection of larger-than-life statues that began near the old city limits with Robert E. Lee and ended a mile and a half later with tennis star Arthur Ashe. The street itself was gorgeous, with stately antebellum homes peeking from behind rustling leaves, the shadows cast by the spires at First English Lutheran Church growing long in the evening sunlight. I rolled down the windows and took deep, calming breaths.

Les would have to eat those words when I exposed the corruption at the police department. And I would very much enjoy watching him do that.

Feeling more sociable and remembering my date with DonnaJo, I followed Monument until it turned into Franklin, then turned on Ninth, passing city hall and the library before I stopped in front of the John Marshall Courts Building, which housed the CA's offices. I flipped the mirror down before I got out, dabbing on lipstick and straightening my hair.

"Let Shelby have her fun," I said aloud to my reflection. "It won't matter. Les is just a jackass on a power trip. Just beat Charlie to the punch here, and it won't matter one little bit."

Since I had no way of knowing what Charlie had or didn't have, I needed to work fast and make sure I got it right.

I took the elevator up to DonnaJo's practically deserted office and found her staring at her computer, which was streaming Charlie's coverage of the press conference, though it still hadn't started.

"I didn't expect to see you." DonnaJo's blue eyes widened when I tapped on her doorframe. Judging by the red rims on those eyes and her smeared makeup, my beauty-queen-turned-hardass-prosecutor friend had taken the news about her colleague badly. "Why are you not over at the press conference? You heard about Gavin?"

"I'm so sorry, honey." I shook my head. "I was at his house when they called his wife. I stayed with her after she got the call, so the asshole who's filling in for Bob sent a copy editor to the press conference instead."

"Ouch."

"It stings, I admit." I sat on the gray velour sofa near the door. "But it's not the end of the world. It's one press conference. Though, good of the paper be damned, I hope she chokes."

DonnaJo laughed. "May Charlie Lewis wipe the floor with her."

"Charlie will eat her for breakfast," I said. "But hey, she wanted to play with the big girls."

DonnaJo spun the screen so I could see it, too, and my stomach turned as I watched Deputy Police Chief Dave Lowe take the podium outside police headquarters.

Lowe cleared his throat and faced the cameras, squaring his narrow shoulders as he gripped the sides of the podium with both hands, his dark, curly hair shellacked so the wind whipping the flags behind him didn't budge it. He wasn't a big man, probably shorter than me with a slight build. Looking into his round brown eyes, even on TV, gave me chills.

He began by telling the small group of reporters that Assistant Commonwealth Attorney Gavin Neal was found dead, his body weighted down in the James River after an apparently fatal gunshot wound. Two guys out fishing found Neal's body after one of them dropped a wristwatch in the water.

I made a mental note to get their names from Jerry and waited for Lowe to get to something else I didn't already know.

"No official cause of death yet from the coroner. We will know more after he completes Mr. Neal's autopsy," Lowe said. "The hearts, thoughts and prayers of the Richmond Police Department are with the Neal family today and in the weeks to come."

He nodded to the new girl from Channel Ten, who started with the obvious. "Do you have any suspects yet, chief?"

"We are pursuing a number of leads in this case, and we have been building a list of suspects for nearly a week now," Lowe said. "Mr. Neal worked within the criminal world for many years, and he may have recently gotten involved, through a case he tried, with a very dangerous part of that world. Our strongest lead, given the circumstances surrounding his death, includes ties to organized crime. That's all I'm going to say about that today."

My mouth fell open. Somewhere far away, I heard Shelby's unmistakable high-pitched drawl, asking if there was evidence of foul play.

"Aside from the gunshot wound and the weights holding him under the water?" Lowe kept a straight face as he spoke, but Charlie's mike picked up her own chuckle at the reply. "There was not."

"That's your girl?" DonnaJo asked.

"She used to cover the garden club, now she wants my beat." I felt a little sorry for Shelby. But only a little.

"Nice."

Charlie hit Lowe with a barrage of questions about the exact time and place of the discovery, and how long they thought the body had been there, but I only half-heard, my mind looping back through Lowe's first answer like a scratched record.

"What do you make of that, DonnaJo?" I asked her as Lowe thanked the reporters and disappeared. "What he said about the mob?"

She shrugged, a thoughtful gaze narrowing her swollen eyes.

"I don't know what to make of any of it," she said. "I mean, the Mafia is, well, full of bad guys. But this sounds like something out of a black and white movie. We put people away all the time. We don't generally end up dumped in the river, though. What the hell is going on here, Nichelle?"

It sounded absurd even in my head, the idea that the cops killed Neal and were trying to frame the mob, so I just returned the shrug and kept my mouth shut.

"I'm not sure," I said. "But we're smarter than your average bear. Why don't we have that drink and see if talking helps us figure it out?"

She got up and moved toward the door.

"I'm going to stop in the ladies' room," she said.

I followed, leaving my bag on the floor in front of the sofa.

"Where do you want to go?" she asked.

"Capital Ale?"

"Works for me," she said, pushing open the bathroom door.

Drying my hands a few minutes later, I snapped my fingers.

"Damn," I said. "I forgot my bag. You go on down and I'll catch up."

DonnaJo eyed me sideways and shook her head slightly. But she didn't object. "Where'd you park?"

"Right outside on the street. You can't miss it." I turned back toward her office as the elevator chimed. "Be right there."

When the doors closed, I sprinted back to her office and grabbed my bag, teetering on my eggplant Nicholas Kirkwoods when I turned toward the door with Neal's name on it. I took a deep breath and darted inside, no time for second thoughts.

I jerked open file drawers one after another, finding only folder upon folder of numbered cases. Damn, there was a lot of crime in this city.

Dropping to my knees, I flung open the credenza doors, already afraid DonnaJo would come back looking for me if I didn't go downstairs shortly. In the back corner of the cabinet, almost hidden by two reams of paper, I saw the corner of a red file folder.

I wriggled it free and flipped it open. My article on the Darryl Wright murder lay on top of a small stack of papers, two paragraphs highlighted and a question mark in the margin.

Jackpot. I wanted to make photocopies, but I was seriously out of time. I stuffed the folder into my bag and ran back to the elevators, smoothing my ivory linen tank dress and taking a few deep breaths while I waited. Before that week, I'd never violated anything worse than a traffic law. In two days, I'd trespassed on a cop's boat and stolen a file from the prosecutor's office. If I hadn't been so focused on the story, I would've felt guilty.

DonnaJo arched an eyebrow at me when I walked outside.

"You get lost?" she asked.

"I had to pee again," I clicked the button to unlock the doors and stowed my bag in the back. "Too much water this afternoon, I guess."

"Uh-huh." She climbed into my passenger seat. "Glad to hear you're hydrating properly."

We politely shoved our way through the after work crowd at the bar and settled into a polished oak booth in the back of the long, narrow dining room. As tables of power-suited professionals dove into platters of gourmet hot wings and fancy hamburgers amid discussions of politics and the stock market, DonnaJo and I sipped Virginia chardonnay and talked about Neal and the police department and the Mafia for two hours. DonnaJo dissolved into tears twice during the conversation, and while I wanted to be invested, I was itching to go through the file I'd swiped from Neal's office.

As the stars became visible overhead, I stopped the car and told DonnaJo goodnight in front of her office building, offering my condolences again as she stepped out of the car.

"Hey Nichelle? I know you're onto something, and I know you don't want to tell me what it is," she said, holding the door open. "I'm okay with that. But Gavin was a good friend and a damned fine lawyer. So don't screw this up, okay? I want to see the guilty bastards put away. And you let me know if I can help you."

"You already have, honey," I said, easing my foot off the brake. "Get some rest. I'll talk to you soon."

She shut the door and disappeared into the parking garage.

Snuggling Darcy and sipping another glass of wine, I settled on my sofa and slid my heels off before I opened Neal's file.

My story on Darryl was first. He'd highlighted the paragraphs about the similarity in the crime scenes, with drugs being left at both of them, and inked a big question mark in the margin.

I kept flipping, finding more articles about drug arrests, a copy of his civil service complaint, and several police and lab reports. The upper corner of one page caught my eye, and I pulled it to the top of the stack. I scanned the data at first, then read again with more care, my jaw dropping as a big chunk of my puzzle fell neatly into place.

"Holy shit, Darcy," I said, and the dog's ears perked up. "They've been getting away with this for…well, for God knows how long. How many hundreds of thousands—or millions—of dollars are we talking about here?"

Hours later, my brain refused to stop running questions in circles, and I gave up on sleep. I fiddled with the five-thousand-piece rendering of *The Scream* that I'd picked up at the Virginia Museum of Fine Arts' expressionist exhibit when I'd gone with Jenna in May, but couldn't concentrate enough to finish the border. I gave that up after ten minutes, flipping open my laptop instead.

I checked my email and then scrolled through shoe listings on eBay, bidding on a pair of aubergine Manolos with transparent silk flowers on the ankle straps and hoping no one else would notice them before the auction's end on Friday night. I couldn't afford to go much higher, and they were the cutest pair I'd seen in my size in months. My feet are anything but dainty—a European size forty, which is about a nine in U.S. sizing. Secondhand ones that big can be hard to find.

Nothing made sleep any easier, though. I ended up staring at my ceiling fan until dawn, mentally paging through Gavin Neal's secret file.

By a quarter to seven the next morning, I was dressed to kill for my interview with Chief Nash: black pencil skirt, powder blue silk tank and my favorite black patent Louboutins giving my strut a little extra oomph as I rang Bob's doorbell.

"Come to apologize for the earful I got from Les last night?" Bob said when he pulled the door open. He'd traded the pajamas for khakis and a golf shirt, which he favored year-round even though he hated the game.

"Yeah, yeah. I'm sorry I'm not the kind of person who abandons a distraught wife when she finds out her husband turned up dead in the river." I stepped inside and followed him to the kitchen. "But wait 'til you see what I have!"

"It better be damned good," he said, pouring me a cup of coffee and pushing the sugar bowl across the high granite bar. "Les is pushing to give Shelby full rein on this thing with the lawyer."

"It's fantastic is what it is." I handed him a copy of the lab report I'd found in Neal's file. The originals were tucked under a loose floorboard in my coat closet, which made me feel both ridiculous and important at the same time.

He squinted at the places on the report where the ink was faded, thanks to my aging scanner, and then looked back at me.

"What the hell does pancake mix have to do with heroin?"

"Everything, when you're talking about cops running drugs out of the police evidence room. How's that for a sexy story?" I bounced on the balls of my feet. "This is what I've been looking for—well, it's a big part of it, anyway. Look at the dates on the tests. There was a bag of heroin entered into evidence last summer, and the results of the lab tests to confirm that it was heroin got lost at the courthouse.

"The ACA on that case asked for another test, and the lab said it was pancake mix. Pancake mix! Then the PD claimed there was a mistake by the lab and sent another sample to be tested, and that time it was drugs again."

I stopped to take a breath, the hope this nightmare of a story might have a happy ending—for me, anyway—sending adrenaline through my veins in waves.

"It wasn't a mistake," Bob's thick eyebrows shot up.

"No." I sipped my coffee. "They are replacing the drugs in the evidence locker with ordinary stuff, but only after the samples have been sent to the lab. Heroin looks like beige powder, just like pancake mix. And no one would look too closely after it's been tested. It's brilliant. And foolproof, except when someone loses their paperwork. This—" I shook the paper. "This is their mistake."

I remembered the copy of my story Neal highlighted, sudden certainty about his reason for going to police headquarters the day he disappeared making me shudder.

"Neal knew it," I whispered. "He was down there to test the drugs from the dealer murders, to see if they were still drugs. He figured they were selling the drugs, and probably guessed that his guns were being sold, too. I'd bet my entire shoe collection I'm right."

"This is great stuff, kid," Bob smiled and pushed the paper back across the bar. "But where'd you get it?"

"Where?" I dropped my eyes to the counter, pretending to be fascinated by the random onyx and cream flecks in the stone.

"Where." He drew the word out.

"I found it at the CA's office."

"You found it? Or you stole it from the dead lawyer's files?"

"Does it matter? We've finally got something concrete. It doesn't link Lowe to the actual drugs disappearing, but it shows what they're doing with them."

"It's good," Bob said. "And you're definitely onto something, but there's two things: one, since I didn't think it was necessary to spell this out for you before, you can't steal evidence from the prosecutor's office. Especially not when the prosecutor in question has just turned up murdered. You could get in serious trouble for this. Two, this is good, but it's not concrete. It says right here that the third test showed a mistake by the lab on the second one.

"And your guy Lowe isn't mentioned on it anywhere. We can't accuse the deputy chief of police of being a drug lord on something this thin. You have to get more."

Nice how he could burst my bubble so effectively, yet be kind about doing it.

"Of course I do." My shoulders heaved with the sigh that rushed from my chest. "Dammit. That's why Neal was down there looking for more evidence."

Bob patted my hand. "You're doing good work here, Nicey. I know it's frustrating, but you really are. Here's the thing: they've barely cleared me to leave the house, and I'm not supposed to drive yet. Les is determined to make you look as incompetent as he possibly can. And while Shelby didn't exactly earn herself a Pulitzer yesterday, her story was more than decent, and she was there, which is his big argument right now.

"I pushed back as much as I could and told him you were in a very unusual situation, but he's going to go over my head if you screw anything else up, and the suits like him better than they like me. I'm just a dinosaur who's won some awards. Good to trot out for the old folks on the board who remember when I covered Vietnam and civil rights, but that's about it.

"Charlie had ten minutes this morning with the fishermen who found the lawyer yesterday. Go find them, get something new out of them, and shut Les up for today. I'm begging you. When you've done that, get to the bottom of this, pronto."

I opened my mouth to protest and he put up a hand and shook his head.

"I know it takes time to get something like this right, but your clock is ticking and I can't do much to slow it down from here." He sighed. "We need this story, Nicey. Every bit as much as you need it for your portfolio. Nail it down. Just keep me in the loop, and don't fuck up again."

I didn't think I'd fucked up before, but since my opinion didn't seem to be the popular one, I nodded and promised to toe the line in a timely manner.

"I'm going to interview Chief Nash this morning, and then I'll find the fishermen," I said. "You do me a favor and get better. Les and his girlfriend are getting on my nerves."

He smiled. "I'm doing my best. And Parker brought me dinner last night. He asked about you. Apparently Shelby put on quite a show on her way out to the PD yesterday. I told him you were with the lawyer's wife, and he said to tell you to ask if you need help with anything. Might be nice for you to have a friend in the newsroom."

If the friend wasn't Dave Lowe's college buddy, sure it would. I half-smiled and nodded, spinning back toward the front door.

"Thanks, chief."

I left the copy of the lab report under my seat in the car when I went into police headquarters to interview Nash.

His office was cavernous, the walls decorated with certificates and medals. A tall bookcase held copies of the criminal justice code, the Virginia Constitution, a smattering of legal thrillers, several coffee mugs emblazoned with logos from different police departments, and a Gators pennant.

"Miss Clarke." Nash stood when his assistant showed me in. He offered a Parker-worthy grin from behind a polished cherry desk, putting a hand out.

He was bigger than I remembered, taller than me with broad shoulders and a thick, solid chest under his trademark charcoal jacket. While most of my non-uniform cops favored a more business casual dress code, I had never seen Nash in anything but a suit.

Not that I saw much of him. The head of a big-city department rarely has reason to talk to the press unless they just like seeing their name in the news, and Nash wasn't a limelight hound.

"Forgive me, but I'm going to have to make this quick," he said. "You've caught me on a very interesting day."

"I won't take too much of your time, and I appreciate you seeing me." I shook his hand. "We'll just jump right in, if that's okay with you."

He nodded and settled back into his tufted red leather chair. I took a black armchair across from him and pulled out my notes, firing questions and scribbling his answers.

He seemed fond of Lowe. Nash said though it wasn't part of Lowe's responsibility to train officers for the river unit, he had an interest in the water patrols thanks to a Hampton Roads upbringing, and often went above and beyond.

"He's invaluable," Nash said. "Spends hours outside his regular duties mentoring promising young officers."

How generous of him.

"To come back from his youthful indiscretions and be the kind of officer he is shows extraordinary determination," Nash continued.

"Youthful indiscretions?" I echoed, furrowing my brow and looking up from my notes.

Nash smiled. "I assumed you knew. Dave doesn't make a big secret of the fact that he had a bit of a wild streak when he was young. A couple of brushes with the law: drugs, misdemeanor theft. When he was arrested, it served as a wakeup call. He's really turned his life around."

Hot damn. I slowed my scribbling, mostly as an excuse to keep my face hidden behind my hair as I bent over my notebook. It took supreme control to refrain from jumping up, shouting "eureka," and sprinting back to my office.

I switched gears, moving the topic to the boat crash.

Nash didn't have much to say about the FBI investigation, which I expected, and his comments about the accident itself were restricted to things I already knew, but I needed the conversation to have more than one focus. The discovery of Neal's body was the hot news of the day.

"Chief Lowe mentioned yesterday that the department thinks the murder of Gavin Neal could be the work of organized crime," I said, thinking of Joey's smile and hoping it wasn't in spite of myself. "Can you elaborate on why that is?"

"I've taken a personal interest in that investigation." Nash shook his head. "We're working several leads, but given Mr. Neal's instrumental role in the New York trucker trial last year, we'd be remiss to ignore the possibility that this was a Mafia payback."

I nodded. There should be a course on cop doubletalk in every college journalism department.

On a whim, I asked him about Mike.

He frowned. "That's troubling, to say the least," he said. "Sergeant Sorrel is one of our best officers. We hope to have an answer for his family very soon."

I nodded as I scribbled, wondering if Mike really could be in on whatever had gotten Gavin Neal killed—or if he was in the river somewhere, too. Either seemed possible, and I honestly wasn't sure which I preferred.

"It's been a pleasure meeting you, Miss Clarke," Nash said, standing when I closed my notebook and smiled at him. "I enjoy the work you do, even when it doesn't make us look like the smartest cops around. The *Telegraph* is lucky to have you."

I smiled. If I was the type, I might've blushed.

"Thank you for your time, chief," I said. "I appreciate your fitting me in. This was very helpful."

Nash hit a button on his desk phone and the assistant came to show me out.

I cranked up the stereo and ran through my suspects as I drove back to the office. Though I had more on Lowe, Nash hadn't offered anything that substantially changed my list. Nor had he given me any real answers.

I made my living asking other people questions, but I was so tired of them I didn't care if I never thought of another one.

A copy of the morning paper, Shelby's story on Neal blocked off in pink highlighter, lay on my desk with a big red "thank you" scrawled across the top of it. Nice. Stuffing it in the recycle bin, I looked up a phone number for one of the fishermen who'd discovered Neal's body and dialed.

They were both there, already drunk at noon and way too excited about having their angling interrupted by a corpse. It was macabre. But also sort of funny, and I needed some levity in my day.

Jake Holly and Tony Ross had decided to spend the day together after they'd been on the early show with Charlie, Jake's wife said, "and they've been sitting on my deck drinking beer and reliving their adventure."

She put Jake on the phone and a nanosecond later, Tony picked up an extension.

I asked them to get further away from each other to avoid feedback from the cordless handsets screaming in my ear. They reminded me of a couple of little boys who'd caught a big fish. Creepy, but in a "Scooby Doo Meets the Redneck Brigade" sort of way.

"Which one of you jumped in the water to get the watch?" I asked, interrupting their race to tell me loudest and fastest what had happened.

"I did," Jake said. "Tony was afraid he'd get caught in the current. I'm a better swimmer."

"You wish," Tony snorted.

"Why didn't you jump in there, then?" Jake hollered.

I could hear the effects of the Budweiser and didn't want the nice woman who'd answered my call to have to break up a brawl in her kitchen, so I moved to the next question.

"Then what happened, Jake?" I asked. "Were you looking around for the watch, or did you see the body right away?"

"My watch landed right next to it. Er, him," Jake said. "I thought at first it was some sorta joke. Like, somebody had dropped a dummy down there, you know? But I got closer and I could see the man's eyes, and I knew it was a real person."

"He came up outta the water screaming like a little girl," Tony chortled. "I thought he was pulling my chain, but he kept screaming at me to call the cops and get him the hell outta the water."

"And then the police came?" I asked.

"Yeah, they brought a boat and scuba gear and went down there and brought him up, and the coroner's office took him away. There were chains with weights around his feet and his middle and his neck. It was pretty gross," Jake sounded less than excited for the first time since he'd picked up the phone.

Charlie hadn't asked about the weights. True, Charlie wasn't quite as invested in the details of this story as I was, best I could tell, but I'd take whatever advantage over her reporting I could claim.

"Weights? What kind? Did you see?"

"The kind you use to exercise," Jake said. "They were pretty big ones, too. I didn't know they made those things that big."

I pictured the shiny rows of dumbbells in the weight room at the police department and wondered if I'd just gotten a break. Surely they'd replaced them by now. Still, it wouldn't hurt to check. Everyone made a mistake somewhere.

They asked me in stereo if their names were going to be on the next day's front page. I assured them they would, then clicked the phone off while they were still hooting at each other about that.

I thought about the lab report from Neal's file, which I had read enough times to commit to memory, and dialed the state forensics office. When the tech who'd analyzed the pancake mix picked up, I introduced myself and asked if he remembered the case, crossing my fingers under the desk.

He laughed. "Yeah, I do. We don't get a lot of stuff through here that's not what it looks like. I knew when I opened that bag that whatever was in it wasn't heroin. The smell wasn't right. I played around with it for a while, trying to see if maybe it was some kind of new street drug, but the compounds in it were all wrong. I was curious, and eventually, I started testing stuff out of my pantry against it. That's how I figured out it was baking mix."

"But then the next sample wasn't," I said, still scrawling the last of his comment on my yellow legal pad.

"I don't want to speculate on that, if you don't mind," he said. I kept my hand moving, not missing a word. "I didn't test the third sample, and I can't speak to what happened with it. All I can tell you for sure is that my analysis was pretty thorough. More thorough than it had to be, because I was curious. There's no way I was mistaken."

"Would that be easy? To fake the appearance of an illegal drug with something else?"

"It wouldn't be hard," he said. "Clumps of baking soda tinted with a little food coloring come close enough to looking like crack cocaine, and any white or off-white powder could pass for cocaine HCL. As I said, pancake mix outwardly resembles heroin. Even the prescription stuff would be doable, if you were doing it right. Lots of stuff, from baby aspirin to mints, comes in little tablets, in just about any color you could want. A dealer could make a killing as long as he didn't want repeat customers. People would be fooled pretty easily until they actually took the stuff."

Except I was pretty sure the fake stuff wasn't being sold. I thanked him for his help, smiling as I cradled the phone.

The smile faded when a voice from behind me interrupted my thoughts.

"Bob is convinced that you're going to redeem yourself today." Les sounded less than convinced. "What do you have, since you skipped out on the meeting this morning?"

I spun my chair around to face him. I'd been avoiding him all day, but Nash was an excellent excuse for missing the meeting.

"I wasn't in the meeting because I was interviewing the police chief. I told you about that yesterday, remember?" I flashed a Shelby-like fake smile.

"Did you get anything good out of him?"

I bit my tongue. I wanted to tell him I knew exactly why he was giving me such a hard time, and it was a shitty thing for him to do no matter how good Shelby was in bed. But I wanted to keep my job, so I swallowed the words.

"I did," I said instead. "Turns out Lowe has a record. I'm going to see what I can dig up on that, and I already talked to the fishermen, too."

"Woohoo. So has everyone else." He leaned against the edge of the cube and folded his arms over his chest.

He stared at me for a long minute. I didn't look away.

"I hope you got something new from someone," he said finally. "You still have a regular job to do around here, and I bet you haven't even looked through today's police reports yet. This big investigative reporter act you're pulling won't play much longer if you don't come up with something to show for it, just so you know." He turned and stalked off.

Dammit. I spun the chair back to the desk and cradled my head in my hands. Shelby made a newbie mistake at the press conference because she was nervous and desperate to ask a question, but her story was good, I had to admit. And with all the unanswered questions swirling around me, Les breathing down my neck waiting to hand her my beat if I missed an apostrophe was crazy-making.

I called Jerry to ask if the PD had released any new information on Neal, the boating crash, or Aaron and Mike. Not surprisingly, he had nothing. And I had less than that in the way of excuses to ask for tour of the gym at police headquarters, so I hung up.

I flipped my computer open and wrote up what I had on the fishermen, which wasn't fantastic enough to impress anyone but should be sufficient to keep me at the crime desk for another day.

Filing the story with Les, I paged through crime reports. Nothing interesting, and my thoughts kept straying to the weights Jake Holly described.

Someone would have to be strong to heft a grown man chained to huge dumbbells into the river. Lowe was about as likely as Jenna to be able to pull that off. There wasn't exactly a shortage of biceps at the PD, but Parker's Polos—tailored to show off the hours he spent in the gym—blipped up in my thoughts, and I wondered if he was the muscle that sank Gavin Neal to the bottom of the James.

"Bob said you had quite a day yesterday." Parker's voice came from behind me and I whacked my bruised knee on the underside of the desk again when I jumped. Did the mere thought of him conjure his presence out of the ether?

Turning the chair toward him, I fixed a big grin on my face.

"Just the man I wanted to talk to today," I said, and his eyes widened.

"Does this mean you read my column?"

Aw, hell. I really would have to get to that at some point.

"Not yet," I said. "Quite a day, remember? But I do have a question, and you're my best bet for a straight answer."

"Shoot."

I leveled my gaze at his face, watching for telltale signs that something was bothering him as I spoke. "Dumbbells."

He cocked his head slightly.

"Pardon?"

"Dumbbells," I repeated, studying him carefully. "The kind someone like you lifts at the gym. How big do they make them?"

Google could have told me that easily, but I wanted to see his reaction to the question.

"There is an actual question." He laughed. "I thought for a second I was being insulted. My gym has them up to 75 pounds."

"And would three of those hold a grown man under the water?"

"Your lawyer that turned up in the river." He narrowed his eyes and nodded. "I'm no physicist, but I would say yes."

I murmured a thank you, a sinking feeling in my gut. If anything else about him jumped out at me, I'd have to say something to someone. If for no other reason than so they'd know who to blame if I turned up chained to a fridge at the bottom of a lake.

"Thanks. I think I have an idea."

"I'll let you get after it, then." He stepped backward and smiled. "Glad to help."

I went back to my computer and clicked into the browser, typing what I assumed was the web address for the area's most popular sporting goods store. I got a popup, courtesy of the paper's pornography filters (who decided to name a business after that particular unit of the male anatomy, anyway?), and hastily clicked back into the address bar, wondering if there was some sort of porn offender IT list I'd just ended up on.

All I needed was for Les to get the idea that I was looking for penis photos online at one o'clock in the afternoon. I didn't want to imagine the fun he'd have with that. Shaking my head, I added "sporting goods" to the URL, landed in the right place, and scrolled through product categories.

Dick's carried large dumbbells. I had a sudden yen for a little shopping.

14.

Out of the frying pan, into the fire

"Three seventy-five pound dumbbells? You sold them Monday?" It took work to keep my voice even, and I flashed the pimply kid behind the counter a grin. Though he didn't look like he regularly lifted anything heavier than a video game controller, he did look like he was a fan of my smile. And my legs, from the way his eyes kept wandering to the lower half of the glass counter between us.

The two locations nearest police headquarters were of no help. This one was farther out, but that didn't necessarily mean it wasn't what I was looking for. I asked who he sold them to.

"We don't have a record of that, but they paid with cash."

I shifted my stance, hiking my hemline up the tiniest bit, and smiled again.

"I know it's not the kind of question you get every day, but I really need to know." I frowned slightly. "There's no magic you can work on that computer that will help me?"

"I don't think so." He pulled his eyes away from my quads and looked at his screen again. "Wait, maybe." He touched a few keys.

I held my breath.

"Well, I don't have a name, but I have an address. There were only two of those in stock. We shipped the other one." He rolled out a blank strip of register tape and scribbled on it, then handed it to me.

I glanced at the address. I didn't know where it was, but it was not police headquarters. Damn.

I smiled and tucked the slip of paper into my bag.

"You have no idea how much better you just made my day." I checked his name tag. "Jesse, I could just kiss you."

"I wouldn't stop you." He smiled and leaned across the counter. Gutsy, for a skinny kid with skin problems. I couldn't help admiring his moxie.

"Something tells me your mom might not approve," I winked. "But thanks for your help."

"Come back anytime," he called as I hurried to my car, silently lamenting my lack of a GPS.

My Blackberry binged the arrival of a text as I unlocked the door, and I smiled when I saw my mom's picture on my screen. "Love you more, kid," the message said. A game we'd played when I was a little girl, now resurrected for the digital age.

"Nope. I love you more," I texted back before starting the engine. "Call you later. Been crazy this week."

Before I made it back to the office, my scanner bleeped an all-call for a bad wreck on the Powhite. Jackknifed big rig and possible fatalities. Shit. I didn't have time for that, but damned if I'd give Les an excuse to send Shelby to something else. I made an illegal U in the median and headed south, leaving Les' voicemail a heads-up that we might have an accident story coming as I drove.

I had barely gotten out of my car at the scene when Charlie Lewis tapped me on the shoulder.

"There's my friend from the print side." A tooth-bleaching commercial smile beamed through the thick layer of peach lipstick that matched her tailored Nicole Miller suit. "I was worried about you, Clarke. You didn't show for the lawyer yesterday."

"I was busy." I peered over Charlie's shoulder at the truck, which at first glance appeared to be peeing on the tollway. "What the hell?"

The smell from the amber rivulets running across the pavement wasn't right for gasoline, and the troopers would've long since cleared the scene if that much gas was running across the road. I breathed in deep and giggled. It was beer.

I wondered how long that would have the Powhite shut down and turned my attention from the truck to find Charlie staring at me, one perfectly-waxed eyebrow raised.

"Busy with what?" she purred.

"A little less obvious next time, Charlie," I laughed. "Not that I'm suddenly in the business of giving you leads, but that was half-hearted, at best. I'm insulted."

"Then we're even. I was insulted by that neophyte you sent to the press conference yesterday," she snapped. "What the hell kind of reporter asks if there's evidence of foul play in a murder? Don't you dare bail on me like that again. You keep me on my toes."

"The feeling is mutual," I patted her shoulder a little too hard, moving her out of my way as I spotted a state trooper I knew in passing. "Speaking of, I have work to do. Nice chatting with you, hon."

I made a beeline for the trooper before Charlie could get turned around and collect her cameraman.

No one died at the scene, Trooper Staunton said, but there were serious injuries, some of them to children. That warranted a story. I checked my watch. It was already three. Double shit.

The trucker swerved to avoid hitting a sofa that wasn't properly secured to the back of a pickup. Out of control, the big rig turned over, began spewing beer, and got hit by a minivan and an SUV. All the occupants of those vehicles, three women and five children between them, had been loaded into ambulances and taken to St. Vincent's before I arrived.

"Can I talk to the driver of the pickup?" I asked Staunton. "Are you charging him with anything?"

"The trucker said he took off when he saw the commotion in the rearview." Trooper Staunton shook his head. "The sofa he dropped is over there, and we're pulling camera feed from the tollbooths a half-mile back to see if we can get a look at his plate. It looks like reckless endangerment. Unless one of those little ones don't pull through. Then it's manslaughter, and he just ruined his whole life because he was too lazy to hook a strap over that couch."

I scribbled his quote down and thanked him, texting Les as I walked back to my car. Charlie pounced on Staunton as I pulled away, and my Blackberry popped up a one-word response from my pseudo-boss: Hurry.

"When do I ever get to do anything else?" I sighed and aimed the car toward the office, the hard-won mystery address waiting in my bag.

It was after five by the time I got the accident story ready to go and noticed an emailed shot of the crash scene, courtesy of Larry from photo. He'd framed the lighter side of a heavy story perfectly: the slightly mauled but still recognizable brewery logo on the truck, the river of beer running over the concrete, and a small band of onlookers waving straws.

I shot back a quick smiley face and sent my story to Les. It was on the website before Charlie went on at six, which saved me from another ass-chewing.

Channel Four led with the wreck and I watched Charlie's report, relieved she didn't have anything I hadn't. She was right. She did keep me on my toes. And if the *Post* and the Mafia and doing the right thing weren't motivation enough, I had to admit the idea of the look on her face when my investigative piece hit the racks was smile-worthy.

I grabbed a turkey on rye from the deli across the street and settled back at my desk for the night.

Google Maps told me the extra dumbbell was delivered to what appeared to be a warehouse near Shockoe Bottom, though whether it was still used for that was anyone's guess. Many of those had been refurbished in recent years, turned into everything from trendy apartments to hot yoga centers.

Maybe it was just a gym. I clicked over to the city's property tax records and typed in the address, renewed hope turning up the corners of my mouth.

A Brandon Smith was listed as the sole owner. Another quick search told me the place didn't hold a business license of any kind. Hmmm.

A DMV records search revealed hundreds of Brandon Smiths in Virginia. I tried Google and came up with an insane number of hits. Gotta love common surnames. Refining the search to include the word "drugs," I clicked on the first link that popped up.

And found something. Even though I didn't quite know what it meant.

"Officer arrested in evidence case takes plea deal" read the headline of an old news story from Miami, with a subhead revealing that the evidence in question had never been found. I scrolled through it quickly.

Eight years before, a cop in Miami had been fired and arrested after more than a million dollars in drugs and cash went missing from their evidence locker. The cop's name was Brandon Smith. The story quoted the DA as saying Smith had a brother who was a small-time dealer with a record. The brother's fingerprints were found in the lock-up after the theft.

"Hot damn." The pen I was tapping fell to the desktop.

Noah. The brother's name was Noah Smith. I flipped to the police report on the first dealer murder to be sure, but I knew I was right.

A cop who'd been arrested in a strikingly similar case in Miami now might very well own a warehouse in Shockoe Bottom. And his brother's murder was likely the catalyst for all this craziness.

That was way too much coincidence to actually be coincidence.

But who the hell was Smith, and where did he fit into my story?

I thunked my head onto the desk, a screaming crick in my neck from the hours of research. I wanted answers, not more questions. At that moment even one answer would've tickled me pink.

"Everything all right?" Parker's voice interrupted my thoughts.

I raised my head and looked around, noticing the silence for the first time. It was dark. And there was no one else around.

"Fine. Just tired," I said, my tone too bright. "These hours are murder."

"Your whole world is murder lately, isn't it?" he leaned on one side of the cube door and put a foot up on the other. I'd never been claustrophobic, but evidently there is indeed a first time for everything.

"It stays that way a lot of the time," I said, my eyes on his hands. They rested easily on his knees, and I didn't see any Magnum-shaped bulges on his person. I took a deep breath, catching a whiff of the same clean-smelling cologne he'd been wearing Saturday. "This has just been a very long week."

"Seems like it, doesn't it?" he said. "I was just thinking I didn't even really know you last Friday, and here it is Friday again, and I feel like we're old friends."

I had thought on Tuesday I might like that, but by Friday night, not so much. He had some old friends I wanted to keep my distance from.

"This story has had its share of weird twists." I smiled, easing the chair backward. Dammit, our cubicles were tiny.

"Anything new?" The question sounded light, but Parker's eyes were serious.

I saw two possibilities: I could play dumb, which I was lousy at, or I could maybe get an answer to one of my big questions. Curiosity trumped nerves, and I scooted the chair as far from him as I could get it and stood.

"Why do you ask? I don't recall you being so interested in my work before." It came out sharper than I intended.

He furrowed his brow.

"I read your stuff all the time. You're good," he grinned and held up his hands in mock-surrender. "I thought you knew that. But if you don't want to share, that's all right. I just wondered if I could help."

Perplexed, I studied him as he stepped backward into the walkway. I knew my murder mysteries. The bad guy wasn't supposed to flash a grin and back off when you pushed back. I opened my mouth to reply and my Blackberry bleeped a text notification.

"Got a date?" Parker asked.

I laughed in spite of myself and shook my head, figuring my mom wanted to know why I hadn't called yet. Parker was still close, and I didn't want to take my eyes off him. Until I glanced at my phone and completely forgot he existed.

"Or yes," I said, shoving my laptop, files, and phone into my bag. "Maybe a hot one. Gotta run, Parker."

He called a goodnight as I ran for the elevators, killing two birds by getting away from him and to whoever had sent that text.

"RPD officer with answers. Meet me at the beanery on Parham in 20 if you want them."

I wanted nothing more.

Who does this guy think he is, Deep Throat? Why is he parked back there in the trees? Unease fluttered in my stomach as I turned the corner a second time and stopped in a spot near the shadow-shrouded police sedan, far from the light spilling out of the coffeehouse despite the relatively empty parking lot.

"Officer?" I called, taking a step toward the car.

The middle-ageduniformed cop in the driver's seat opened the door and unfurled a hulking form that towered over even my height.

The butterflies in my stomach morphed into bats.

I stood up straight and called up my most confident smile before I looked up at his dark eyes and extended my hand. "Nichelle Clarke. Nice to meet you."

Officer McClendon (according to the shiny nameplate on his uniform) had hazel eyes, but they looked darker because they had curiously little depth. It added to the nagging in my gut that something was off, and I was glad he didn't hold my gaze long.

"Nice to meet you." He mumbled, ducking his head.

I took a big step backward and asked if he'd had a chance to eat dinner yet. My instincts about people were almost never wrong, and everything about him screamed at me to get to a place where we weren't alone in the dark.

I considered sprinting back to my car, but dismissed the thought almost as quickly as it occurred to me. I wanted the story worse than I'd ever wanted anything.

Eyes on McClendon, I planted my feet and curled both hands into loose fists. My right hook had sent my trainer staggering a few times, and he was a pretty big guy.

"Um, no," McClendon said, staring at his shoes.

I knew that voice from somewhere. The hesitancy and soft tone were unusual for a cop. I tried for a better look at his face, but he kept it pointed down.

Maybe hearing him talk some more would help.

"Let's go inside, then. Have you ever tried their blueberry scones?" I took another, shorter step backward.

He shook his head and fidgeted with his hands, and I wondered if I was getting paranoid. Parker turned out to be less than threatening. Maybe his weird vibe stemmed from the fear of revealing something he wasn't supposed to.

"Are you okay?" I smiled again, trying to catch his eye. "Whatever you want to talk to me about, you don't have to be on the record. At least not at first."

"Thanks. I've never talked to a reporter before." He looked up and to one side, toward The Beanery's windows, and something clicked in my head.

He was the cop from the beheaded accountant trial, the one who'd forgotten to read the accused his rights.

Shit. How did he still have a job? There was only one answer for that, and it meant I wasn't paranoid after all.

I spun on my stiletto and started to run. I didn't get two steps before something hit the back of my head, and everything went black.

15.

Of crooked cops and car trunks

Not even a week as an investigative reporter and people were already trying to bash my head in? That had to be some kind of record.

Pitch black surrounded me like a cloak on all sides, but I was pretty sure I was in the trunk of McClendon's cruiser. And the car was moving. Trying hard not to panic, I focused first on deciphering why I was there. I wasn't certain I knew anything too incriminating, but someone sure thought I did.

First the mysterious Mr. Smith, now this guy. The only way for him to still be a cop after losing a murder case to such a stupid mistake was for him to be in on something—or with someone—pretty powerful. Like David Lowe?

But I didn't have anything on Lowe that I could prove. Did I? I pondered that for a minute.

My stomach lurched as we took another corner and I decided none of what I'd compiled would mean squat if I didn't figure out how to get away from McClendon. I had no experience with being cracked over the head and tossed in a car trunk, but his intentions couldn't be good.

I remembered a salesman showing me the release handle inside the trunk of my old car. But they were supposed to glow in the dark, and I saw nothing. I ran my hands along the side walls. The lining was rough, the metal and plastic beneath it hard. I felt a thick, textured metal cable roll under my fingers, but it didn't lead to anything. Damn.

In the absence of an escape hatch, I needed a weapon. Maybe surprising him when he opened the trunk lid would give me an advantage. I was unsure exactly how I'd manage to hold my own with the Jolly Green Giant's cousin out there, but I damn well had to try.

Mostly, I counted on the fact that Officer Felony didn't know I had such a hard head. Whether it was conditioned or just a God-given gift to offset my uncanny ability to get brained by any object flying through the air in my vicinity, my skull seemed more resistant to damage than the average.

Which was nifty, given that I needed my brain at full speed if I wanted to see Saturday's sunrise.

Think, Nichelle. I had a sudden flash of slipping my Blackberry into the small pocket in my skirt as I jumped out of my car.

Please, be there.

My fingers grazed smooth plastic when I slid them into the slit at my hip, and my heart leapt as I sifted through everyone I knew, trying to think of anyone I might be able to call for help.

Not the police ("Hello, 911? I've been abducted by one of your officers and am in the trunk of his cruiser on my way to certain doom. Please come save me." I could practically hear the click of the operator hanging up on me). Not Jenna. Not Bob. Agent Starnes at the FBI came to mind. Did I have a cell number for her?

I touched a key and the screen lit up.

No bars. Not even a fraction of the little one.

Most coverage in the country, my ass. I stared, willing the icon to change. The flashing "no service" verged on mocking.

I pointed the LCD away from me like a flashlight.

The metal cable I had felt during my tactile exploration appeared from the ragged end to be what was left of the safety cord. Fantastic. McClendon was a planner.

I moved the phone slowly, looking for anything I might be able to inflict pain with. A short steel bar strapped to the side-wall over my head looked promising. Probably part of a small jack for changing a tire.

I jerked the bar loose, grimacing at the ripping noise it made as the Velcro holding it to the wall gave way.

I shoved the phone back into my pocket and gripped my makeshift club with both hands, waiting for the car to stop.

After several corners and some brain-rattling bumps, it did. I had no idea how long I'd been out, so I wasn't sure where we were. Apparently, somewhere that wasn't on Verizon's big red map.

I waited for McClendon to come for me.

The air felt thick.

Stress, or an actual shortage of oxygen making it harder to breathe? I couldn't tell.

Bob could've been in the trunk talking to me, I could hear his words so clearly: "You're crossing into the world of investigative reporting, here…That means you're going to be in every bit as much danger as any cop working a case would be."

I thought of the hundred or so times I'd watched *All The President's Men* and imagined investigative reporting to be glamorous. Right. I'd be young and beautiful in my casket. And I even knew where mom could get a good deal on a "gently used" one. A stray hubcap wouldn't bother me.

A door slammed.

Fear obliterated the greater good I'd always wanted to serve.

I wished I could turn the clock back a week and do it all differently. I'd never cared less about a scoop.

Charlie was probably on her third sangria of the night, and I was locked in a car trunk. I failed to see where that meant I was winning anything.

I wanted desperately to be curled up on my mother's sofa in Dallas, watching trashy TV and eating chocolate and laughing.

I hadn't even called her back. What if I never saw her again? I'd been so scared of that when she was sick, that a can't-breathe-can't-eat-oh-my-God-I'm-going-to-vomit dread washed over me every time a monitor beeped or she shifted in her bed.

In a thousand tearful prayers, I'd begged and bargained, offering God anything and everything in trade if he would please just not take my mommy away. And he hadn't.

And McClendon would not take me away from her. Not without a fight, anyway.

Squashing the terror, I shifted my knees toward the back of the trunk so I'd have a clear shot with the tire tool.

Footsteps on…gravel? I held my breath and listened. Maybe. That would explain the rough ride at the end. So I'd have to watch my footing in my characteristically impractical shoes. If I got a chance to get my feet under me at all.

I gulped a lungful of heavy air and choked up on my steel club, preparing to swing for whatever vulnerability I could see when the trunk lid popped.

The footsteps stopped.

Would he take me out of the car first? My stomach knotted. Surely they didn't want blood all over the trunk of the cruiser.

I heard the gravel crunch under his shoes as he turned.

Showtime.

I steeled myself.

The key scraped into the lock.

I said a very fast prayer.

The pop of the latch letting go was heart-stoppingly loud, and I gripped my weapon tighter to keep from dropping it.

Blinded by the security lamp on the back of a nearby building, I stuck the pole straight out of the trunk and swung skyward as hard as I could, praying I would hit something.

From the scream, I did better than I'd hoped.

I fluttered my eyelids, and when my pupils constricted significantly I saw McClendon, doubled over, groaning, and holding his crotch. Bullseye.

I reached behind my head and grabbed the edge of the trunk opening for leverage, flexing my ankles and thrusting both heels at McClendon's face.

He screamed again. Blood spurted down his left cheek, but he moved too fast for me to guess its source.

Staggering backward, he groped for his sidearm. Shit. My stilettos were no match for a police special.

I shoved with my arms and twisted my hips, rolling out of the trunk and catching my balance blessedly quick, though pain shot through my skull when I came upright.

I blinked away the dizziness, matching the pounding in my head with the memory of the upbeat training music from body combat as I stepped forward. The moves were almost second nature, though the target was new.

Punch, punch. Two to McClendon's midsection. He took another step back.

I bounced forward, then delivered a swift *ap-chagi* to his chest, stumbling only slightly because of my shoes.

He tumbled over backward, but managed to unholster his gun.

I looked down for just long enough to see that the blood came from his left eye, which was pinched shut. Aiming with his right, he fired as I dodged sideways. The bullet went wide.

I spun and sprinted across the wide gravel parking lot, no idea where I was or where I was going.

I should've stayed at the office with Parker. At least if he'd turned out to be a psycho, my car was there.

I zigzagged in an attempt to avoid the half-blind shots McClendon was popping off, then rounded the corner of the closest building and found a narrow street. Possibly an alley. The sprawling, boxy buildings all looked to be warehouses.

I tried the nearest door, but of course it was locked. Why wouldn't it be?

I started for the next one, afraid to look over my shoulder and also afraid not to, imagining McClendon as my very own lumbering slasher-movie villain: limping behind the running girl, yet somehow catching her anyway.

Except I wasn't in a movie, and my stalker had a gun. He didn't have to catch me. All he had to do was make it around the corner and get off one good shot.

As if on cue, his shadow stretched across the mouth of the alley.

"There's nowhere to go, bitch," he called.

I ducked behind a dumpster, peering into the dark. I couldn't even tell if I'd run into a dead end.

McClendon shuffled closer.

I tried to squeeze between the dumpster and the wall and succeeded only in ripping my skirt and slicing my thigh open on a rough piece of metal. I bit blood out of my lip to keep from screaming.

The chirping that meant I had an eBay alert might as well have been a bugler playing *Revelry*, it was so loud in the stillness. I whacked my elbow on the side of the dumpster, but managed to fumble my Blackberry out of my pocket and shut the alert off, resisting the urge to fling it into the nearest warehouse wall.

Of course it had a signal now. And look, I was winning the Manolos I'd bid on the night before with only a few minutes to go. Fantastic. I could be buried in them.

"Such a pretty sound," McClendon called. "Where, oh where, has this little birdie gone?"

Another gunshot. This one sounded like it zinged off the dumpster. Double fuck.

"Come out, come out," he cackled.

My breath coming fast and loud, I could still hear the shuffling inching closer.

I closed my eyes and prayed. I opened them to headlights flooding the far end of the alley, followed by tires squealing around a corner and the roar of an engine.

Way to be on top of your inbox, big guy.

Mouthing a thank you to the heavens, I stared at the Lincoln emblem racing toward me and straightened my spine, trying to flag down the driver without leaving my hiding place.

The passenger window lowered as the car slowed, and I jerked the door open and jumped in without waiting for an invitation. I figured the likelihood I was in one alley with two murderers was pretty low.

"Drive, please," I crouched in the passenger floorboard, my voice raspy from ragged breath. "Now. And keep your head down. I'll explain when you get me out of here, I swear."

"My, my, Miss Clarke," Joey clicked his tongue, giving McClendon a once-over and gunning the engine. "Remind me not to piss you off."

16.

Heroes and villains

I heard one more shot as the sleek sedan leapt forward, the alley fading quickly behind us. Sinking into the cool leather seat, I stared at my mobster "friend," the familiar sardonic smile on his face and his dark eyes on the road.

"It's bad that I'm not even surprised to see you, isn't it?" I asked. "This week has completely robbed me of my ability to be shocked."

"Damn. And I wanted to save the day and sweep you off your feet." He chuckled. "Fucking D.C. traffic. Apparently, everyone and their cousin leaves that town on Friday night."

"I'm not easily swept. But you could take me by the ER if you want some brownie points," I poked gingerly at my still-bleeding thigh, and his eyes widened when they strayed to the gash there.

"Ouch." He held the wheel with one hand and pulled off his cornflower blue tie with the other, tossing it to me. "Tie that just above the cut. Pull it tight. You need stitches. I know my flesh wounds."

Of course he did. So much for two murderers not being in the same alley. But at least this one didn't want to kill me. I didn't think, anyway.

I hiked up my skirt and cinched the length of blue silk—Brioni, no less—around my thigh. The bleeding slowed and I studied Joey as he drove us easily out of the maze of warehouses. His expression was the polar opposite of stressed.

"How did you know the day needed saving?" I asked when he turned onto a better-travelled road and I recognized the less-touristy, more-industrial area of Shockoe Bottom.

"I didn't." He chuckled. "Though I would like to have a go at that sometime. I was looking for you. Glad I found you when I did. But I gotta say, it looked like you handled that guy pretty well. And he was a big fella." He glanced at me and arched an eyebrow. "There's nothing sexier than a woman who can fend for herself."

"I feel about as sexy as a saddle shoe right now," I said, sucking a hissing breath between my teeth at the pain in my leg and fighting the urge to smile.

This was not good, Joey Soprano over there flirting with me. I didn't need encouragement on that front. I needed to stop thinking he was hot. Remembering the headless accountant helped.

"And nice sidestep, but how exactly did you know where to find me?" I narrowed my eyes, looking for any tell that he might be lying and wishing I knew who to trust.

First I'd ditched Parker for a trigger happy cop who'd turned out to be a nutcase, and now I had escaped from him into a speeding car with the Mafia. If I was going to have to bail out, I needed to know it.

I believed his theory about the boat crash, mostly because everything I'd learned since Monday pointed in that direction, and his presence indicated that he knew something, maybe even more than he'd already said. And I still didn't get the same run-now-and-run-fast vibe from him I had from McClendon.

"Again, I didn't." He cut his eyes toward me and shook his head, turning the car onto East Cary. "Not like you think, anyway. You weren't home, so I went to your office. I ran into a big blond guy in the garage, and he told me you got a text about a huge story you've been killing yourself on and took off.

"I was going to go back to your house and wait for you, but I wanted to have a look at something down here first. It's what I came to tell you about, actually. I heard gunfire and went to check it out. I sure as hell didn't expect to find you in the middle of it."

"What were you looking for?"

"Open the glove box," he said, the smile returning.

"There's not an accountant's head in there, is there?"

He shot me a look from the corner of his eye as he weaved the car through traffic, the normal people around us stalking nonexistent street parking for the restaurants and nightclubs that lined this part of the slip.

Wishing I was out there with them, I kept my eyes on Joey's face, daring him to deny it.

He just shook his head, then chuckled. "You are one very smart lady, Miss Clarke. I like that."

"That's great," I said. "Though it would be more great if I didn't have a rule against becoming involved with felons."

"Even never-once-convicted ones with impeccable timing?" He winked, and I ignored the flip my stomach did in response.

"Even then."

"Rules were made to be broken. It's sort of a personal philosophy of mine."

"Not this one." The words sounded a lot more convincing than they felt, but that was good.

I had a whopper of a mystery it suddenly seemed my life depended on solving, and for all I really knew Sexy McDarkEyes here could be a decoy dispatched by the bad guys. I still wasn't sure why he was helping me.

"There are no body parts in my car." He chuckled, and I really hoped it was a sign of sarcasm. "Getting the smell out can be a real bitch, you know. But you might want to have a look at what's in the yellow envelope in there."

I pulled the latch on the glove compartment, which appeared to hold mostly the usual: a pair of Ray Bans and a black leather owner's manual, plus a manila envelope. I plucked it from the pile and ripped it open with the flair of an Oscar presenter, then sighed when I saw the articles about Brandon Smith I'd found earlier in the evening.

"I know this already," I said. "There aren't many reporters who aren't on a first-name basis with Google. I call her Gigi."

Joey laughed and I glanced at him from beneath lowered lashes, hoping he had more than a handful of old news.

"Do you know what happened to this guy? It would seem that he should be around, since I'm fairly certain his kid brother was my first drug dealer victim."

"It would seem." Joey nodded, turning the car into the ER drive at St. Vincent's. "I don't know where Mr. Smith ended up, though. I was hoping you might. My friends in Miami tell me he disappeared suddenly several years back, but they weren't sorry to see him go."

He did have one thing I didn't, and I studied the grainy copy of a half-decade-old mug shot, unable to place the round, bearded face scowling back at me. The guy was vaguely familiar, but I saw a hell of a lot of people every week, and he might bear a resemblance to any dozen of them. Nothing jumped out, at any rate.

"He wasn't working with your…friends…in Florida?"

"Not even close. They had about the same situation we have here." The corners of Joey's mouth turned up in a wry half-smile. "The cops were taking product off the streets and this guy was swiping it and selling it. It's a bit frustrating, having someone else pocketing our money."

So that's why he was pissed.

"But you wouldn't have made money on it if it had stayed in the evidence room and gotten burned up," I said.

"Call it the principle of the thing." Joey parked the car and turned to face me. "Losing to the cops every once in a while is expected. A cost of doing this business, you might say. But this is unsportsmanlike. Let's put a stop to it."

"Why does someone like you need my help to do that?" I asked. "I may be forgetting my manners, but I've just very nearly been turned into fish food over this. Why can't you just find this guy and…" I threw up my hands, unable to think of phrasing that didn't sound like I was enlisting a hitman. "And, well, do what you do?"

He stared for a second and I fidgeted, not wanting to think too hard about the fact that he'd probably killed people. Maybe many people.

Without a word, he got out of the car.

I opened my door and he stepped up to it, offering a hand. I latched onto his forearm, wincing when my leg—absent the stalked-by-a-killer adrenaline rush—protested the weight I put on it.

"What I do, contrary to popular characterization, is not run around 'whacking' people left, right, and center," he said quietly, walking slowly next to me as I hobbled to the door.

"Taking someone's life is not an easy thing to do. It's a mortal sin. Something that stays with a man long after he's done the requisite 'our fathers.'"

I stopped walking and looked at him, feeling a bit like a child who'd been reproached for an accidental slight. The whole Mafia thing notwithstanding, I did like him. And I hadn't meant to hurt his feelings.

"I'm, um, really sorry," I stammered.

"For what? Figuring out something about me and thinking bad things?" He smiled, his lips tight and his eyes locked on mine. "No need for apologies, Miss Clarke. I am who I am, even if sometimes I wish I weren't."

His eyes said everything he wasn't, and I looked away.

Not. Happening.

He cleared his throat.

"Just so you know, I didn't have anything to do with that accountant. I know people who did, as you have already deduced. But that wasn't my handiwork, if that's what you were thinking.

"A lot too much, what they did to that guy. I'm trying to resolve this differently. Call it an ideology shift. A savvier organization that uses technology and information, and those who purvey that information," he winked, "to work more around the edges of the law than outside it."

When he put it that way it didn't sound so bad. But not so bad was still bad enough.

I turned back to the door and resumed limping toward medical care.

"So, you really don't know who Smith is?" I asked.

"You don't, either? Logic dictates that he's either a cop here, or he knows someone who is. At least, from what I've read this week. Nice work, by the way."

"Flattery will get you nowhere."

"Honesty is not flattery."

The doors slid open and the harsh fluorescent light revealed a left leg that looked worthy of a slasher movie. Blood had run clear down into my shoe, drying brownish-red on my skin. My favorite skirt was trashed.

Looking at the gash seemed to make it throb more, and I felt a little sick. The petite gray-haired desk attendant jumped to her feet and pushed a wheelchair over.

"Oh, honey, what happened to you?" She clucked like a mother hen and wheeled me through to the treatment rooms.

"It's just a cut," I said. "I think."

I looked up to see that Joey had followed. Mother hen lady disappeared and a nurse swept in, tossed me a hospital gown, and smiled at him.

"Help her into the gown and onto the bed," she said. "I'll be right back."

She shut the door behind her with a loud click and Joey grinned and stepped toward me.

"I've got it, thanks." I held one hand up. "Could you excuse me for a sec?"

"I'm happy to help."

"Thank you, but I've been dressing myself for quite a while. I can manage."

He made a big show of turning his back.

"And they wonder why chivalry is dead," he said. "What were we talking about?"

"Smith." I kept my eyes on the back of his head as I kicked off my shoes and managed to get clumsily back to my feet. "Who he is and why you want my help."

"Ah, yes," he said. "Well, Miss Clarke, I find that the court of public opinion is far more influential in the actual courts than it should be, most of the time. If you get to the bottom of this and write about it, I get a double bonus: I know who to blame for it, and they've been exposed in the press.

"A news story lives forever on the Internet. And if enough people are upset about it, it can't get swept under any proverbial rugs no matter who's behind it. *Capisce?*"

I grunted agreement as I wriggled out of the skirt, which was stiff with dried blood, and dropped it on the tile. My silk tank top came off with a little work, and I jerked the gown on and tied it, hobbling to the bed and pulling up the covers.

"All right. I'm decent."

"Damn." Joey turned, the grin back in place, and I rolled my eyes. More at myself than at him, though I didn't want him to know that.

Before I got a chance to reply, the door opened and Dr. Schaefer came in.

"Hello there," she said. "I didn't expect to see you again so soon. What did you do?"

"I stumbled into a rusty garden tool and got a nasty cut," I said, figuring the actual details of my evening would either get the cops called or me a first-class ticket to the psych ward, neither of which sounded like fun.

She eyed the bloody Louboutins and slashed linen skirt.

"Gardening?"

"No, garden tool." I stressed the last word, dismissing the golf-ball-sized lump on the back of my head, because it was hidden under my hair and I didn't have a fake explanation for it. "I was on my way out."

Joey nodded when she looked at him.

"I see." She pulled the blanket back and examined the cut. "This is going to need a few stitches. When was your last tetanus vaccine?"

Shit. I hated shots. And since I couldn't remember the last one, I was due.

She bustled off and returned with the nurse and a tray holding two hypodermics and several other pointy medical things.

I took a deep breath and clamped my fingers around the railing on the right side of the bed, studying the cream wallpaper and trying to think of anything but needles and murderers. I felt the doctor remove Joey's tie from my leg and gripped the rail tighter.

"You all right, Xena?" Joey's voice was closer and a quick glance revealed that he'd walked to the foot of the bed. He stepped up beside me and leaned his head down, so close I could feel his breath on my ear. "Guns, kidnapping, overgrown maniacs. That doesn't faze you and this is what gets to you?"

I clenched my teeth and glared at his smirk.

"Shut up," I said, without moving my jaw.

"No judgment," he grinned. "Just trying to figure you out."

"Because I'm such a mystery." The sarcasm I intended to inflect on the words was lost in a hissing intake of breath when the doctor stabbed my leg with one of the needles.

"Lidocaine," she said. "It'll burn a little for a second, but you won't feel the stitches go in. That hurts a lot worse."

Apparently "burn a little" meant "set your entire thigh aflame from hip to knee," but it faded quickly. Feeling odd pressure where the cut should've been, I glanced over to see her prodding it, squirting it with first a clear solution, then a rust-colored one. Although it looked disgusting, it didn't hurt.

"How about that?" I muttered.

She asked about Bob as she scrubbed dried blood off my thigh, and I told her he was stubborn, but improving.

When my wound was decontaminated to her satisfaction, she picked up a pointy doohickey that could only mean she was about to start sewing me up, and I looked away again. Deadened nerves or not, I couldn't watch that.

Joey could, though. And did, giving me the color commentary as the doctor closed up the unsightly souvenir of my crazy night. Seven stitches. The scar would limit my skirt-length options, but it'd make a respectable war story for the whippersnappers someday.

Dr. Schafer dressed the freshly-sewn cut with loose gauze as the nurse stuck a little round band aid on my arm over the blood drop from the tetanus vaccine. She smiled at my grimace and began cleaning up.

"You should be healed in about ten to fourteen days." Dr. Schafer pulled her gloves off and tossed them into a bin in the corner, picking up my chart and laying a hand on the doorknob. "Keep it covered until day after tomorrow, then let it air out as much as you can. Clean it with antiseptic solution twice a day, and put some antibiotic ointment on it after you do that.

"Your general practitioner can remove the stitches for you. After it's healed, make sure you use sunblock every day for six months to minimize the scarring, and if it swells up or gets red or oozes anything, come back here."

I thanked her as she left, signing a stack of papers for the insurance company while the nurse finished picking up. I handed her the papers, eyeing my bloody skirt with distaste.

"Why don't I see if we have a pair of scrubs you can wear home?" She asked, following my gaze. She took the paperwork and the tray of pointy things with her and returned shortly with a clean outfit, such that it was. I thanked her.

"Be more careful around your garden tools." She patted my shoulder and smiled at Joey. "Take good care of her."

I opened my mouth to tell her I could take care of myself, as evidenced by Burly McGiant the one-eyed cop, then snapped it shut. That's why I don't lie. My big mouth tends to get me caught.

I shooed Joey into the hallway and pulled on the pea green PJs before I settled back into the wheelchair and let an orderly push me to the car.

Joey insisted on driving me home, and since asking for help picking up my car would give me a good excuse to catch up with Jenna the next morning, I didn't argue.

The short trip to my house was mostly silent, me scrutinizing Smith's photo and trying to place him, and Joey drumming his fingers on the wheel in time to Kenny Chesney.

A Jersey mobster who liked country music. Of all the crazy things about my week, that one might be the most unbelievable.

I looked up as he turned onto my street, still just a nagging familiarity about Smith's face dancing in the back of my brain. Maybe sleep would float whatever it was to the surface.

"Get your head down," Joey said in a low voice, throwing an arm behind me and yanking my torso over into his lap.

"Have you lost your mind?" I struggled to sit up, but he was strong. My heart rate took off like Earnhardt roaring out of a pit stop. Dammit, was no one trustworthy?

I didn't want to die in a Lincoln with Kenny crooning about tequila and toxic love in the background. I shimmied my shoulders, trying to get an arm free to swing at Joey.

"I count three cars that weren't here earlier, all close to your place. And your lights are on," he said tightly. "I know this isn't terribly comfortable, but would you be still?"

I froze. They were in my house? I didn't feel so ridiculous about having hidden Neal's folder under the floorboard anymore.

"Darcy." I swallowed a sob.

"No reason to hurt the dog unless they're just douchebags," Joey said, stomping on the accelerator once we passed the house and letting go of me a second later. "I'll handle that. She likes me. You have to get somewhere safe."

I told him to take me to a hotel and laughed when he reeled off the name of the poshest place in town.

"You might be able to afford The Jefferson, Captain Armani, but those of us who don't have unlimited offshore accounts tend more toward Holiday Inn."

"Fair enough. Where is one? Far from here, preferably, and no using a credit card for that or anything else. We'll get you some cash."

Off the grid. Fan-fucking-tastic Friday I was having. At this rate, I'd be hacking off my ponytail and bleaching my hair by Sunday. I glanced at my reflection in the dark window, hoping it didn't come to that. Brassy hair and washed out skin would make me a shudder-worthy blond.

I directed Joey to a bank and emptied my checking account, which netted me a pitifully small stack of twenties, then navigated to a suburban hotel in my price range, turning to tell him goodnight when he stopped outside the revolving glass door.

"Thanks for your help." I said. "How do I get in touch with you if I do figure out who this guy is, anyway?"

"I'll be around," he said. "And I'll look for your byline. Try to stay out of trouble."

"That seems to be difficult for me this week."

"All you can do is the best you can do." He smiled, staring at me for a long minute. Not liking where that could go, I kicked the car door open with my good leg and climbed out, watching the taillights until they were out of sight.

17.

Two and two isn't five

Morning didn't bring me closer to a match on Brandon Smith, but staring at Google Maps gave me an idea of what might.

Though I didn't remember exact details—owing to the darkness and the running for my life—the satellite view of the warehouse Smith owned in Richmond looked disturbingly similar to where McClendon had taken me. Which would also give me a reason for Joey's never-fully-explained cameo in the alley.

What if I'd been a hundred and eighty degrees wrong and this was all a criminal ex-cop who'd hooked up with a crazy patrolman looking for some extra cash?

I ran mentally through Mike's evidence log, but I didn't remember McClendon's name. For the first time, I wondered if Mike had brought me the actual documents, or if the ones I had were doctored versions designed to finger Neal as the bad guy. My stomach wrung like an old dishrag, uncertainty swimming through my head.

I pulled out a notebook and made a list of everything I knew and everything I didn't. The latter was much longer. And Les' timer was running out.

"A week of busting my ass, and I still don't have the first clue," I said to no one.

As much as I wanted a sounding board, the only people I trusted were Jenna, Bob, and my mother, and I wasn't about to worry any of them with my near-death experience.

I stared at the lists until the letters blurred, instead, then tossed the notebook to the foot of the bed and sighed. Loads of suspicion, but very little actual fact.

And Brandon Smith's warehouse was the only place I could think of to find a few facts, whatever they might be.

It was early, and I was willing to gamble cab fare on a hunch McClendon had been so preoccupied with his injuries he'd forgotten about my car. I called a taxi to the hotel and forked over two of my dwindling stash of twenties when we pulled up next to my sporty little SUV. It was still at the coffee shop, my bag resting in the backseat. Hooray for tiny awesomes.

Thanks to the deserted Saturday morning streets, it took less than twenty minutes to get to the warehouse. I circled it three times. The steel double doors that served as the main entrance were on the side of the building that faced the big gravel parking lot.

When I was reasonably sure no one was there, I parked in the alley around back next to a hulking green dumpster. An inspection of its back corner revealed a piece of jagged metal decorated with dried blood and black linen.

Bingo.

In the daylight, without a maniac chasing me, I could see a large bank of windows high on the wall above the dumpster.

I looked around for a stepping stool and spotted a big plastic crate at the far end of the alley. Dragging it over, I slid the side door on the dumpster open and clambered up onto the lid. The four Advil I'd gotten from the hotel desk kept the pain in my leg to a dull ache, though I still leaned heavier on the uninjured one.

Reaching the other side of my perch, I gripped the bottom of the window frame and pressed my nose to the glass, taking a deep breath as the interior of the building came into focus.

Boxes. Hundreds, maybe thousands, of stacked plastic crates like the one I'd used to climb up, their contents not discernible from the outside.

I groaned under my breath as my eyes swept the room again. A whole lot of nothing. Just a massive expanse of concrete floor, white walls, white and gray steel ceiling beams, and boxes.

I stood there for a long minute, contemplating the door, but knowing there was only so far I should push it. There was investigating, and then there was just plain asking to be murdered. Going inside that building looked like an excellent way to jump from one to the other.

Just as I turned to get down, I heard the low purr of an engine.

I froze for a split second, then nearly gave myself whiplash searching for the source of the sound.

Shit.

I started for the edge of the dumpster, but couldn't help wondering if I'd be able to see what lurked in the mysterious boxes if someone went inside.

The engine shut off, the alley still empty.

I was still out of sight.

"All or nothing," I whispered, spinning back to the window. *That curiosity that killed the cat is about to help the crooked cops whack the nosy reporter*, the little voice in my head that sounded a lot like my mother warned. *Guns. River. Sleep with the fishes. Anything unclear?*

I held my breath as the door on the opposite wall swung outward, and a large man I didn't recognize walked into the room. It could've been Smith. It could've just as easily been the tooth fairy for all I could tell from so far away. I tried to focus on his face, looking for the features from the grainy mug shot.

He had a scar on one cheek I could see across the considerable distance, and his dark features looked frozen in a perpetual scowl. He was probably as tall as Parker and maybe even more muscular, sporting an expensive-looking tailored leather jacket in the middle of summer.

He jerked the big metal door closed behind him and walked to a small office, emerging with an empty plastic crate much like the ones that were stacked halfway to the ceiling throughout most of the room.

He stopped in front of a tower about ten yards from the door and pulled the top box down. Taking a large plastic bag of white powder out, he added it to the box he was holding.

I blew my breath out forcefully and thanked my lucky stars, every fiber of my being zeroed in on Mr. I'm-Too-GQ-For-This-Heat.

He chose another crate and peeked inside it before he lifted the lid and moved a smaller bag, this one full of little yellowish pebbles, into his box.

I wondered if my mystery man was getting ready to make a delivery, already contemplating whether I was stealthy enough to follow him without getting caught.

The next box was full of guns, and he pulled two out and added them to his cache.

"Jesus," I whispered to myself. "Welcome to Costco for criminals."

Replacing all the lids carefully and straightening the boxes, he turned to take the one under his arm outside and froze.

I clutched the window frame, forgetting to breathe. In all my excitement over a building full of proof that I was right, I hadn't heard another car, but a long shadow stretched across the concrete floor in the light from the high windows.

Someone else was there. A very large someone.

And I couldn't see them because they were standing behind a tower of plastic crates. Shit.

Mr. Box o' Drugs and Guns shook his head hard, setting his loot on the ground and backing up three steps.

I wished I could hear what they were saying, and I would've traded my shoe closet for a camera. From the side of the discussion I could see, it appeared that maybe someone was taking things that didn't belong to him.

Which shouldn't surprise people who employed criminals, in my opinion.

Leather jacket man fell to his knees, and inspiration struck me seconds before a bullet struck him.

Clenching my eyes shut and flinching at the faint scream that was cut off by a muffled gunshot, I snatched my Blackberry out of the hip pocket of my baggy scrubs and hit the camera button.

Raising it to eye level, I pushed the selector and then the save key over and over, capturing the death of a drug dealer and wondering again if this was Smith. Whoever he was, he'd just become the story of the year.

The body slumped to the left onto the concrete, blood ebbing outward in a nearly-black circle on the smooth silvery floor.

The shadow moved.

I held my breath, my thumb still clicking automatically.

The shooter stepped out from behind the crates, sunlight glinting off the gun in his hand.

My entire body went numb. Clinging to the window frame, I managed to keep clicking the camera and tried not to throw up.

Tucking the gun under his pinstriped navy suit coat, Police Chief Donovan Nash surveyed the warehouse with a satisfied smile before his attention turned back to the hemorrhaging form at his feet.

The body shuddered once and fell still. Nash's lips curved up and he pulled one foot back and sank his shiny wingtip into the man's midsection before he disappeared into the office.

Oh. My. Fucking. God.

Not Lowe. At least, not just Lowe.

I stumbled backward and clapped one hand over my mouth, the metal under my feet strangely less than solid all of a sudden. But even my shaking knees and roiling stomach couldn't keep me from getting the hell out of there.

I whirled, scrambling on all fours as I stuffed the phone back into my pocket and half-jumped, half-fell back to the concrete, my leg protesting through the double dose of painkillers.

Diving behind the wheel, I started the engine and steered stealthily out of the alley, then squealed the tires when I got past the next building.

Shaking, I gulped deep breaths, the adrenaline fading fast. My stomach lurched and I groaned, barely getting the car stopped and the door open before I vomited Friday night's turkey sandwich into the grass between the road and the river.

When my insides were empty I sat up, fumbling in the console for a napkin and a stick of gum. The image of the police chief kicking the dying thief would haunt my nightmares forever, no doubt. I'd been so focused on Lowe that I hadn't even considered the possibility that Nash was involved.

I dug my Blackberry out of my pocket. *Please, God, just let the photos be recognizable*, I thought.

Before I could call up the pictures, my phone started ringing, Bob's office number flashing on the screen.

"Clarke," I sighed as I picked up. I wasn't obligated to work Saturdays, and I really wasn't in the mood for Les' bullshit.

"Charlie Lewis has a nice interview with the FBI about how they've ruled your boating crash an accident," Les barked. "But it's the damnedest thing—being the managing editor of a daily newspaper, I'm getting tired of getting my news from Channel Four. So haul your ass out of bed and get me a story I can put online before three."

I barely heard him, my eyes resting on the printed copy of the story from the Miami paper Joey had brought me the night before.

Nash's cold smile and something I'd seen in his office the day before zipped through my thoughts. I put Les on speaker and opened my Google app, tapping Nash's name in.

It took less than twenty seconds for my Blackberry to make me swear I'd background every cop I ever worked with for the rest of my career.

Nash had come to Richmond from heading the narcotics unit at the Miami PD eight years earlier—about two months before the date on the article in my passenger seat. I'd seen a Gators pennant on his office bookshelf, but by the time I'd found the story about Smith, I'd forgotten all about it.

"Clarke? Are you even listening to me? I can send Shelby over to interview the FBI if you'd like," Les' voice blared from the tiny speaker in my phone.

I contemplated telling him to fuck off. But I'd pissed him off enough for one week and, exclusive of the year or no, Bob was right about Les. At his core, he was bitter and spiteful, and he could hang onto a grudge like a bride with a hundred-dollar Vera Wang at a Filene's basement sale.

"I have something better," I said. And I needed to let the feds know there was a dead guy in that warehouse, anyway. "And I have to talk to the FBI about it, so I'll get your story while I'm at it."

"You have something better than the FBI concluding the crash that killed five people was just bad luck? What'd you do, witness a murder?"

"As a matter of fact, I did." My lips turned up slightly, picturing his face when the line went silent. "And I have art. Charlie will be chasing my byline for the foreseeable future."

I actually shut him up for so long I thought I'd lost my signal.

"Les?"

"You have what?" he asked finally.

"You heard me. Murder. Art. It'll be ready in two hours. Just watch for an email from Bob and don't say anything to anybody. Please."

"Don't tell me what to do," he snapped. "But I'll be waiting. It better be good."

"You won't believe it." I hung up on him and stood, physically unable to sit still despite the injured leg that burned with every step. Pacing the length of the car, I waited for my actual boss to answer his phone.

Something so monumental was not going on our presses without Bob seeing it first. Les could bite my ass. No way he was touching this story.

"Bob, oh my God," I began when he picked up, the story tumbling through my lips so fast I wasn't sure I got the words in the right order.

"Jesus, Nichelle," he whistled when I stopped for air. "That's…Wow. I'm not often at a loss for words, but I don't know what to say. When will you have it done?"

I turned back toward my car and opened my mouth to ask him if I could go to his house to write. Before I got the words out, a silver sedan shot out of a side street and lurched to a stop near my back bumper.

I let out a short scream and dropped the phone, my battered leg giving way when I tried to leap for my door. Sprawled in the grass, I threw a glance over my shoulder, but the glare from the sun obscured everything except the barrel of what looked like a rifle in a pair of very large hands.

I should have called Agent Starnes first.

Shoving hard with my good leg, I made it back to my feet and tried to spin toward the rifleman.

He was faster.

I heard a harsh huffing noise, like air being forced through a tube too fast.

Something stung my right hip.

I didn't even get my hand there to see what it was before I was lost in the darkness.

18.

Exclusive of the year

My head was bigger and heavier than I remembered, and my eyes opened to a world painted in watercolor, blurred and fluid at the edges.

I tried to remember where I was and how I got there, but the closest I could get was an odd urge to run. Except I couldn't muster the energy to get up. Everything seemed floaty and far away. Was this what dying felt like?

Voices filtered through the fog. I strained to hear the conversation, but it was akin to trying to listen to a television with the volume too low. I could make out syllables here and there, but nothing that made sense. And I couldn't hear them well enough to tell who they belonged to. One rose in pitch and volume, angry. The other remained flat.

Blinking too-fat eyelids, I looked around. White, industrial-looking walls, exposed metal ceiling beams, and a corrugated tin roof.

So I wasn't dead. While I'd never given much thought to what waited beyond the pearly gates, I was pretty sure the hereafter didn't resemble a warehouse.

A warehouse. There was something important about that.

Then I saw the boxes.

Fuck.

My heart took off at a gallop, adrenaline blazing a trail through the haze in my brain. Stacks and stacks of plastic boxes, in a warehouse where I'd just witnessed a murder.

I preferred the view from outside.

I tried unsuccessfully to lift my arms and legs. I was lying on hard, cold surface, but from the distance I perceived there to be between my body and the ceiling, it wasn't the floor. I tried to calm myself with a few deep breaths and caught a whiff of something that stung my nostrils.

The voices got louder.

"We certainly can't stay here." Donovan Nash's booming tenor wasn't a huge surprise, but that didn't make it any less terrifying.

"Why not?" The reply was barely audible.

I closed my eyes and focused. Nash's friend sounded familiar, but I couldn't place the voice.

"I caught her before she got more than three blocks from here, didn't I?" the mystery man argued. "No way they have a story yet. We get rid of her, and we've contained the situation."

"Didn't you say she was on the phone when you caught up to her?" Nash boomed. "How stupid do you think this girl is? If she figured out enough to come here, don't you think she told someone where she was?"

I wished. It hadn't occurred to me to mention my location as I spilled the murder story to Bob.

"So check her phone," Captain Mystery said. "See who she talked to and we'll take care of that."

"Yes, because disappearing in the wake of the murder of an assistant CA and half the city's newspaper staff is not at all suspicious," Nash snapped. "Not to mention, we still don't know where the hell the Boy Scout brigade got off to. What if Sorrel and White know more than I gave them credit for?"

I sighed, a small smile breaking through the insanity surrounding me. I knew my guys couldn't have been crooked. And if he didn't know where they were, then they probably weren't dead.

"The FBI said they were done for now," Nash continued. "I don't need them poking around anymore. We need to clear out of here and I need time to figure out our next move. Make those biceps useful and haul boxes out to the truck. If we can get out of the state, we can buy a little time."

Biceps?

And the voice. Damn. Mr. Mystery didn't really sound like Parker, but I'd never heard Parker sound mad.

"Rise and shine, sleeping beauty," Nash clapped his hands, the sound echoing in the cavernous space.

I turned my head toward him and bit back a scream, full-on panic drawing acid to the back of my tongue.

I was tied up and surrounded by at least two very large, armed men who wanted to "get rid of me."

Objectively, I didn't like my odds.

"Nichelle, I didn't expect to see you again today." Nash took two more steps and stared down at me with the same cold smile I'd seen from the window. Up close it was a thousand times more frightening, and a hundred and eighty degrees different from the charming grins he'd flashed in his office the day before.

"I knew you were working on a story about this." Nash waved a hand at the surroundings. "But I was pretty sure you suspected Lowe."

"And I thought I was being so secretive."

"I'd give you a solid B," he said. "I was impressed with your roundabout questions yesterday. I thought having McClendon arrange a meeting with you last night would keep you from tying anything back to me. It appears I was wrong, on a couple of counts. Notice the ropes. I won't be losing an eye to one of those pretty shoes."

I raised my head and peered at my ankles. Like my wrists, they were bound to a big metal table with medium gauge, white rope.

"I'm sure you're wondering why you're here," Nash said.

I concentrated on keeping my breathing even, trying to slow my pulse. I refused to let him see that I was about to pee myself.

"That crossed my mind," I said. "Why not shoot me in the alley and be done with it? The river was right there."

"I need to know how you put this together. I already had to deal with an unpleasant situation this morning. You showing up here was not something I expected."

Killing a man was an 'unpleasant situation'? I'd hate to see what really got him upset.

"Who tipped you off?" he asked.

"Why should I tell you anything? You're going to kill me anyway." I nearly choked on the words. Saying it aloud made it real.

"There are many ways to die, Nichelle," Nash smiled and wrapped a hand in my hair, jerking my head to one side and removing a few strands. "Some of them are less pleasant than others."

I stared, keeping my silence.

"I suspect you've been talking to Mike Sorrel." Nash said, his hand still in my hair. "Since he's jumped ship, I can't ask him, so I need you to share."

"I'm an only child. I suck at sharing." The words slipped out before I could stop them.

"You have a knack for sarcasm." He wrenched my hair harder, and I gasped as I felt a clump give and a warm trickle down the back of my neck. "I don't particularly care for it. Who told you?"

"No one." It was the God's honest truth, unless someone promoted Google to personhood. Too bad he didn't believe me.

He snapped his arm backward. White stars of pain exploded behind my eyes and I screamed. Nash flung a bloody clump of my hair onto the concrete behind him.

"Don't make me ask again," he said.

I closed my eyes and took slow breaths, trying to mimic the Lamaze breathing Jenna had used when Carson was born. When I could speak, I focused on Nash.

"There is no mysterious trench coat-clad source." I said, blinking back tears brought on by the pain. "Only my computer. Tax records are boring as hell, but they're often a reporter's best friend. So is Google."

Nash didn't appear to know about Joey, and I wasn't about to tell him. Too bad I didn't have some kind of mobster bat signal. Joey could probably get me out of the warehouse without scuffing a wingtip.

"Is that a fact?" Nash held my gaze and appeared to relax, his grin returning as he pulled out his cell phone. "Nice detective work. Have you ever considered going into law enforcement?"

"Ugly shoes." I tugged at the restraints on my wrists, which were snug, but not too tight. My double-jointed left thumb could probably help me slip a hand out of them if I could stretch them a bit. Trying to look relaxed, I kept pressure on the rope and my eyes on Nash.

"Aren't you supposed to uphold the law?" I asked.

"There's not as much money in being a good guy." He didn't look up from his phone. "Look where it got Gavin Neal."

"Do you know he had a sick little boy?" I asked, already sure he didn't care.

"And if he'd kept out of my business, the sick little boy would still have a father. If you'll excuse me, I have some calls to make." He smirked. "Don't go anywhere."

He disappeared into the dwindling stacks of boxes, and I stared at the ceiling, contemplating a way to save my ass while Nash tried to cover his. The back of my head burned with what would've been all-consuming pain in any other situation.

Flexing my forearms, I strained the ropes against the table. They cut off my circulation when I pulled, but I could've sworn they felt looser every time I relaxed. How the hell could I get out of the building without getting shot?

Bob must have heard the commotion when I'd dropped my phone. I didn't want him to come riding to the rescue, but I hoped he'd call someone. Jerry. Starnes. Spiderman. I wasn't picky, though it might help if the someone had a gun.

I popped my thumb flat and tried to wriggle my hand free. I almost had it when Nash's voice came closer again. I shoved my wrist back into the rope.

"Good news," he said, sticking his phone back into his pocket. "Things are going my way again. And in a way, I owe you my thanks for forcing my hand."

"You're welcome. I'll take a ride home in lieu of a card, if you don't mind."

"I'm not that grateful." Nash's eyes skipped around the warehouse and he nodded, appearing satisfied with the progress.

Faint chatter and the sliding, slapping thud of the crates being moved were the only sounds. From what I'd seen earlier, there was no one in earshot who'd care if I screamed.

"Hey, if you didn't know I suspected you, how did you know I was here this morning?" I asked.

"A combination of luck and brilliance." What could only be described as a shit-eating grin crossed his face. "Your copy editor wants your job."

"You've got to be kidding me." I stared, waiting for him to go on. That back-stabbing bitch. She better hope Nash finished me off before I had a chance to practice my *ap-chagi* on her.

"She called police headquarters this morning asking for information on a murder. Of course, that murder hasn't been reported to the proper authorities." Nash said. "But she insisted that a *Telegraph* reporter had witnessed it. Since we LoJacked your car, it was easy to see you were nearby."

"How very Orwellian villain of you. When did you do that?"

"McClendon said you left it at the coffee shop, so Brandon went by before dawn and put in a tracking device. It came in pretty handy." He grinned like a father whose son had just scored the winning touchdown.

"Brandon Smith?" If my minutes were numbered, I had to find out who that guy was. "Why would he LoJack my car for you after you killed his brother?"

"Noah got greedy. He and his friend were trying to blackmail me, and after I paid them very well for the effort I asked of them."

From his tone, he could've been talking about the weather or his golf score. "I wasn't sure what to do, because I couldn't afford to lose Brandon," Nash continued. "But he was surprisingly reasonable."

"I even went to Noah's house and explained it all to him. Right before I shot him." The voice Nash had been arguing with earlier came from behind a stack of crates to my left.

Except closer, with a more conversational tone, I recognized it instantly.

I clenched my eyes shut. No way.

"Brandon," Nash boomed. "How are we doing out there?"

"Almost done."

I opened my eyes just as Jerry Davis' face came between my head and the ceiling.

Smith was in much better shape than he'd been in when he left Florida, with darker hair. His clean-shaven face looked younger, too. But Jerry Davis was the man from the mug shot, plus one extreme makeover.

"Brandon?" I whispered.

"Yes, Nichelle?" He leaned over me and batted his lashes, his laugh low and disturbing.

How many times had I talked to him that week, with him "filling in" for Aaron? Christ on a cracker, as Eunice would say.

"You didn't know." He grinned. "How about that?"

"You're quite the thespian," I said. "I suppose that helps when you're trying to get away with murder."

"I was sure you'd pegged me when I let it slip that I was watching the Seminoles in the college series," he said. "I knew you had to know where Noah was from. Isn't that why you turned me down when I offered to help you?"

Strike two. Nash's Gators pennant and Jerry's college world series. Fat lot of good it did me to put it together now.

As long as they were giving answers, I figured I'd try for a few more. The way Nash's eyes flicked to his phone every four seconds, he was waiting for a call. And the boxes were disappearing fast. Maybe I could buy a few minutes if I could get them bragging about their cleverness. Not that I knew what I'd do with more time, but I wanted it anyway.

"Why put the drugs on a boat?" I blurted the first question I thought of. "Doesn't that limit where you can take them?"

"We used to use trucks," Nash said. "But for the last couple of years, some friction has made that difficult. This spring, the river level rose enough that the water allowed us access to the coast, and I didn't need to fight anyone over transportation. No one was the wiser until that baseball player lost control of his speedboat."

"Friction. With the mob." Gavin Neal's guns had come off a truck, so it followed that Joey's friends had been involved.

"We tried to work a deal with them," Nash said. "I even had McClendon perjure himself during a murder trial and say he hadn't read the defendant his Miranda rights so their guy would get off. But they're stingy bastards."

Greedy crooks. Imagine that.

"And the guys who died in the boat crash, Freeman and Roberts? Did they know what they were hauling?"

Nash shook his head, staring at his phone again.

"They weren't the type," he said. "Which is what made them the perfect cover."

The phone binged and Nash turned his back, studying the screen and muttering to himself.

I turned to Jerry/Brandon, the crime scene stills of Darryl and Noah flashing up from my memory, both of them relaxed in the face of death. Because they knew him.

"You knew I was here because you tracked my car." I said, talking to keep from panicking as Nash waved an arm in a wrap-it-up gesture at whoever was carting off boxes. "It was you with the rifle. A dart, right?"

He grinned.

"I tried to aim for your hip. They hurt a lot more when they hit you in the neck. I do what I can for the pretty girls." He leered, trailing one finger down my arm, and I clenched my jaw to keep from spitting in his face.

Brandon turned his attention to something I couldn't see, and I tried again to yank my left hand free.

Success!

And not a minute too soon, if I could just think of some way to capitalize on it.

Arm still at my side, I looked around, noticing a muted splashing sound had now replaced the slapping of the crates moving. The sharp scent in the air was suddenly strong enough to make my eyes water. Shit.

"What's going to happen to this place?" I fought to keep my voice even, because I already knew the answer.

"You don't smell the gasoline?" Nash spun back toward me, cold smile in place. "Enough chit chat. You've had a fine last interview, and we have somewhere to be."

His phone rang and he raised it to his ear.

"Are we good?" he asked.

He shot Brandon a thumbs up.

"Excellent." Busy swallowing nausea and tears, I wasn't sure which of them said it.

Nash slid his phone into his pocket and pulled a gun out of his jacket.

"Bullets are much quicker than flames, Nichelle," he said. "What's it going to be?"

19.

Here comes the cavalry

I closed my eyes as Nash prodded my shoulder with the gun when I didn't answer him. Before I opened them again all hell broke loose around me. The door slammed open with a metallic ringing. Nash and Jerry/Brandon whirled in two different directions as a barrage of sharp cracks split the stillness outside.

I froze for the tiniest fraction of a second before I wrenched my right hand out of the rope, losing a good bit of skin in the process. Clawing at the binding around my left ankle, I got it loose, then used the heel on that shoe to lever the rope and jerked my right foot free. Swiveling on my tailbone, I pulled my knees to my chest and slammed both feet into the small of Brandon's back.

The stilettos on my battered black Louboutins sank into his kidneys, and he let out a strangled cry and pitched face-first onto the concrete. He didn't move to get back up.

I somehow rolled over, flipped backward, and managed to land upright on the far side of the table.

Though his attention was on the commotion outside, Nash still stood less than ten feet away. Between me and the door. Leg throbbing and head wound burning, I stumbled back two steps, looking around for another way out.

"Not so fast," Nash said as he whirled on me.

I planted my Louboutins and shoved the table with all the strength I could muster.

It flew at him, the casters beneath it gliding across the concrete. The wind left his chest in a *whoosh* and he staggered backward when the steel edge hit him squarely in the sternum.

A gleeful cackle came from somewhere. Maybe from me. I wasn't sure of anything but the relief that washed over me as the building filled with bodies encased in black tactical gear.

Brandishing large guns, the cavalry took its orders from a tall man in a bulletproof vest whose face was mostly obscured by a two-way radio.

"Watch the woman," he ordered, striding to the middle of the nearly-empty room. "Donovan Nash, you are under arrest."

I took my eyes off Nash long enough to see that Captain Rescue had a gun in his other hand. He didn't move the radio, but the ice-blue eyes peering over the top of it widened when they met mine.

I didn't process that before Nash raised his gun, swinging between me and Officer Cool. He settled on the easy target.

"Give my regards to Gavin Neal, won't you, Nichelle?"

The room was empty. Nowhere to hide.

A shot fired.

I screamed. But the pain didn't come.

Nash crumpled to the ground, a dark spot blooming across the middle of his tailored navy suit coat. A pair of SWAT-clad officers pounced on him.

I locked eyes with Captain Rescue, who holstered his sidearm as the radio handset fell away from a face I could never forget.

Adding shock to the adrenaline and sedatives was too much. The room wavered, the floor seeming to buckle under me as I fell.

But I never hit the ground.

Kyle Miller, ex-love-of-my-life, sprinted across the dozen feet of concrete between us and caught me as I drifted back into the fog.

More voices. I lifted my eyelids, but couldn't focus on the backlit figure next to me for a full minute.

"Bob," I mumbled. "My story."

"That's the Nichelle Clarke I remember. Bleeding. Nearly murdered. But always thinking about the story."

Not Bob.

"Kyle?" I blinked.

His voice had a commanding edge I'd never heard. He leaned forward, no longer silhouetted by the summer sun flooding the ambulance. The white sheet over my lap reflected flashing blue and red from the emergency vehicles crowding the parking lot around Nash's warehouse.

I probed gingerly behind my ear, finding hamburger where a sizable chunk of my hair had been. It hurt. And was still bleeding.

If I was dreaming, I had to award points for realism.

"Don't take this the wrong way, but what the hell are you doing here?" I asked. "Am I dead? Because when I heard your life flashes before your eyes, this is not what I had in mind."

"No, Nicey, you're not." He chuckled, gentle hands smoothing the hair I still had off my forehead. "All things considered, I think you're okay. But I want someone to check you out."

"How? Where did you come from?" I stared, even reaching a hand up to touch his face lightly.

He was older, with a neat goatee the same auburn color as his hair. But I'd looked into those eyes a thousand times in another life.

"I work for the ATF." He smiled. "And I guess you work for the Richmond newspaper, right? We got a tip from the FBI that a reporter was taken hostage by a group of crooked cops who've been moving guns and drugs all over the east coast. We've been trying to trace something back to Nash for a long time. I came up a month ago to help with the investigation."

When my mom said "law enforcement," I assumed Kyle had joined the Dallas PD with his dad, but the Bureau of Alcohol, Tobacco, Firearms, and Explosives made more sense in the context of him being sent out of state, which didn't happen often in local police work.

"Small world," I said. "Lucky for me, I guess."

"I'm a pretty good shot." He handed me my Blackberry. "Is this yours? My guys found your car, too. The bag that was in the backseat is right here." He pointed to the floor.

"Thanks." I smiled.

"Nicey!" Bob's it's-four-o'clock-where-the-hell-is-my-copy shout rattled the windows, and Kyle turned to the open ambulance bay doors.

"Bob?" he asked.

I nodded. "My boss."

He stood. "I guess that's my cue. I have four corpses out there and a shit-ton of paperwork to do, anyway."

"She's in here," he called, sticking his head out of the back of the ambulance and waving one arm before he disappeared.

"Goodbye to you, too," I said. "Thanks for saving my ass."

Bob climbed into the ambulance, the lines in his face deeper than I recalled.

"Are you all right?" he asked.

The medic shooed at him from her perch behind me. "Sir, I'm sorry, but we're going to have to go," she said. "You can meet us at St. Vincent's if you want to visit with the patient."

"No." I tried to look at her, but succeeded only in scraping my injured scalp on the sandpapery pillowcase.

"No, what?" Bob asked, ignoring the medic and laying a meaty hand over one of mine.

"No, I'm not going to the hospital. Not until my story is done. Get me a computer."

"Excuse me?" The medic leaned forward, her red hair brushing my face. "Ma'am, you've been drugged, you have a bleeding head wound, and you've been in the middle of a police firefight. You have to see a doctor."

"I will. As soon as my story is done." I looked at Bob as I spoke. "My laptop is in that bag. There'll be TV trucks out there from everywhere between here and Fredericksburg in a half-hour, and I'll completely lose my shit if I almost got killed twice so Charlie Lewis could break this story."

Bob laughed, bending to retrieve the computer and laying it across my lap.

"That's my ace," he said. "Always worried about the scoop."

"Miss, we really can't—" the medic began, but Bob cut her off.

"You might as well let it be," he said. "She won't sign the treatment consent until she gets her way. Besides, it looks to me like she's earned it."

The paramedics huddled behind me, muttering. Apparently, people don't often demand to finish work before being ferried to the hospital. Not that I cared—I already started typing.

"Just tell Ryan to be ready to get it on the website and Facebook and everywhere else he can throw it as soon as I'm done," I said. "Get the pictures off my phone over to photo. And then hush up and let me work some magic for you."

"Get after it, kiddo." Bob sat on the bench Kyle had vacated and picked up my Blackberry. "This is going to be one hell of a story."

The keyboard and my thoughts drowned out his conversation.

Hands in the air, an unknown man with a scar on his left cheek dropped to his knees on the concrete floor of a warehouse in Richmond's river district Saturday, begging for his life. His pleas fell on deaf ears, surrender not altering Richmond Police Chief Donovan Nash's plan.

Nash fired a single shot, then stood over his victim, kicking him in the ribs as the man lay in a growing pool of his own blood on the concrete.

Nash, in his ninth year as head of the RPD, confessed the murder to a Telegraph reporter he and RPD Detective Jerry Davis drugged and took hostage Saturday. The journalist became a threat when she uncovered a drug ring operating out of police headquarters.

Nash and Davis, formerly known as Officer Brandon Smith of the Miami PD narcotics unit, used the RPD river unit to move drugs and guns throughout the mid-Atlantic.

Assistant Commonwealth's Attorney Gavin Neal, whose body was found in the James this week, was suspicious of oddities in the RPD's evidence procedures, his widow said.

"Gavin swore to me something fishy was going on at the police department," Grace Neal said Thursday. "From that point

on, he made weekly random checks of the evidence room. Then Sunday, he never made it home."

Nash confessed to involvement in Neal's death, among other crimes, including trafficking drugs and weapons and accessory to perjury that set a confessed murderer free.

Nash was shot Saturday by Bureau of Alcohol, Tobacco, Firearms, and Explosives Agent Kyle Miller while threatening Miller with a gun. Two additional people were killed in the fire-fight between criminals and ATF agents, but their names were not available at press time.

I continued into the conflicting lab reports on the heroin, Smith's conviction in the drug thefts in Miami, and Roberts and Freeman's innocence.

Since I was the only person who knew the story of my kidnapping, we could hold it for the next day, but I tossed another teaser into the end.

I flipped the screen around and Bob read it silently, touching the keys only twice before he looked up at me.

"You have outdone yourself." He smiled and handed the computer back. "Just don't jump ship when Washington comes calling. I gave you a shot when they wouldn't, and don't you forget it."

I smiled, the pricking in the backs of my eyes telling me tears were coming whether I wanted them or not.

I brushed them away, grinning as I read.

I'd really done it. We had the story of the year. Grace Neal would know why her husband died. So would Valerie Roberts.

Hot damn.

"You want to do the honors?" Bob asked.

I turned on my Blackberry's Wi-Fi hotspot and opened an email to Les.

"Bite me, you asshat," I muttered as I clicked send. He'd no doubt find a reason to be unimpressed.

"What a colorful—and accurate—description." Bob laughed, nodding to the medic. "I think she'll behave now."

She put a blood pressure cuff on my arm and Bob's grin dissolved into a glare.

"You scared the shit out of me, kid," he said. "I heard you scream, then a scuffle, and then nothing—well, let's just say those pills must be working, because I'm still sitting here.

"Why the hell would you go after this guy without any help?" He shook his head. "I told you Parker said to let him know if you needed anything. He's a big guy. And he would've come with you."

"Which would have been great, if I was sure he wasn't in on it."

"If you what?" Bob stared. "What are you talking about?"

Sighing, I waited for the medic to decide I wouldn't expire on the ride to the hospital. When she returned to her seat, I pulled a copy of the photo of Lowe and Parker out of my bag, waving it under Bob's nose as I explained a suspicion that suddenly sounded far-fetched. Especially given that Lowe wasn't actually the big bad.

"Oh, good Lord," Bob chuckled. "You have to remove *The X-Files* from your Netflix immediately. Impressive conclusion you jumped to. Did that take a springboard?"

"I didn't jump to anything," I argued, ticking off points on my fingers. "The designer bike, the flashy cash. And then the photo. Plus, he-who-has-never-spoken-to-me has been all into my story this week. It's weird. A long step, or a hop, maybe, but no jumping."

"Did it ever occur to you that he might respect you?" Bob asked. "And I imagine he was asking about the drug dealers because he had a friend from college who blew out his knee catching for the Cardinals not long after Parker wrecked his shoulder. Except his buddy got addicted to Oxycontin, then to heroin. Hung himself. Sad story.

"Parker's got a real thing about it. He gives speeches to school kids on the evils of drugs. And he has more money than you because we pay him more."

"What? How much more?"

"Grant Parker is a bona fide local hero," Bob said. "According to Les' focus groups, his column generates nearly a third of our daily subs and almost that much of our ad revenue. And he saves me paying a baseball reporter. He's also a good writer, which you would know if you'd ever read that column he's been begging you to critique for him. We can't afford to lose him. He makes more money than I do."

My eyes dropped to my lap under his reproachful stare. Bob and my mother were the only two people in the world who could make me feel so effectively chastised.

"Oh," I said.

"Oh, indeed. You may owe him an apology."

"Well, why didn't he mention knowing Lowe?" I cringed at what Parker must have thought of my insane behavior the night before.

What if he really was a decent guy who just wanted to be my friend? Though he probably wouldn't once he heard I'd labeled him a murderer.

"The cop was the water boy, right? Didn't you go to high school? How many star pitchers knew the water boy's name?"

Everything he said made perfect sense, which irritated me.

"Forgive me for being a newbie at the 'everyone's trying to kill me' platinum edition," I huffed. "Maybe next time I'll get to the bonus levels."

"Let's not have a next time," Bob said as the ambulance rolled to a stop outside the emergency room. The medic ordered him to the registration desk, and he took my bag and eased himself out the back doors.

I snatched up my Blackberry.

"Miss, you can't make a call right now," the medic sighed. "You really do need medical attention. Everything else can wait."

"I'm not calling anyone," I smiled, clicking the browser open and looking for Parker's name on the *Telegraph*'s mobile site. "But while I'm stuck here, I have some reading to catch up on."

20.

Overnight sensation

It turned out Bob was right. Parker was a hell of a good writer, and while I'll admit to being emotional when I read it, his piece on the basketball coach brought tears to my eyes.

I emailed my mom a link with "Read this, but get tissues first" in the subject line, and copied Parker. Maybe that would begin to make up for suspecting him of murder.

The doctor who patched up my scalp assured me my hair would grow back eventually and admitted me for observation because of the sedatives.

I watched Charlie's coverage of the day's events and learned that Nash was one of Kyle's corpses. I didn't know how to feel about that, but couldn't say I was sorry.

Since I knew my name and who was president, they let me go Saturday night.

Jenna came to pick me up, listening to the tale with wide eyes before she stopped in my driveway. Leaning across the console, she hugged me, mumbling something into my shoulder about boring being a good thing. I could go with that. I climbed out and waved as she drove off.

"The dog is glad to be home." The voice floated out of the darkness and I smiled.

"Nope. Still not surprised," I limped up the steps and seated myself next to Joey on the white wooden swing that was one of the best things about my house. "Maybe it's you, because my old beau showing up with the cavalry this morning shocked the hell out of me."

"I used it all up on that first night." He snapped his fingers. "Damn."

"That must be it. To what do I owe the honor of this visit? You could've left the dog here. I do it all the time."

"I wanted to thank you," he said.

"Shouldn't I be the one thanking you? You called the FBI and tipped them off, right?" I knew Bob hadn't, because he'd told me as much while we waited for the ER doctor. Joey was the only other logical assumption. "Which saved my life. Again. But how did you know?"

"I went snooping around the warehouse." His teeth flashed white in the darkness. "I thought I'd be in the clear, going early on a Saturday. Instead I found them moving stuff out and hosing the place down with gasoline. I found your car a couple of blocks away and called the FBI. They showed up while I was debating the best tactic for a rescue mission."

"You were?" It made me smile, though I didn't know why.

"Of course. I drug you into this. At least part of it."

His eyes held mine and my hospital-issue broiled cod flopped around in my stomach like it was still alive.

"I never wanted you to get hurt. I had no idea it went all the way to the police chief. But I also didn't want a shootout with a truckload of cops. I was outnumbered, and wouldn't have come out of it well no matter how it went down. So I called it in. Working around the edges of the law, remember?"

The edges. It still didn't sound so bad. I stared at his lips and wondered if he was a good kisser. Something told me that was a given. And something else told me the answer was there for the having if I wanted it.

I took a deep breath and leaned back into the throw pillows, not sure enough to stay so close to him.

"Was it you the first time, too?" Focusing on business seemed like a good bet, and I had a flash of what seemed like a long-ago conversation with Agent Starnes that made me wonder. "The boating accident? You set the FBI on him then, too, didn't you?"

"Nothing gets by you, does it?"

"I wish some things did," I said, more to myself than to him, but he heard me anyway.

"Me, too." It was little more than a whisper.

"Thanks for taking the dog," I said, out of questions and beginning to fidget. "I should go say hi to her."

"Seemed like the least I could do." He stood up. "Goodnight, Miss Clarke."

"Goodbye, Joey."

He nodded, staring at me with an unfamiliar sadness. "I can't say I blame you. But I can be persistent." His lips turned up slightly. "And I'm not sure I'm ready to give up."

"I'm stubborn." I couldn't help smiling back.

"So am I." He disappeared into the night.

I got out of bed on Sunday only for coffee or food. Monday, I walked into the staff meeting to white chocolate chip banana bread and a lecture from Eunice about being more careful. From Bob, who was back for half-days because he was just that stubborn, I got a bear hug.

I stayed put when everyone filed out. Eunice paused to hug me, squeezing so long I smelled like patchouli the rest of the day. When she was gone, too, I tucked a wayward lock of hair behind my ear and smiled at Bob and Parker.

"Nice to be missed," I said.

"We're just glad you're okay," Parker said. "I would have come to help you if you'd called, you know. I wouldn't have even asked for a byline."

Bob cleared his throat with way too much fanfare and shot me a pointed stare.

"Hey Parker, about that," I said. "I owe you an apology. I was up to my ears in crooked cops and dead people and I found this old picture of you online and I sort of thought you might be in on it. A little." I held my thumb and forefinger a half-inch apart.

"In on what? Murder and theft with your crooked cops?" He shook his head and laughed. "I'd love to know what the hell kind of photo you found that made you think that."

He snatched it out of my hand before I got it all the way out of my bag, and laughed harder as he explained that he didn't even know Lowe.

"Someone told me that." I shot a glance at Bob and smiled at Parker. "Sorry I thought you were a murderer."

He grinned. "Glad you didn't get yourself killed."

"And what a story!" Bob leaned back in his chair. "Ad revenue hasn't been so high since Clinton was in office, and our page count has gone up 25 percent. Les even shuffled in here with a half-assed apology this morning. And every TV personality from Charlie Lewis to Anderson Cooper is quoting your story five times a day. This is great."

And it was. The only part of the RPD scandal's aftermath I didn't care for was the instant celebrity. I'd arrived at work to messages from reporters as far away as Los Angeles requesting interviews.

In the middle of the media storm, Kyle called to offer me an exclusive with the ATF in exchange for some company at dinner.

"How could I turn down a real-life hero?" I asked. "I heard from a little birdie on the TV that you're some sort of supercop."

"I don't know about that." The years had done nothing to his laugh. "But I do all right."

I gave him my address and told him to be ready to spill everything at seven-thirty.

Aaron and Mike were back at the PD and said they had a long story for me when I had time for it. All was right with my world again.

Bob just nodded when I told him about my date with Kyle.

"Promising," he said. "And if anything breaks tonight, Shelby can cover for you."

I shot him a glare that would've scared anyone else. "Not amusing."

He laughed. "I thought it was."

"Yeah, Clarke," Parker chimed in from the doorway. "We're all one big helpful family around here: cheapskate uncles, backstabbing cousins and all."

Funny for Parker to put into words how I'd always thought of the staff as my family.

"And friends?" I smiled.

"Friends." He winked. "I meant to tell you before, thanks for that email about my column. Not bad for a murdering drug pusher?"

"Not bad at all." I grinned. "For a jock."

Turning back toward my desk, I smiled at the bustle of the newsroom, not even a little sad that my call from the *Post* hadn't come.

I had a job. I had friends. I had great shoes. And I had a home. There might be mobsters in my living room or coffins in random driveways, but life was rarely boring. And every beep of my scanner promised a new adventure.

Reader's Discussion Guide

1. Have you ever discovered something unexpected in the course of your job? What happened?

2. Was there anyone on Nichelle's suspect list you were sure was innocent? Who and why?

3. Have you ever worked with anyone like Shelby? Did you dislike her, or feel sorry for her?

4. Which of the male characters made a strong romantic fit for Nichelle? Why?

5. Though her heels prove to be less than practical a few times, Nichelle has a utilitarian side, too. What elements in the story showed it?

6. Have you ever had a group of friends or coworkers who felt like a family to you?

7. Have you ever wanted something for so long you began to want it out of habit? Do you see that in Nichelle?

8. What are the differences between Charlie and Shelby? Which of them did you have more respect for?

9. Have you ever had a boss who could make your week with a compliment? What was the best one s/he ever gave you and how long ago was it?

Photo by Sarah Dabney-Reardon

LynDee Walker

LynDee Walker grew up in the land of stifling heat and amazing food most people call Texas, and wanted to be Lois Lane from the time she could say the words "press conference." An award-winning journalist, she traded cops and deadlines for burp cloths and onesies when her oldest child was born. Writing the Headlines in Heels mysteries gives her the best of both worlds. When not writing or reading, LynDee is usually wrangling children, eating barbecue or enchiladas, or trying to walk off said barbecue and enchiladas. She and her family live in Richmond, Virginia.

IF YOU LIKED THIS HENERY PRESS MYSTERY,
YOU MIGHT ALSO LIKE THESE...

Diners, Dives & DEAD ENDS

by Terri L. Austin

As a struggling waitress and part-time college student, Rose Strickland's life is stalled in the slow lane. But when her close friend, Axton, disappears, Rose suddenly finds herself serving up more than hot coffee and flapjacks. Now she's hashing it out with sexy bad guys and scrambling to find clues in a race to save Axton before his time runs out.

With her anime-loving bestie, her septuagenarian boss, and a pair of IT wise men along for the ride, Rose discovers political corruption, illegal gambling, and shady corporations. She's gone from zero to sixty and quickly learns when you're speed-ing down the fast lane, it's easy to crash and burn.

PORTRAIT of a DEAD GUY

by LARISSA REINHART

In Halo, Georgia, folks know Cherry Tucker as big in mouth, small in stature, and able to sketch a portrait faster than buckshot rips from a ten gauge -- but commissions are scarce. So when the well-heeled Branson family wants to memorialize their murdered son in a coffin portrait, Cherry scrambles to win their patronage from her small town rival.

As the clock ticks toward the deadline, Cherry faces more trouble than just a controversial subject. Between ex-boyfriends, her flaky family, an illegal gambling ring, and outwitting a killer on a spree, Cherry finds herself painted into a corner she'll be lucky to survive.

BOARD STIFF

by Kendel Lynn

As director of the Ballantyne Foundation on Sea Pine Island, SC, Elliott Lisbon scratches her detective itch by performing discreet inquiries for Foundation donors. Usually nothing more serious than retrieving a pilfered Pomeranian. Until Jane Hatting, Ballantyne board chair, is accused of murder. The Ballantyne's reputation tanks, Jane's headed to a jail cell, and Elliott's sexy ex is the new lieutenant in town.

Armed with moxie and her Mini Coop, Elliott uncovers a trail of blackmail schemes, gambling debts, illicit affairs, and investment scams. But the deeper she digs to clear Jane's name, the guiltier Jane looks. The closer she gets to the truth, the more treacherous her investigation becomes. With victims piling up faster than shells at a clambake, Elliott realizes she's next on the killer's list.

DOUBLE WHAMMY

by Gretchen Archer

Davis Way thinks she's hit the jackpot when she lands a job as the fifth wheel on an elite security team at the fabulous Bellissimo Resort and Casino in Biloxi, Mississippi. But once there, she runs straight into her ex-ex husband, a rigged slot machine, her evil twin, and a trail of dead bodies. Davis learns the truth and it does not set her free—in fact, it lands her in the pokey.

Buried under a mistaken identity, unable to seek help from her family, her hot streak runs cold until her landlord Bradley Cole steps in. Make that her landlord, lawyer, and love interest. With his help, Davis must win this high stakes game before her luck runs out.